The Alpha List

'So the crooks could have known about it for some time—and just waited for the right moment?'

'That's how I figured it.'

'What did you say?'

'I told her I'd have to think it over, and to come here in the evening. I got her thinking I was scared. Actually, I decided almost straight away that the only thing to do was to go and give myself up. So when she came I was ready for her.'

'What did you do?'

'I asked her in and then I started kicking her.'

Palmer stared. 'You did what?'

'I started kicking her. I'd put on a pair of shoes with very hard, square toe-caps. I waited until she was in the middle of the room and then I let her have it.' She spoke dreamily. 'Do you know, I must have got in fifteen or twenty really good hacks before she managed to get out. I started on her ankles and worked my way up. Her legs must have been quite a sight for the next couple of weeks. I've never seen anyone so surprised. I don't think she'd ever been kicked before. You should have heard her screaming. Have you ever kicked a really repulsive person, Inspector Palmer? It's a strangely satisfying experience.'

Palmer laughed. It was the first laugh he'd had out of these investigations, and he laughed long and loud.

Other titles in the Walker British Mystery Series

JAMES
ANDERSON
The
Alpha
List

WALKER AND COMPANY · NEW YORK

First published in the United States of America
in 1973 by the Walker Publishing Company, Inc.

This paperback edition first published in 1985.

ISBN: 0-8027-3129-5

Library of Congress Catalog Card Number: 72-80525

Printed in the United States of America

10 9 8 7 6 5 4 3 2 1

1

British Members of Parliament do not as a general rule appear in obscene photographs.

So Mr Gordon Hemmings was something of a rarity.

Most people would shrink from having to admit this to several Scotland Yard detectives. But not, apparently, Mr Hemmings. When the blackmail had started he had gone straight to the Commissioner of the Metropolitan Police. And the Commissioner had summoned the Assistant Commissioner, who had summoned Detective-Chief Superintendent Malcolm Phillips, who had said: 'Detective-Inspector Palmer's my best man on blackmail, sir.'

So Bob Palmer was stuck with it.

He listened silently, letting the M.P. tell the story in his own way, before asking: 'And what's the price, sir?'

'Oh. Er, five hundred pounds.'

'Hm. Very modest.'

Mr Hemmings looked annoyed. 'That may be a modest sum to you, Inspector Palmer. But not to me. I am not a rich man.'

That's funny, Palmer felt like saying. I just looked you up in Who's Who: you're a qualified accountant, a director of an advertising agency, principal shareholder in a big public relations firm, and you've got interests in a supermarket chain, consumer research, even a firm of bookmakers; all quite apart from your M.P.'s salary. So why aren't you rich?

But he couldn't say that.

'I think it's monstrous,' Hemmings snapped.

No, Hemmings, it's not monstrous. You're a middle-aged married man and a public figure with a carefully-nurtured reputation. You've been playing around on the sly with a girl half your age. You've had your fun and now you're being asked five hundred quid to preserve your image. I'd say it was cheap at the price.

But he couldn't say that, either. Because he was the Best Man on Blackmail. A Specialist.

It was not a reputation he relished. And not at all what he'd visualised when he'd joined the force twelve years before.

Palmer sometimes cursed the effort he had put into those three blackmail cases which, purely by chance, had come his way just after his promotion to inspector. He'd secured three convictions. And found himself labelled.

Since then too many men and women had sat in the chair now occupied by Hemmings and told their sordid little stories. They had all been the same. All in a blue funk because their sins had come home to roost. And all expecting him, Bob Palmer, to do something about it.

He always had done something about it. He would do this time. But he had heard it all too often to have any sympathy left for this petty politician. Hemmings was no different from any of the others. Except . . .

Except that he wasn't really scared like them. Nor was he the least embarrassed. He had just told a story which showed him to be a lecherous, hypocritical, and rather stupid person. Yet his air of perfect self-satisfaction had not abated. It was clear he firmly believed himself to be a good and clever man, and nothing would shake this.

It was a belief that must rub off on others. It had certainly fooled thirty thousand voters in one of the most puritanical constituencies in the country for the past twenty-five years.

But it wouldn't fool them again if this story got out. So why was Hemmings so nonchalant?

'I'm sorry, sir,' Palmer said. 'I know it's very upsetting for you; and I don't mean it's a trivial sum. It's simply that these villains usually ask more than that. They imagine they're dealing with wealthy people, whatever the true position may be.'

Mr Hemmings was somewhat mollified.

Palmer said: 'And I suppose it's the usual routine: used £1 notes, brown paper parcel to be left somewhere?'

'Yes. He's going to give me exact instructions next time he rings.'

'About these photographs of yourself he sent you: may I see them?'

'No.'

The reaction was to have been expected but the abruptness was surprising.

'But look, sir, it's very . . .'

Hemmings interrupted. 'I know what you're going to say, Inspector. You want to examine them for fingerprints and send them along to your laboratories for all sorts of tests. But my objection is that you or one of your colleagues might recognise the young lady, and that would hardly be fair to her. She knows nothing about any of this. I'd rather see if we can catch the criminal by some other means first. If not, then I may reconsider the position later on.'

Palmer opened his mouth with the intention of pressing the point. Then he decided it just wasn't worth it. So he shrugged and said: 'As you wish, sir. But perhaps you can tell me something about the photos. Where were they taken?'

'I really couldn't say.'

'Oh come, sir, surely . . .'

'Inspector, you must understand that in my position I had to be very discreet. The young lady and I were forced to meet in various places.'

'But is there nothing in the pictures – no extraneous detail – that tells you where these particular ones were taken?'

'I'm afraid not.'

Palmer sighed. 'Or when?'

'No.'

'Can you give me the names of anybody who might have known of your – your friendship with this lady and of your movements at any particular time?'

'I'm sorry, no.'

'Do you know of anybody – not necessarily by name – whom you think might have been in a position to take them?'

Hemmings shook his head.

'They were sent to you at the House of Commons?'

'That's right.'

'No note?'

'No.'

'What about the envelope?'

'I didn't notice it, I'm afraid. And unfortunately it was thrown away.'

Palmer took a deep breath, then said quietly: 'Tell me about your 'phone call.'

'Ah, that was at home. The same evening.'

7

'What did he say?'

'Simply that he had the negatives of the pictures I'd received and that he wanted five hundred for them or copies would be sent to my wife and my constituency party. He told me to get used notes made up into a parcel and be ready for instructions about where to leave them.'

'How would you describe the voice?'

Hemmings considered. 'Well, not an educated man, but not completely illiterate, either. He had a slight cockney accent.'

There was silence while Palmer finished writing his notes. Then he said: 'And that's all you can tell me, sir?'

'I'm afraid so.'

'Right. Then it's just a matter of waiting. We can't really make any plans until you hear from him. Please let me know as soon as you do.'

'Very well.' Hemmings stood up.

'I feel I ought to warn you, sir,' Palmer said, getting up himself, 'that although you've behaved perfectly properly in coming to us, you have taken a risk. It's possible the villain's been having you watched and now knows you've come to us. In which case he'll probably call the whole thing off. But he might go ahead with his threat just the same.'

Hemmings made a gesture of resignation. 'Of course I realise that. It was a risk that had to be taken.'

'And the possibility doesn't alarm you. Is your wife . . . ?'

'My wife found – my wife *knows* about my friendship with this young lady. She is divorcing me.'

'And what about your constituents, sir? Don't they have the reputation of being rather strait-laced?'

'That's true. But fortunately I need not concern myself with them any longer. You see, Inspector, there is one thing the blackmailer doesn't know. In fact, very few people know it so far, so please keep it to yourself. The fact is' – he lowered his voice – 'I shall not be contesting the seat again at the next election.' He squared his shoulders. 'I have given twenty-five of the best years of my life to public service, Mr Palmer. Now I think it's time I started looking after my own affairs rather than the whole country's.'

So one mystery was solved, at least.

A couple of hours later Bob Palmer was driving out of central London, on his way home. He was a squarely-built, powerful-looking man of thirty-four, serious-minded, abstemious, almost ascetic, a man who neither smoked nor drank, who was happily married and who never gave a thought to other women, and who had never been heard to swear.

Now he accelerated and changed into top gear as there came a momentary break in the traffic. 'He's a slimy little devil,' he said. 'On this occasion my sympathies were rather with the black-mailer.'

In the passenger seat, Detective-Inspector Andrew Thompson laughed. 'Careful. Those are not words which should fall lightly from the lips of the C.I.D.'s foremost authority on the subject. Blackmail's moral murder, isn't it?'

'Rot,' Palmer said forcefully. 'Ninety per cent of blackmail victims deserve all they get. Don't waste your sympathy on them. They've always done something dirty or malicious or sly or downright bent – and got away with it. The blackmailer's just somebody who's tried to make them pay. You could almost say he dispensed justice.'

'Hey, you're supposed to catch blackmailers, remember? Not give a commercial for 'em.'

'Oh, I'll catch 'em, all right. I've caught my share already. But don't expect me to get all steamed up about them. There are worse villains around than the average blackmailer.'

Palmer and Thompson had joined the police during the same month twelve years previously, had gone through training school together, and their careers had kept pace ever since.

Thompson, the elder by a year or so, was a tall, blond bachelor with a deceptively lazy air and a cheerful and easy-going manner. He was a contrast to Palmer in nearly every respect. Yet six years before he had been best man at Palmer's wedding, they had remained close ever since, and two or three times a month, as now, Thompson went to dinner with Palmer and his wife.

Yet in spite of knowing him so well, Thompson sometimes realised how little he really understood Palmer. This was such a time. Surely this surprising defence of blackmailers wasn't to be taken seriously? If so, Thompson thought, it could change a lot of things. Yet he was sure Palmer would never go easy on a real villain. And, thinking it over, he decided that what Palmer had said was not basically so much out of character. He remembered a conversation they'd had many years previously when they had both been raw trainees. He had asked Palmer why he wanted to be a detective. Palmer had thought for a moment and then said: 'People have got to pay – and be paid – for what they do. That's what it's all about. I want to help see people pay a fair price.'

And that, thought Thompson, explains what he means about blackmail. It occurred to him, not for the first time, that to certain people Palmer could be a dangerous man. The thought made him a trifle uneasy. He asked: 'Got any leads in the Hemmings business?'

'C.R.O. came up with a few names – Shorty Rodgers, Johnny James, Harry Edwards, Carlo Spinotti. They've all tried their hand in the past – using about the same *modus operandi*. But it's just as likely to be someone quite clean up to now. Blackmail's often an amateur's crime – or a sideline for a pro when the chance comes along.'

'If you say so,' said Thompson. 'You're the expert.'

Palmer just grunted and pulled out to overtake a bus. He didn't, Thompson thought, seem too happy.

Two minutes later Palmer turned into the driveway of a small modern house and stopped. They both got out of the car and went indoors.

As Andrew took off his coat, he looked round with pleasure. He liked this house. Not that, on the surface, there was anything really special about it. On the contrary, there were thousands outwardly similar. Furniture and décor were all quietly conventional.

Yet there was *something* that made this house different – though it was difficult to put your finger on anything in particular. It may have been the way the furniture was arranged; or certain unexpected combinations of colour; or a slight, almost indiscernible originality in the choice or positioning of a lamp, a picture, or a clock.

But it went deeper than that. There was a warmth about the place that was quite indefinable. And Andrew knew that it could only be explained in the personality of one individual.

The door to the kitchen opened and Jill Palmer came into the hall. Andrew was conscious of his usual stab of pleasure on seeing her. He thought: it was quite unintentional. She didn't set out to create any special effect. She had a free hand and she just followed her own inclinations. Perhaps she doesn't even think there is anything special about it.

Jill went up to Bob and kissed him. 'Hi. Hard day?'

'Routine. You?'

'Uh-huh.'

Jill Palmer was an American from Wisconsin. She was twenty-eight, small and slim, auburn-haired, hazel-eyed and softly spoken. Her father was a colonel in the United States Air Force who, seven years previously, had been commanding a base in England. Jill had been spending the summer with her parents after majoring at college. Bob, then a detective-constable, had visited the base in connection with some petty crime. Twelve months later he'd married the C.O.'s daughter. Colonel and Mrs Orville Forbes had returned to the States a year after that. Jill had settled down as the wife of an overworked English police officer. There had been no children.

Jill turned to Andrew. 'Hi, Andy. Good to see you. How are you?'

She really means it, thought Andrew. She *is* glad to see me. And she really does want to know how I am. You always feel that with Jill.

'Hullo, yank,' he said. 'You're looking more beautiful than ever.'

'Don't be silly, Andy.'

'Silly? Is it silly to praise the beauty of a lovely woman? Was Shakespeare silly? Was . . .'

'It's silly if it's completely untrue.'

'Who says it's untrue?'

'I do.'

'How dare you insult my best friend's wife?'

'I practise a lot. Now go get yourself a drink.'

Andrew followed Bob into the sitting-room and poured him-

11

self a whisky and soda from bottles he sometimes thought were kept exclusively for his use.

Bob was deep in a chair, an unopened newspaper on his lap and a faraway look in his eyes. Andrew sat down opposite him.

Bob said: 'You know, I've been thinking about that Hemmings business . . .'

'Stuff it, Bob.'

'Oh. Sorry.'

'Give it a rest sometimes. Forget the job.' He put down his glass and leaned forward. 'You know what's the trouble with you? You and Jill?'

'You're going to tell me, aren't you?'

'I am. You are getting dull. Both of you. You're ageing before your time. You work all day, then you come home, eat, sit in a chair, watch the box, Jill reads, then it's bed and the same thing all over. You need some variety.'

'I get enough variety at work, thanks.'

'But what about Jill? Stuck in the back rooms of that poky little reference library every morning, housework every afternoon, and this room every evening.'

'Oh, Jill's quite happy.'

'But she ought to see more people. When did you last take her to a night-club? When did you last go to a party? And you get asked to plenty.'

'She doesn't like night-clubs or parties. I've told you before.'

'I know you have. But I've never believed you. She's just being self-sacrificing because you're such a moribund slob.'

'All right: ask her.'

'O.K.'

He got up and strolled out to the kitchen.

Jill looked at him quizzically as he came in and perched on the edge of the table. 'Now what?'

'A straight answer to a straight question.'

'Oh, Andy, I'm in the middle of getting a meal.' She gestured helplessly round the kitchen.

'Carry on. I like watching you. Just listen and then answer me truthfully.' He repeated what he had said to Bob and put his question.

She stopped what she was doing and looked at him. 'I ap-

12

preciate it, Andy, I really do. But you're wrong, honestly. I'm perfectly happy. I've never been much of a one for night life. Don't worry about me.'

'But I do. You seem so much alone always. I mean all your folks are three thousand miles away, and you don't seem to make friends very easily, and you hardly see anybody in your job. You don't even belong to any clubs or things.'

'I don't like clubs – night, tennis, country or anything else. I don't like suburban social life any more than the West End variety.'

'You get on with English people all right, don't you?'

'Not really.'

His eyebrows went up. She laughed. 'But quite as well as I do with Americans. It's just that I don't like people much *en masse*. I don't care to be forced into the company of people I've nothing in common with. So my job suits me fine. Besides, I like books. I'd hate to do the sort of job you and Bob do.'

Andrew stared at her silently for a moment, then smiled and shrugged. 'So be it. You know what you want best, I suppose. In future I'll keep my big mouth shut.'

'Don't. Say what you feel always. I'll never mind. But we're both quite content. Good thing, really. We couldn't afford much social life, we're saving up so madly.'

'Oh – for that trip to the States next year? It is on, then?'

'Well, things look fairly hopeful at present, but it's going to be a struggle. Bob's so silly, really. He's determined we pay every cent ourselves. And my father's begging to help out.'

'You're looking forward to it?' he asked quietly.

She nodded, her eyes bright. 'There are so many places I want to show Bob, and folk I want him to meet. And of course I haven't seen my parents in five years.'

'Have they never thought of coming back to see you?'

'Heaps of times. But something's always come up at the last minute to stop them. Now,' she added more briskly, 'if you want a home-cooked dinner tonight get out of my kitchen.'

Andrew went back to the sitting-room. Bob raised his eyebrows.

'You win. Sorry.'

'I thought like you for a long time,' Bob said. 'For quite a while after we were married I used to come home dead beat and pretend I was really keen to go out again. At last it sunk in that she genuinely wasn't interested. I still get worried about her sometimes. I know she gave up a lot to marry me – material things as well as her family. But I can't make it up by giving her things she doesn't want. Only do my darndest to see she gets what she does want.'

'The American trip? She was just telling me about that. Think you'll be able to make it?'

'We'll make it. That's one thing I'm determined about. I owe Jill that trip.'

Andrew looked amused. 'Owe? See it as a debt, do you?'

Bob didn't smile. 'Yes. A debt. That's exactly what it is.'

The next day Palmer had a telephone call from Gordon Hemmings. The M.P. sounded quite excited. 'I've heard from him, Inspector. He obviously doesn't know about my seeing you.'

'And where do you have to leave the money, sir?'

'Up a tree on Hampstead Heath.'

Palmer blinked. 'Did you say up a tree?'

'Well, in a hole about seven feet from the ground. He explained very carefully which tree.'

'Tell me, sir, will you?' He listened for a minute or so, writing rapidly. Then he said: 'Right, sir, then I think we'd better play along with him. Would you be prepared to make up a convincing parcel and carry out his instructions to the letter?'

'Why, certainly. Er – not real money?'

'It's hardly necessary in this case. Sometimes a villain will say money has to be left in a place where it's conceivable an innocent person could find it by chance. Then it can be advisable to put actual cash and give the blackmailer a chance to take it away and hang on to it for a short time. Then at the very least you can get him for theft. But if we can pick this bloke up immediately he collects, he won't have a prayer. I'd rather like to hear him try to explain why he was poking his hand into a hole in a tree on Hampstead Heath.'

Just seventy-two hours later a rather disgruntled Palmer was again on the telephone to the M.P.

'I'm sorry, sir. Something went wrong.'

'What do you mean?' Hemmings asked sharply.

'He didn't show up. The parcel's been where you left it for three nights and two full days.'

'I see.' Hemmings seemed relieved – perhaps because what had gone wrong was no worse than this. 'Do you think perhaps he saw your men?'

'I'm quite sure he didn't, sir.'

'He might come yet, though, might he not?'

'Doubtful, sir. Well give it another twenty-four hours, then we'll call it a day. I'd like you to collect the parcel, if you'd be so kind – just in case he's ultra cautious and is still watching. Then if he sees you remove it he's sure to get in touch with you again. You can explain that you just went along to make sure he had collected it and that when you found it still there you assumed he'd given up. Offer to put it back immediately and ring me straight away.'

The next day Hemmings collected the parcel. Palmer got on with other work. He telephoned Hemmings two days after that, but the M.P. had heard nothing.

'Why do you think he backed out, Inspector?'

'I don't know, sir. I admit I expected him to go through with it after I heard he'd made the second 'phone call to you. Probably he was a first-timer and just got cold feet.'

'So I may hear nothing else from him?'

'Impossible to say, sir. It's a chance. Anyway, there's nothing more I can do now, I'm afraid, unless you can think of anything else you didn't tell me before – or let me have those photos. You said you might reconsider your position if all else failed.'

There was silence for a few seconds before Hemmings said: 'I don't think so. I feel I've done my bit. There's no call to carry public-spiritedness to extreme lengths and as long as my friend and I are reasonably safe from embarrassment, I think I'll let sleeping dogs lie.'

Palmer rang off. So that seemed to be that.

2

THE PERSON WHO BLACKMAILED MR. GORDON HEMMINGS, M.P. WAS JOHNNY JAMES.

The words had been written on a piece of cheap white paper with a black ball-point pen, in very square block capitals.

Palmer's eyebrows went up. 'Who was this sent to?'

The young constable who had brought the anonymous letter to him said: 'The Assistant Commissioner, sir. He passed it on to Mr Phillips. *He* said you were to see it before it goes to finger-prints and handwriting. And Mr Phillips would like to see you in half an hour, sir.'

Palmer stared at the letter for another ten seconds, then, being careful not to touch it, he closed the folder in which it reposed and handed it back to the constable, who left the room.

Palmer sent to the Criminal Records Office for the file on Johnny James and when it came studied it carefully for fifteen minutes. Then he went to see Detective-Chief Superintendent Phillips.

'What are you going to do about it?' Phillips asked.

'It gives us grounds for questioning James, I think, sir. He fits the pattern – two previous convictions for blackmail. Each time he'd got hold of information about an illicit love affair. Once he asked for three-fifty, once for four hundred – so he's not too greedy. He made all his demands by 'phone and his instructions for handing over the money were very similar to those Mr Hemmings received.'

'Why didn't you question him before? C.R.O. gave you his name, didn't they?'

'Yes, sir, but they gave me several other names as well, all of whom have used the same m.o. – as seven out of ten black-mailers do.'

'I read your report on the case. Been meaning to speak to you about it. Bit of a foul-up, wasn't it?'

'I'm afraid so, sir.'

'You didn't suggest to Mr Hemmings that we tapped his incoming 'phone calls?'

'No, sir.'

'But a recording of a man's voice could have been crucial.'

'Yes, sir.'

'You didn't see if he recognised the faces of any of those men C.R.O. gave you in the rogues' gallery?'

'I'm afraid not, sir.'

Phillips puffed at his pipe for a few seconds. Then: 'Made a bit of a hash of things, didn't you, Palmer?'

'In a way, sir, yes.'

'What do you mean – "in a way"? The elementary things you ought to have done. Things you've done as a matter of course in other cases.'

'Yes, sir, I know, but – well, to take the second point first. None of those men were strictly suspects – just villains who had pulled this sort of stunt before. We didn't have a scrap of evidence against any of them. Secondly it didn't look as if it would be necessary – I thought we'd pick up the bloke when he went to collect the parcel. Then that fell through and Mr Hemmings didn't seem very interested in carrying on with the complaint. Quite frankly, sir, he wasn't very co-operative at all – not from the start.'

He explained about Hemmings' reluctance to give information, and then went on: 'It did occur to me to ask if we could tap his 'phone, but he was so unhelpful it seemed like asking a favour and I didn't feel like asking any.'

'That's as may be,' said Phillips, 'but you weren't investigating this case as a personal service for Hemmings. An offence had been committed. It was your duty to do everything in your power to arrest the criminal. You know that, Palmer.'

'Yes, sir. Of course. I'm sorry.'

Phillips gave a grunt and eyed him keenly. 'Not losing interest in the job, are you?'

'No, sir. Definitely not.'

'Because if you are there's no room for you here. Or maybe the pace is too hot for you . . .?'

'It's not that, sir. Far from it.'

'What then?'

17

Palmer drew a deep breath and took the plunge. 'It's just the cases I've been getting.'

'What d'you mean?'

'All this blackmail, sir.'

'But that's supposed to be your speciality, isn't it?'

'I never planned it that way, sir. It just happened. It started with the Clawson affair. I think you considered I handled it quite competently. Then I got that business with the actor fellow. Since then it's snowballed.'

'And you don't like it?'

'Somehow, sir, they all seem so petty.'

'They're all crimes. They've got to be investigated.'

'Of course, sir, and I'm quite happy to do my share. But I've been getting so many of them. I'd just like to spread my wings a bit.'

'Hm.' Phillips re-lit his pipe. Then he asked: 'Well, what about this tip-off? What are you going to do?'

'I thought we might pick up James and ask Mr Hemmings to come along and listen to his voice. Then we'll take it from there.'

'Right. Do that. Keep me posted.'

'Yes, sir.' Palmer stood up.

'And I'll think about what you said, Bob.'

'Thank you, sir.'

Palmer, Gordon Hemmings, and Detective-Constable Gerald Cochran sat in a room at a divisional police station in north London. They were listening to two voices coming through an intercom on the table in front of them. One of the voices was that of a local detective-sergeant. The other was that of Johnny James, who was being questioned about his movements at the time of a recent burglary. Nobody had mentioned blackmail to him yet.

After five minutes of listening, Hemmings leaned back. 'That's enough.'

Cochran switched off the machine.

'Good idea, that,' Hemmings said, pointing to it. 'It flattens the voice – makes it sound more like it would on the telephone.'

'Is it him, sir?'

'Yes. There were one or two phrases there that gave him away.'

'Would you swear to it, sir?'

'Ah, now that's a different matter, isn't it? I mean, I've no real doubt in my own mind but, of course, there could be another voice identical with his. Even if I said yes, you couldn't prosecute on the basis of that alone, though, could you?'

'Not with any real hope of a conviction. We need some evidence. If we could prove that he'd been at the same place at the same time as you and your friend, and had an opportunity of photographing you . . .'

'No. I've made up my mind about that.'

'Then, unless when I question him, he just suddenly confesses, we are not going to be able to nail him. And he won't confess. There's no reason why he should.'

'I don't want to appear to be trying to teach you your job, but have you thought of searching his flat?'

'If there's no other way, sir, we'll try it. But he's too much of a pro to have left anything incriminating lying about. A search will be only a formality.'

No other evidence against James was forthcoming. Palmer questioned him at length, but he flatly denied even having heard of Gordon Hemmings. So as a last resort Palmer obtained a warrant, and he and Cochran went with James to his flat and searched it in his presence.

In a drawer in the living-room they found a folder containing about six different photographs, negatives and prints, of Hemmings and a very attractive blonde girl.

Shortly afterwards James was charged with making unwarranted demands with menaces, contrary to Section 21 of the Theft Act, 1968.

'Of course, they were planted there,' Palmer said later. 'Johnny was as surprised as we were when you took that folder out of the drawer. I'd swear he wasn't acting.'

'You don't mean he was framed?' Cochran said. He was a lanky, dark-haired young man, intelligent and eager to learn. He had worked on several cases with Palmer, who liked him.

'No! Didn't you notice he recognised the folder? He knew what was inside it before you opened it, and more or less caved in there and then. Poor little rat. I felt almost sorry for him.'

'You think he was double-crossed, then, sir?'

'Yes. And I'd bet on a girl. He probably gave her the photos to mind. Then she sent us the tip-off, waited until we picked him up, slipped into his flat and left the folder in the drawer, knowing we'd be bound to make a search. Quite neat, really. Wonder what Johnny did to get her back up.'

'Are you going to look for her, sir?'

'No. Why should I? She helped us. There's no law against sending anonymous letters to the police, provided you tell the truth. I'm grateful to her.'

'I reckon Hemmings can count himself pretty lucky. Hope he remembers all this next time they debate police brutality in the House.'

'He won't be there after the next election. He'll be devoting himself to making money.'

'I'm not surprised if he's going to have to keep that bird in the photos. A dish, but a very expensive one, I'd say.'

'Do you speak from personal experience, Gerry?'

'Oh no, sir. Just a guess. She wouldn't really be my type.' But he sounded a little regretful, nonetheless.

'It was strange about that James tip-off,' said Palmer.

'Too professional, you mean?' said Phillips.

'Exactly, sir. I've been looking at the reports. She – if it was a girl – used a Bic fine-point, which is probably the most widely-used ball pen in the country. The paper was a type sold in thousands of stationers. Now that's obvious enough. The writing was all in very square block capitals, if you remember – again an elementary precaution. But Handwriting say it's completely characterless: all straight lines and all of them exactly the same length – five-sixteenths of an inch; uniform pressure was exerted all the time; and the pen seems to have been held perpendicularly. They say it's almost certain some sort of mechanical aid was used.'

'Interesting.'

'Add to that the fact that the paper was quite clean and not only free from prints but also from any traces of sweat, and that the envelope was sealed and the stamp moistened with tap water – not licked – and taken all in all you get a picture of someone very careful indeed – and pretty knowledgeable about the sort of things we can find out from a letter. Somehow I wouldn't have expected any girl friend of Johnny James to have shown so much finesse. Anyway, why should she care so much about not being traced? She must know we wouldn't give her away to Johnny – even if he doesn't know quite well already who was responsible.'

'Doesn't have to have been a *girl*, does it?'

'Oh no, sir. Johnny may have had a male accomplice – a pro who knows all the ropes and who had a grudge against him for some reason. But if that's the case why doesn't Johnny shop him in return? He must realise by now he's going back inside. So why doesn't he at least give himself the satisfaction of getting back at the other bloke? Apparently he always talked the other times – once he saw the position was hopeless.'

'Give him a chance. Perhaps he's making up his mind to do that right now.'

But James didn't change his defence. He was found guilty and sentenced to three years' imprisonment.

Palmer didn't like loose ends. But he had to accept some in this case. He was too busy to do anything else. He'd been assigned to some enquiries that had nothing to do with black-mail.

Harry Edwards was feeling very pleased with himself as he went into the pub. He ordered a double Scotch to celebrate and stood at the bar quietly sipping it, as he went over in his mind the recent conversation. There was a smug curve to his thin lips.

He'd told 'em. They knew now they couldn't push Harry Edwards around. Bloody cheek. What was it the bloke had said? 'Stay away from him, Edwards – for your own good. He's our property.' *Our* property! What a nerve! He'd got hold of this dirt just as soon as they had. He'd got just as much right to put the squeeze on. Besides, the old guy was loaded. There were plenty of pickings for everybody. But he was going to get his pickings first.

He stayed at the bar for another hour; then, somewhat un-steadily, made his way outside. It was later than he'd thought and already dark. He'd have to get a move on. A short cut. Yes, he'd go along the alley. There wasn't any light, but he knew it well enough.

He felt his first twinge of uneasiness when he heard heavy footsteps behind him. The uneasiness turned to fear when he realised there were two of them. He started to walk faster. The next moment a torch shone straight in his eyes.

'Hullo, Harry,' said a voice from in front of him.

Then they were all around him. He felt a surge of terror. He opened his mouth to shout. But nothing but a gurgle came out because at the same instant a metalled fist crashed into the pit of his stomach. He doubled in agony, only to be grabbed by both arms and forcibly straightened up.

'We've been told to teach you your manners, Harry. We didn't think you were going to make it so easy for us.'

Harry gave an imploring whimper. But it did him no good. Many, many more blows landed before unconsciousness brought blessed oblivion.

'How is he, doctor?'

'He's had an extremely bad beating, Sergeant Miller. He's got multiple bruising and three fractured ribs. There's been internal haemorrhage and he's got severe concussion from that blow on the head. He'll live, but it's the psychological effect of an experience like that which is really lasting. It was a very professional job.'

'He's not conscious, I suppose?'

'Not yet. He might come to any time – or it might take several days.'

'I'll leave a man by him, if that's all right with you.'

'As you wish, sergeant.'

'Has he said anything, Coles?'

'Nothing really coherent, sarge. He's been delirious – just rambling. I got it all down, I think. But I doubt if it'll be much use to anybody.'

'Good practice for you, anyway. Get it typed out. You never know what might come in useful.'

'I had a talk with Harry Edwards today, sir.'

'Oh yes, Miller. How is he?'

'Physically he's over the worst. They're discharging him in a week or so. But he's a nervous wreck. You remember how cocky he used to be, sir? He's like a ghost now. And absolutely scared stiff.'

'He's not saying anything, I take it?'

'Not a peep.'

'Have you got anything at all to go on?'

'Afraid not, sir. There's just no lead of any kind.'

'So there's not much more we can do, is there? Oh, well, if he's in such a bad state it means one more pest out of our hair, I suppose.'

'I'd rather not have got rid of him this way, sir. It was about the worst beating there's ever been on this patch. Even Harry Edwards didn't deserve a going over like that.'

Bob Palmer happened to hear about Harry Edwards. He remembered that Edwards had been one of those considered as possible suspects in the Hemmings case; and the unexplained elements in that affair were still nagging at the back of his mind. Although no connection between the two men were known, it occurred to Palmer that Edwards might have been the accomplice who betrayed James, and that James himself, now in prison, had arranged to have Edwards done over. If James had been planning this revenge ever since his own arrest, it would explain his refusal to involve Edwards. In such a set-up he naturally wouldn't want his connection with Edwards known to the police.

The weakness of the theory was that Palmer could not conceive of James, an unpopular little man even in his own circles, having friends willing to do such a job for him; or being able to afford to pay to have it done. But the only alternative seemed to be that Edwards and James, both known blackmailers, had got themselves enemies at about the same time – enemies powerful, unscrupulous and smart.

Logically, there was no reason for Palmer not to forget all

about it. But like every good detective he had developed a kind of sixth sense for recognising unusual patterns in crime. And for some reason he couldn't let this thing drop.

So he got hold of the notes taken at Edwards' bedside during his delirium. Most of it had been either gibberish or obviously irrelevant. But a few phrases, uttered over a period of several hours, caught Palmer's attention. He extracted them and wrote them down separately.

'Nothing to do with you – between him and me . . . If I can get it from him you can't stop me . . . He can afford it . . . You haven't got any bloody monopoly . . . I can put the squeeze on anybody I like – it's a free country . . . I'm not stopping you trying it on too if you want . . . Plenty of pickings to go around . . . Tell your boss to go to hell.'

Put like that it was coherent and told a story. This beating up had presumably been the boss's reply to being told to go to hell. Palmer put out of his mind the theory of James having been responsible for it, and went on to another tack.

Edwards had been putting the black on somebody whom another blackmailer already considered his property. Edwards had been warned off, had refused to take any notice, and had been punished. This other blackmailer had to be a professional and in the business on a pretty big scale. Suppose he'd also had his eyes on Gordon Hemmings – but Johnny James had got in first? That could explain who had framed James. He was a man who didn't like being crossed. And Johnny might know who he was but be genuinely scared to talk. Palmer thought of the mechanical aid used in the tip-off letter. It suggested a crook who took his blackmail very seriously indeed.

Yet the whole hypothesis seemed quite to change the nature of the crime as Palmer had known it. It would mean that a big-time professional criminal had moved in and was starting to get it organised. One such man would mean others. Blackmail would no longer be 'an amateur's crime or a sideline for a pro'.

Palmer had little real evidence to support this suspicion. But he kept his eyes and ears open nevertheless.

3

It was two weeks later that Joshua Kendall and his wife were arrested in Spain.

Kendall was one of the country's best-known businessmen. A bluff, outspoken character, he was famous for his take-over bids and his pithy, highly quotable comments on virtually every public issue. He had risen from comparative obscurity in about seven years until he was the controlling power behind scores of companies, and a millionaire several times over.

Then a batch of documents, accompanied by a short anonymous note, had been received at the office of the Director of Public Prosecutions. They were mostly photo-copies of letters to and from Kendall and of various contracts, share transfers, proofs of cash payments or receipts, and the like. They were examined closely by lawyers and accountants, and it seemed that if they were genuine Kendall might well be guilty of embezzlement on a huge scale. Detectives from the Fraud Squad were sent to interview him. But he and his wife had disappeared.

A week of intensive investigations into the affairs of the Kendall Group followed. And it was proved that the photocopies were genuine. A warrant was issued for Kendall's arrest. Shortly afterwards he and his wife were discovered by the Spanish police, living in a small village in the Pyrenees. Extradition proceedings were started, and eventually the Kendalls were flown back to Britain, where Kendall was charged with embezzlement. After consideration, no charges were made against his wife.

The affair shook the City, made the front page of every newspaper, and provided Bob Palmer with the next link in his chain.

Palmer was not personally involved in the case, but his interest was aroused when he heard about the nature and contents of the letter sent to the D.P.P. This was conventional of its kind, as it was made up of letters cut from newspapers. It read:

THE ENCLOSED DOCUMENTS PROVE CONCLUSIVELY THAT MR. JOSHUA KENDALL HAS, FOR SOME YEARS, BEEN ENGAGED IN THE MIS-APPROPRIATION OF COMPANY FUNDS.

Palmer managed to get a look at the letter and at the reports on it. A strange feeling of excitement gripped him and he immediately sought an interview with Phillips.

First, Palmer briefly explained his feeling about the James and Edwards cases and the possible existence of a professional blackmailing ring. Then he said: 'Now, sir, I know there are differences, but I'm convinced that this Kendall tip-off letter came from the same source as the James one.'

Phillips raised his eyebrows. 'Why?'

'It's the wording and the punctuation, sir.' He produced copies of both letters. 'Look, sir. Take the general style first. In each instance it's very formal and needlessly involved. The word *person* in the first one, *conclusively* and *misappropriation* in the other; *Mr.* Gordon Hemmings, *M.P.*; *Mr.* Joshua Kendall. The *M.P.* was quite superfluous and so were both the *Mr.'s*. Then there's the punctuation. I've never seen anonymous letters like it: there's not one point left out – commas between *Hemmings* and *M.P.*, after *has* and *years* in the second one; full stops at the end in both, after the *r*'s in both *Mr.'s* and after *M* and *P*. In the Kendall letter he's had to clip out all these marks and stick them on separately. I just can't believe there'd be two people to write an anonymous letter like that.'

Phillips was silent for some seconds. He said: 'And what's it mean?'

'I think it's just an idiosyncrasy on the part of the writer. Perhaps he's not even conscious of it being unusual. It's only significant insofar as it indicates a common source.'

'So – what do you want from me?'

'First of all I'd like to speak to Kendall and ask him straight out about blackmail.'

'He's sure to want his solicitor present.'

'So much the better, sir. If I'm right, *and* if he hasn't told his solicitor about it, then the solicitor will see that it could do Kendall some good to reveal it – gain him a bit of sympathy. If I can't persuade him to say anything then perhaps his lawyer will.'

'Very well. And if nothing comes of it – what then?'

'I'd just like permission to nose around a bit and see what I can pick up.'

Philips smiled. 'And the other day you were telling me you didn't want to be put on any more blackmail cases.'

'Let's say I withdraw that, sir.'

'Very well. You'll need help. Any preference?'

'D. C. Cochran, I think, if he's free.'

'Rather young, isn't he? I was going to let you have a sergeant, you know.'

'Thank you, sir, but I'll stick to Cochran, if I may. He's a bit green but he's going to be good.'

'As you wish.' Phillips made a note. 'I'll try to keep you free from other assignments for a while. Keep me posted.'

Joshua Kendall was a big, red-faced, ungainly man of about forty-five, looking more like a farmer than a financier. He was slumped in his chair and he didn't look up as Palmer and Cochran were shown in by a warder. Kendall's lawyer, a shortish, fat, sleek man called Cadwallader, did all the talking at first. 'Inspector Palmer, I must state at the outset that Mr Kendall has said all he intends to say to the police, as I have already informed numerous of your colleagues. He's completely innocent of these charges, as will be made abundantly clear at his trial.'

'I'm quite prepared at this stage to accept that these charges may be unfounded,' Palmer said mendaciously.

Kendall looked up at him sharply but said nothing.

Palmer went on: 'I know very little about these charges. The case does not concern me personally. I am primarily investigating an entirely different matter. But I think it may have an indirect bearing on Mr Kendall's case. And if I'm right it could in fact help Mr Kendall. I simply wish to ask him one question.'

Cadwallader and Kendall exchanged a quick glance. Then Kendall spoke for the first time. 'Ask it,' he said.

Palmer leaned forward. 'Mr Kendall, who is it who's been blackmailing you?'

The expression on Kendall's face did not change. His eyes flickered slightly but that might have been just surprise. He said: 'Nobody's been blackmailing me.'

Palmer looked at him for another few seconds. Then with a

27

slight sigh he straightened up. Twelve years' experience told him it would be a waste of time to press the question.

Cadwallader said: 'Really, Inspector, I cannot imagine what grounds you have for believing that my client could be susceptible to blackmail. The idea is absurd.'

Palmer looked at him closely. 'There I must differ from you, Mr Cadwallader. I have no doubt at all that Mr Kendall has been the victim of a blackmailer. And he's not the only prominent person to have found himself in that position recently. I recommend, sir, that you urge your client to tell the truth about this. A blackmail victim invariably receives a great deal of sympathy. However unfounded the charges he faces, sympathy is always a valuable commodity.'

He turned to Kendall again. 'If you change your mind, sir, you know where to find me.'

Outside, Palmer asked: 'Well, what do you make of that?'

'You're quite sure he was lying, sir?'

Palmer nodded. 'But why I don't know. Let's go and see Mrs Kendall.'

The Kendalls' town home was a penthouse suite in a new luxury apartment block. Palmer and Cochran were admitted by a plump, nervous-looking *au pair* girl and shown into a small reception-room.

'Tell Mrs Kendall,' Palmer said, 'that we have not come about the same matter as the other policemen, but that I think I may be able to help both Mr and Mrs Kendall. Do you understand?'

The girl nodded slowly and went out.

Marion Kendall entered the room about a minute later. She was a dark, gaunt woman with a haggard expression. Palmer introduced himself, but she hardly waited for him to finish. 'You said you've come about some other business but you may be able to help us? How? I don't understand.'

Palmer said gently: 'It's just this, Mrs Kendall. I am engaged in enquiries into the large-scale blackmail that has been going on recently. I'd like you to tell me everything you can about the attempts at extortion that have been made against your husband.'

Her eyes widened. She opened her mouth. 'You – you know about . . .' She stuttered to a stop.

Palmer's heart beat a little faster. It was almost an admission. Now he had to tread carefully. 'I don't know enough yet, Mrs Kendall – not enough to make an arrest with any hope of getting a conviction. These people are very clever and very careful – as you know. I need all the help I can get if I'm going to nail them.'

Her eyes were fixed on his. Palmer sensed that the words hovering on her lips were, What do you want to know? Then the moment passed. Instead she said: 'I don't think there's anything I can say.'

'Mrs Kendall, anyone who has been the victim of a blackmailer always receives a lot of sympathy. If it were known that you and your husband had been facing this kind of stress – well, it could only do you good.'

'Have you seen my husband?'

Again picking his words carefully, Palmer answered: 'I got permission yesterday to speak to him today.'

'Then he'll have to tell you anything he wants to. If he wishes me to confirm or add anything I will. But I'll have to speak to him or Mr Cadwallader first.'

'Mr Cadwallader knows all about it?' Palmer asked casually.

'I don't know. He knew nothing before the – the arrest. I don't know how much Josh has told him since.'

Palmer said: 'I appreciate you point of view, Mrs Kendall, but it just occurs to me that your husband might try to keep some things quiet in order to save you from what he'd possibly think would be distressing for you – police enquiries, facing the press, eventually having to give evidence against these villains. Now, if I can go to him and tell him that I've already had certain facts from you, that you have already involved yourself in helping me, then he might be much more inclined to talk freely. And that can only be for his good.'

For a moment the issue again hung in the balance. Palmer watched her face intently. Then it was as if a shutter swung down, and Palmer knew he'd lost.

'I'm sorry. I really must talk to my husband first.'

In the lift, Cochran said: 'Bad luck, sir.'

'Yes. We came very close. It wasn't a waste of time, though.

We now know definitely that Kendall was being blackmailed. And even if she had told us all she knew it's on the cards we wouldn't be much forrader. These villains are no fools. I doubt if they'd have informed on the Kendalls if either of them had known anything really incriminating.'

They went back to Scotland Yard. On the way, Palmer said: 'I shall probably be hauled over the coals for what I've done to-day. My behaviour has been a little unethical, to say the least.'

'You mean not telling her that you'd already seen Kendall?'

'Not only that but actually implying I hadn't seen him, and trying to trick her into saying something I knew Kendall didn't want her to say. Quite apart from interviewing her without permission when her husband's already been charged with an offence being investigated by another squad.'

'Still, as you said, it would be to the Kendalls' own good, wouldn't it?'

'Indirectly. If it came out at the trial it would probably help him with the jury. Though heaven knows why. The swindle seems to have been going on for a long time – well before the blackmailing started, I should think. There's no evidence he was driven into it by the blackmail.'

'Mustn't the blackmailer be somebody pretty close to Kendall, sir? I mean to know about his activities?'

'Not necessarily. But it would seem that somebody close to him must have given the blackmailer the tip-off. But let's ask the Fraud Squad people what they think.'

Detective-Superintendent Youngman of the Fraud Squad was in charge of the Kendall case. It was immensely complicated, but he somewhat grudgingly gave Palmer a few minutes. He said: 'I know nothing about any blackmail and quite honestly, Palmer, I'm not really very interested. Naturally we wanted to know who the information had come from, and clearly, to have had access to all those documents, it had to be somebody high up in the Kendall organisation, probably somebody with financial training. Whether this chap passed the information straight to us, or to some third person who sent them, isn't really relevant to my enquiries. I doubt if anybody could have added anything useful to what was in the documents.'

'So you want to find him if it's not too much trouble, but aren't desperate, is that it, sir?'

'Not want – wanted.'

Palmer stared. 'You've found him already?'

'Found out who he *was*. He's dead. Heart attack the day Kendall was arrested.'

'Blast.'

'Yes, I know, very inconsiderate of him.'

'Who was he, sir?'

'Name of Wetherby. Elderly chap. Been with Kendall Holdings, the controlling company, for donkey's years. An accountant. Was retiring in less than a fortnight. Gave four weeks' notice at the end of last month.'

'May I ask how you got on to him, sir?'

'From Kendall himself. He says only Wetherby could have had access to all those papers. We've checked as far as possible and that seems to be true. Kendall was itching to tell us. His claim is that he's been framed by Wetherby, that Wetherby himself was the crook.'

'Any evidence to support that, sir?'

'None whatsoever. But none to disprove it either. Of course, we don't believe a word of it. Everything suggests Wetherby was straight. But now he's dead it's a damn good defence for Kendall. It's going to take some shaking.'

'Did Wetherby have any family?'

'A wife.'

'Would you have any objection to my seeing her?'

'Be my guest. I've finished with her.'

Mrs Wetherby was a faded, wispy woman in her sixties. She displayed all the conventional signs of grief, being dressed in black and frequently dabbing at her eyes with the corner of a handkerchief. Palmer found it difficult to decide how deep was her actual sense of loss.

She said: 'I'm sure I can't tell you any more than I told Superintendent Youngman. I knew nothing about my husband's work. But I *know* Percy wasn't involved in anything questionable. He couldn't have been. He was the most honest of men. He'd even take back a sixpence to Woolworths if he was given too much change, which I think is silly, don't you?'

'It's not really his business affairs I'm interested in, Mrs

Wetherby,' Palmer told her, 'but his private life.'

Mrs Wetherby looked blank. 'What do you mean?'

'Well – had Mr Wetherby changed in his behaviour recently?'
She considered. 'Yes. I suppose you could say he had, in a
way.'

'In what way, Mrs Wetherby?'

'I fancy he'd been less, how can I put it, less *even*. He'd
always been a very placid sort : he didn't get worked up about
anything – good or bad.'

'And this changed?'

'Well, yes. He seemed more up and down. More irritable –
likely to flare up, but he'd get over it very quickly, and at the
same time he was more considerate – he'd do unexpected things,
bring me presents, almost as though he was trying to say he was
sorry.'

'And how long had this been going on?'

'Oh, I don't really know. Six months, a year perhaps.'

There was a pause. Then Palmer said slowly : 'Forgive me for
saying this, Mrs Wetherby. Please don't take it wrong. But could
it be possible your husband was being blackmailed?'

Mrs Wetherby looked scandalised. 'Oh, certainly not! I mean,
how could he have been? He'd never done anything wrong in
his life.'

'It may have been something quite small – something most
people would not think was wrong at all.'

'Oh no, there was nothing like that. He would have hated the
mere suggestion – and this whole business. He had a horror, always, of being involved with the police or the newspapers or anything like that.'

'Do you think he had any money worries?'

'Oh no!' She was even more shocked. 'He always paid his way.
And he took out a very good insurance policy many years ago,
so he's left me well provided for. If you don't believe me you can
go to our bank – Lloyd's, just down the road.'

Palmer changed the subject. 'Tell me, was his death completely unexpected?'

'Oh, of course. It was a dreadful shock.'

'He'd been quite well always?'

'Well, he did have his first heart attack five years ago. But it
was quite a minor one. And he made a wonderful recovery.

32

The doctor said that as long as he took things fairly easily and avoided worry he could live for many years.'

'And he never had any undue worry that you know of?'

'Well, only politics and the state of the country and students and strikers and things like that. But we all worry about that sort of thing, don't we?'

'Did he have any close friend he might have confided in – I mean if he had a problem he didn't want to worry you with?'

'Oh, I don't think he would tell anyone else his problems.'

'But who were his friends – could you tell me?'

'Well, he didn't have any special friend. Just colleagues, you know, and neighbours and men at the Rotary Club. Not what you'd call *friends*.'

She paused, and Palmer waited, saying nothing. Then she went on : 'There *is* Joe Harding, of course.'

'Who's he?'

'He used to play chess with Percy. Once a week. One week he'd come here and the next week Percy would go there. They'd known each other a long time.'

'Thank you,' said Palmer. 'Perhaps we could have Mr Harding's address and also the name and address of your doctor.'

'Well, all right. But you're wasting your time, you know.'

In the street a few minutes later, Palmer said : 'Three jobs for you . . .'

'I know, sir : the doctor, the bank, Mr Harding.'

'Good. Know what you're looking for?'

'I think so. At the bank, general state of the Wetherbys' account, any unusual fluctuations. At the doctor, any possibility that his death wasn't natural, how bad his heart condition was, and what sort of thing would have been likely to cause the final attack. Also, if he knows of any special worry Wetherby may have had. And this question, too, to Harding, plus a general pumping about what he knows of the Wetherbys.'

'Right. Off you go. I'm going back to the Yard.'

When he got there he was told to report to Phillips. He did so and received the expected dressing-down for his interview with Mrs Kendall. However, Phillips was, if anything, somewhat less severe than he might have been; and Palmer wondered if his chief's annoyance was tinged with relief at finding him once more over-enthusiastic about an investigation.

Phillips then asked about his progress, and Palmer told him what he had found out about Kendall and Wetherby.

Phillips asked: 'Was Wetherby the blackmailer?'

'No, sir.'

'Getting a cut from same?'

'I'd say not.'

'What's your theory, then?'

Palmer hesitated.

'Bit nebulous so far, is it?'

'Say unproven. I'd like to wait . . .'

'Very well. I don't want you to commit yourself before you're ready. Carry on. But try to stick to the rules a bit, will you? Keep me posted.'

Cochran said: 'Nothing much, I'm afraid, sir. The bank account's been perfectly normal for years. No deposits of any size other than Wetherby's salary, and no large withdrawals. The doctor says Wetherby's death was definitely due to natural causes. He didn't have a very strong heart, but the doctor was surprised by his death all the same. He admits that a long period of strain could well have aggravated Wetherby's condition, but he tends to think that a sudden shock on top of that would explain it more satisfactorily. Now there's no doubt that Wetherby was under a strain quite apart from any business worries. The doctor told me in strict confidence that Mrs Wetherby's a very sick woman. He gives her about twelve months at the most. Wetherby was told this a little over a year ago and it shook him rigid. The doctor says that if Wetherby had had an attack then it wouldn't have surprised him, but of course you can never forecast that sort of reaction. Wetherby was absolutely adamant that his wife wasn't to be told about her condition. In fact about seven months ago he went back to the doctor and made him repeat his promise that if Mrs Wetherby ever came to him again for reassurance he'd tell her she was O.K. He said he was frightened that somebody might tell her the truth. So you see, sir . . .' He broke off as he noticed that Palmer had stopped listening. 'Sir . . . ?'

'Sorry, Gerry, but that could be it.'

'I'm sorry, I don't . . .'

'No, you couldn't understand. I've just thought of something. It could explain a lot. Just shut up for a couple of minutes, will you? I want to concentrate.'

Cochran gave a shrug and shut up. Palmer suddenly said: 'I must see Youngman again,' and left the room. He was back after ten minutes. 'Right,' he said, 'what were you going to say?'

'Just that Wetherby's knowledge of his wife's condition would explain his changed behaviour.'

'Would it, though? What exactly was it that Mrs Wetherby said about him – did you get a note?'

Cochran got out his notebook and thumbed through it. 'Here we are, sir. Where do you want me to start?'

'She said something about him being more up and down, I think.'

Cochran scanned the page. 'Oh yes. Quote: "More irritable – likely to flare up, but he'd get over it very quickly, and at the same time he was more considerate – he'd do unexpected things for me, bring me presents".'

'That's it. Gerry, that doesn't fit. The second half, yes. He knows his wife is dying, so he's kinder to her, takes her presents, and so on. That's natural. But not the first part. Not the irritability. He's a repressed sort of man, used to keeping his emotions in check. Now, when he learns about his wife he is not going to start getting irritable with her. He's going to take more care than ever to remain placid – outwardly, at least. The irritability is wrong. Something else was causing that.'

'Perhaps his knowledge of Kendall's fraud.'

'I don't think so. If he was an honest man and not involved in the swindle personally but had just happened to find out about it – and we can only go by what Youngman says, which is that he was *not* involved – then he wouldn't be jumpy or irritable. He'd be more likely to brood, to withdraw into his shell, to puzzle out the best thing to do. Now, he wasn't the type of man ever to want to be involved with the police – even at the best of times. And with his wife dying, he'd obviously be particularly loath to get mixed up in criminal proceedings, having to give evidence, and so on.'

'So,' Cochran broke in, 'when he found out about Kendall's

activities, he sent the D.P.P. an anonymous tip-off. What's wrong with that? I reckon the style of the letter fits a man like Wetherby, too.'

'Good, Gerry, but it just won't do. Remember that the tip-off about Johnny James was written in the same sort of style – and I can't imagine Wetherby being mixed up in that business. Then again, Kendall was able to put his finger on Wetherby as the only possible source of the tip-off about his racket. Now Wetherby must have realised that Kendall would be able to do this. And surely, too, the possibility of Kendall trying to pin the blame on him must have occurred to him. But even if it didn't, he was bound to have known that if the authorities were notified, he would stand out as the informer – and would be up to his neck in enquiries. No – Wetherby would steer clear of the police always. And that would make him particularly vulnerable to blackmail himself.'

'And that's what happened to him, sir?'

'I think so. And I believe I know what led up to it. The trouble is I don't see how I can ever prove it. I know what would be strong corroboratory evidence but it would depend on whether he'd talked about his plans to anybody.' Palmer thought for a few seconds, then said: 'Gerry, I want you to go and see Mrs Wetherby again. If my theory's right, then Wetherby very probably decided to retire once before – something over seven or eight months ago – and then stayed on, after all. Ask Mrs Wetherby – What's the matter?'

Cochran was staring at him unbelievingly. 'But he did, sir. You're quite right. He told Joe Harding about it.'

'Harding! Of course! I'd forgotten all about him. What did he tell you?'

'It was back in February, sir.' He consulted his notebook. 'Luckily for us Harding keeps a diary. Wetherby told him he was giving in his notice at the end of the month. The following week he cancelled their chess game – which was very unusual: he religiously kept them up even at the time he first heard about Mrs Wetherby, so that she wouldn't suspect anything out of the ordinary. The next time they met – March 7th – Harding asked him what the firm's reaction had been. Wetherby told him he'd changed his mind and was staying on.'

'Then I'm right. I must be!' Palmer concentrated fiercely for a moment, then said: 'Hang on. I've thought of a snag. The doctor told you about her in strict confidence; Wetherby himself surely wouldn't tell anyone else. Then how ...'

'He told Harding, sir.'

'He did?'

'Yes, sir. Apparently he let it slip one evening towards the end of last year. I fancy he was angry with himself afterwards. He made Harding promise not to tell anybody. But Harding broke his promise.'

'He told you that?'

'Yes, sir. He insisted. I think he's been feeling guilty about it. He was relieved to tell somebody he could trust. He didn't mention what he knew to any of their friends and certainly not to Mrs Wetherby. But he did let it out to a stranger who got into conversation with him in a pub one night. He didn't tell Wetherby about it. They were great buddies and Wetherby trusted him implicitly, apparently.'

Palmer wore an expression of satisfaction. 'Then that's it. No loopholes.'

'I'm afraid I don't understand any of this, sir.'

'I'm sorry, Gerry. I know I haven't been very coherent. What I think happened was that some time – probably towards the end of last year – Wetherby found out about Kendall's racket. Then, as I said before, I think he worried over it – perhaps for a couple of months. He wouldn't go to the police. What he did decide to do was to get himself clean out of the affair altogether by retiring.'

'And he told Harding.'

'Yes, but just after that our friends got hold of him. I think there must have been rumours in certain circles that Kendall was on the fiddle. Youngman's just told me, in fact, that they had heard the merest whispers that all wasn't quite well before the D.P.P. ever got those documents in the post. I think the rumour was picked up by the outfit that framed James and beat up Edwards. And they decided Kendall was ripe for plucking. But they couldn't prove anything against him. So they looked round for someone to provide the proof – and alighted on Percy Wetherby. Percy was contacted and the pressure was applied to make him stay on at work and supply them with the documentary evidence they needed. The dates on the papers sent to the

D.P.P. covered a period of about seven months, the earliest February 28th – the date, remember, that Wetherby cancelled his chess appointment. From then until about the end of last month he supplied the – the organisation we'd better call it – with the stuff they needed. That was the period of his irritability. At last they had all they wanted. Wetherby's job was over. He was free to give his notice to Kendall Holdings. The organisation went to Kendall with their demands. Kendall refused to pay up. We know what happened. It all ended with Kendall arrested. And then, of course, Wetherby saw it all coming out, including his part in it. And coming on top of everything else, the shock killed him.'

'It all fits. But it's pure supposition, isn't it, sir?'

'I'd prefer to call it deduction. But answer me this – and bear in mind that the James and Kendall letters almost certainly came from the same source – does any other explanation fit the known facts better?'

'No, sir, not that I can think of. But there are objections. For instance, what sort of pressure could they have brought against Wetherby? According to your reconstruction he hadn't been guilty of anything when they approached him first – except perhaps not reporting Kendall, and I doubt if anybody could prove that he'd known about it. I can't see what hold they had on him. Or do you know of some guilty secret he had? It seems very unlikely from what we know of him.'

'No, nothing like that. But think. There was something that Wetherby wanted desperately to keep from a particular person, something that he'd foolishly let out to Harding, who in turn talked about it to a stranger in a pub.'

Understanding dawned in Cochran's eyes. 'Mrs Wetherby. They threatened to tell her she was dying . . .'

'Well, that would be my guess. It's an unpleasant idea, but horribly plausible. It came to me when you told me about Wetherby's return visit to the doctor. He believed somebody might tell his wife the truth. That must have been shortly after he was first approached by the organisation. He wouldn't have been worrying about Harding telling, and he'd have hardly talked about it to anybody else. So why should he fear somebody telling her – unless he'd received a specific threat?'

Cochran didn't answer. Palmer crossed to the window and

looked out over London. 'You know, I've never got angry about a case of blackmail before. But I'm getting very angry about this one. An innocent person has been blackmailed. In my experience that's something quite new. And very nasty.'

'Stuck, are you?' Thompson asked sympathetically. He and Palmer were drinking coffee in the canteen.

'I just don't know what I'm looking for, Andy. There's not much point in going back into old records. If the cases weren't cleared up the trail's now cold. Besides, I know of virtually all the more important cases we've handled over the last few years.'

'None of them strike a chord?'

'One of them. A psychiatrist called Woolf had an affair with a married woman patient. He was fool enough to send her some absolutely unambiguous letters.'

'Which somebody got hold of?'

'Exactly. But he wasn't asked for money. They agreed to return the letters if he'd give them some information about one of his big-wig patients.'

'Very much like Kendall and your – what's-his-name? – Wetherby.'

Palmer gave a nod. 'The two-tier system Cochran calls it: Blackmail "A" into giving you information to enable you to blackmail "B". I was a bit slow to see the connection, actually.'

'What happened?'

'Woolf said no. So they sent the letters to the General Medical Council. Eventually he was struck off. He came and told us the whole story. We couldn't do much. Firstly, he'd been approached on the 'phone and didn't know the voice. Secondly, he wouldn't tell us the name of the big-wig patient – which would have enabled us to check with him to see if he *had* been blackmailed after all. And thirdly, he wouldn't tell us who his girl friend was, so we couldn't even question her. We couldn't force Woolf to tell us – he hadn't committed any crime. So that was more or less all there was to it.'

'And that's the only case you can tie in?'

'So far. You see, for anything to be on record the victim must have stood up to them: either come to us like Woolf; or defied them and been exposed in some crime, like Kendall. And if the victims are carefully chosen and not squeezed too hard not many of them are going to make a stand. So unless the villains blunder, we just don't get to hear about it.'

He drained his cup and went on gloomily: 'What I've got to do is locate people who are obviously afraid of us or they couldn't have had the black put on them in the first place.'

'And you've no ideas at all about how to start?'

'Not really.' Palmer stood up. He gave a sudden, unexpected grin. 'I think for a start I'll ask Jill what she'd do.'

Jill stroked her jaw slowly. 'Well, I guess if I was being black-mailed and I couldn't meet the demands there'd be only one thing to do – short of suicide or murder.'

'What's that?'

'Own up.'

'But if you'd broken the law?'

'It might still be the easiest thing to do. Confess before the blackmailer has a chance to report you. That way you'd get off more lightly. I mean, say you're a big financier and you've made phoney tax returns. If you're blackmailed the best thing you could do would be to go straight to the tax people and admit what you've done. Say your conscience had been bugging you, and offer to pay off what you owe in instalments. They're not so likely to prosecute as if you're found out. Or suppose I'm the wife of a rich and jealous husband. I've been playing around on the side, but I don't want to be divorced. My safest bet if any-body started to blackmail me would be to go straight to my husband, tell him tearfully about my affair, and swear it was all over. There'd be at least a chance he'd forgive me.'

'It wouldn't be easy.'

'Nothing would be easy. But I guess it would be the lesser of evils. Appear to repent and you get some sympathy. Be exposed by somebody else and you get none.'

Bob said thoughtfully: 'So I should search for confessions – surprising and apparently unforced confessions – by wealthy or strategically-placed people.'

'Yes, that – and suicides. I mean, there'd be people who couldn't stand up to it at all – they'd just cave in.'

'Suicides of wealthy people – or those likely to know the

secrets of wealthy people. And confessions of old crimes from ditto.'

'It's got to be actual *crimes*?'

'Not exclusively. But it's my best bet. You see, a blackmail victim who's stayed inside the law can usually in the last resort come to us. But if he's being blackmailed by someone who knows he's actually committed a crime, he's in a much stickier position. Now I fancy that to these professionals men and women who are scared of the police are going to be by far the most appealing targets. Besides, confessions of anything else but crimes simply aren't likely to be on record. Take your erring wife: whatever happened in the end, the police wouldn't be involved.'

'Yes, but you could watch out for that sort of thing as regards the suicides. There are some people still vulnerable – even in these permissive days.'

'You mean doctors, politicians, people like that?'

'Or clergymen. I can imagine one of them killing himself to avoid disgrace.'

'Good lord!' Bob sat up suddenly. 'You mean that Catholic priest?'

'*I* don't mean anybody. You're the detective.'

'About six months ago. What was his name?'

'Dooney.'

'That's it. In Brighton. Took an overdose of sleeping pills. Coroner's jury brought in an open verdict. There was a lot of talk . . .'

He fell silent, thinking. Jill smiled. Bob wouldn't consult her again. She probably wouldn't hear another word about his enquiries until they were over. She had played her part.

41

4

The next day Palmer and Cochran began doing some research along the lines suggested by Jill. It was a tedious task and they started off along many false trails. But after about a week's work, including study of police records, old newspapers, court transcripts, and interviews with various colleagues, they had compiled a slim dossier of just four cases which Palmer thought worthy of further investigation.

Geoffrey Hurndall was the owner of a prosperous precision-engineering firm about twenty miles from London. Five months before Palmer began his investigations, Hurndall had walked into his local police station and confessed that eighteen months previously he had run over and seriously injured a child and had driven on without stopping. He had said that the matter had been preying on his mind ever since, and that he had decided to make a clean breast of it. He had been summonsed, tried, banned from driving for five years, given a stiff fine and a suspended two-year jail sentence.

Palmer said : 'We must have a talk with Mr Hurndall.' He rang up and fixed an appointment.

Hurndall received them in his office, a room which seem designed more for show than work. It was unnaturally tidy, with a thick grey carpet and pseudo-oak panelling. Around the walls were dotted a number of glass cases containing the small aircraft components which were the company's chief products.

Hurndall himself was a large man of about fifty, with bushy eyebrows, a moustache, and a forceful, aggressive manner. His dress and hairstyle showed a somewhat unsuccessful attempt at trendiness, and he had a pronounced London accent.

'Inspector Palmer? Constable Cochran? I can give you twenty minutes. Sit down.' The eyebrows went up and down vigorously.

Palmer said: 'Very good of you to see us at all, sir. I'll try to be as brief as possible.' He paused momentarily, trying to decide on the best approach, then continued: 'Mr Hurndall, a few months ago you did a very plucky thing.'

Hurndall looked surprised: 'I did?'

'I think so, sir. You walked into a police station and confessed to a traffic offence committed eighteen months before. That took guts.'

'Oh.' Hurndall didn't look too pleased. 'I don't want to talk about that. It's over.'

'I don't want to talk about it, either. Not directly, that is. You've been dealt with by the courts – very harshly to my mind – and as far as we're concerned that's the end of it.'

'Listen, if you really haven't come to talk about that damn business, get down to brass tacks. Why *are* you here?' But in spite of the words his manner was thawing perceptibly. It was clear he had no objection at all to being told he had guts and that the courts had dealt harshly with him.

Palmer said: 'I'm leading up to that, sir. I have to talk about that unlucky accident of yours, I'm afraid, not because I'm concerned with the case itself but because my enquiries are indirectly connected with it.'

'Oh, Inspector, please – come to the point. What are you after?'

'I'm after the swine who blackmailed you, Mr Hurndall.'

Hurndall's eyes flickered. He seemed nearly to speak, then think better of it.

'I want the man,' Palmer went on, 'who dragged all this affair into the open after nearly two years, who forced you into court and lost you your licence – just for his own gain. Can you help me to nail him, sir? You'd be doing the country a good turn – and getting revenge yourself.'

Hurndall said nothing for a moment. He seemed to be thinking rapidly. Then: 'I never said I'd been blackmailed.'

'No, sir, of course not. It's the sort of thing you can't tell anybody. And I know what a burden it must have been – especially to someone in your position of responsibility.'

Hurndall nodded. 'Yes, it was tough for a bit. Then I had this brainwave about giving myself up. Thought I might get off more lightly if I threw myself on the mercy of the court, you know –

and sort of kick the legs out from under the rat at the same time. And it worked.'

Palmer smiled. 'Very clever idea, sir. But one thing puzzles me. Why didn't you come to us after the case was over and tell us about the blackmailer? The trail would have been much less cold, you know.'

Hurndall shrugged. 'I thought about it. But after swinging that line about remorse and conscience, thought it might look a bit bad to admit I'd more or less been forced into confessing. And the bloke was off my back – so I thought, what the hell.'

'I see. But I'm sure you'll want to help us now, sir. Anything you tell me will be in confidence, of course.'

'I must admit I'd like to get my own back. What exactly do you want to know?'

'Everything, sir. In your own words.'

'Well, then, let me see.' Hurndall leaned back. 'About eight o'clock one Sunday night back early in May a man came to the house. Said he had to see me privately on a very urgent matter. Next thing I knew he was telling me he had evidence that about eighteen months before I'd run a kid down and not stopped. Knew the place and the date and almost the exact time. Of course, it pretty well bowled me over. I was sure after so long I'd got clean away with it. I asked him what sort of evidence he had, and he said proof I'd been in the area at the time – and a signed statement from a witness who'd seen it happen and got my number.

'I'd better explain: at the time I was running a Jag and a little M.G. two-seater, which I'd only had four months, and when I hit the kid I was driving the M.G. I'd swerved and hit a lamp-post – and got a bloody great dent in the wing. But it didn't affect the driving. I was pretty sure no one had seen me, so I just drove straight home and put the car in the garage. A day or two later, as it happened, the tax expired and it was natural enough not to re-tax a car like that for the winter. So I just left it there for about four months and then early in April, when my wife had gone away for a few days, I got it out very early one morning, drove up to Birmingham, and left it at a little back street panel shop.'

'The car was untaxed when you drove it, then, sir?'

Hurndall looked awkward. 'Well, er, as a matter of fact . . .'

'It's all right, sir.' Palmer's voice was reassuring. 'I'm not concerned with a technical offence like that. I just want to get all the facts straight.'

'Oh, that's decent of you. No, it wasn't taxed. That's important, actually. Anyway, I left the car there, came back by train, went up again the following afternoon, collected the car, drove it back in the night, put it in the garage again, and a few weeks later, still without taxing it, put it in part-exchange against a Lotus with the big dealers down the road I'd bought it from in the first place. I've dealt with them for years and they do all my repairs and servicing.'

Palmer nodded. 'I think I'm beginning to get the picture.'

'What the lousy little crook had on me were a lot of small points all adding up to quite a lot.

'Before the accident I'd been at a committee meeting. It was in the Minutes I'd been present – and the time the meeting closed. And leaving then and driving straight home I'd have had to pass along the street where the kid was knocked down at just about the right time.

'The guy said that if he tipped off the cops and produced his eye-witness, they'd be bound to check up. They'd trace the M.G. and examine it. He said they'd have taken samples of paint from the lamp-post I'd hit and they could match it up. They could also tell the car had been repaired, and unless the new owner happened to have had a knock in just the same spot on the car they'd know it must have been damaged when I owned it. So they'd ask me when and where – and where I'd had it repaired and why I hadn't gone to my regular garage. And I wouldn't have the answers. I'd either have to admit I'd taken it out when it was untaxed and driven a hundred miles to have it fixed – and try to explain why; or else tell a load of lies which wouldn't stand up to investigation.'

Hurndall was now quite caught up in his own narrative and even seemed, in a strange way, to be enjoying himself.

Palmer nodded understandingly. 'Tricky.'

'There's more. He said it was possible your forensic boys would even find traces of blood if they examined it closely enough. Now I thought this was pretty unlikely after eighteen months – but I couldn't be *sure*, d'you see? I've heard about some fantastic things they've done in that line. And if they did,

I'd be in dead trouble. Even apart from that, though, and apart from this eye-witness, I'd still be in a mess. There'd be no proof, of course, it'd all be circumstantial. But there'd be no doubt it would look damn fishy and there'd be quite a strong case against me. I was bloody rattled, I can tell you.'

'What did he tell you about this eye-witness?'

'Nothing. But he did let me see a copy of the statement he was supposed to have made.'

'Accurate?'

Hurndall nodded grimly. 'Hundred per cent.'

Palmer frowned. 'Then why should he have waited eighteen months before telling anybody?'

'I asked that. He said the bloke had a perfectly good reason, but *I* was not going to be told what it was. If it was true, all I could think was that he'd been ill – a coronary, say, immediately after he saw the accident.'

'Could you describe this man who called?'

'Not very well. Nondescript sort. Early thirties. Short. Slim. Medium colouring. Clean shaven.'

'We'd like you to come along and look at our rogues' gallery some time, if you can spare an hour.'

Hurndall agreed to this, and Palmer asked him next how much the man had wanted.

'He didn't say.'

Palmer looked surprised.

'I'll be quite frank – I did ask him, but he said not to worry about that yet, that he wouldn't be too greedy, and that if I co-operated that would be the end of it – he wouldn't keep coming back for more. He said he'd call again to talk over the details the following morning. I thought it was strange.'

'It is unusual. Probably he didn't want to risk asking too little or too much. He thought that if he let you worry overnight you might come up with an offer the next day which would give him a bargaining position.'

'Well, I didn't. I did think about it. But I knew that in spite of what he said once you start paying these people it never ends. I'd have to call a halt some time, and then he'd tell the police anyway. I weighed it all up. Discounting the possibility of them finding blood, even discounting the eye-witness, there'd still be a chance I'd be convicted. It was a chance I couldn't afford to take. So I just went and did my George Washington bit. And it worked. The sentence was stiff, but my solicitor said that if the law had found out about it without my owning up, and I'd been convicted, I'd almost certainly have gone inside.'

'Obviously you never saw this man again?'

Hurndall shook his head.

'Is there anybody else at all you could name who might have known about the accident?'

'No.'

'You mentioned it to nobody – not even your wife?'

'Least of all her. And she couldn't have found out. The M.G. was locked in the garage for four months, and I've got the only key. My wife doesn't drive and never goes near the garage. Neither does anybody else.'

Palmer asked him a few more routine questions and arranged a definite time for him to visit the Yard. Then he and Cochran got up to leave. Hurndall walked with them to the door of the office.

They were just going out when he said: 'Inspector, I may have seemed a bit flippant about that accident.' He sounded surprisingly hesitant. 'Believe me, I wasn't really. But I honestly wasn't to blame for it. I hadn't been drinking and I wasn't speeding. The kid ran straight out. Nobody could have stopped in time. And there was nothing I could have done if I'd stayed. It was a residential street – everybody must have heard my brakes. I saw lights going on as I drove off. There was no question of leaving the kid without help. If I hadn't panicked and driven on, I reckon I would have got off completely. But once I had – well, then it was too late. But I went through hell until I read the child was going to recover.'

Jill might well have been correct about the death of Father Dooney.

That, at least, was Palmer's feeling when he'd finished reading everything he could about it. But even then Joseph Dooney was still just a name in a dossier. So Palmer and Cochran went down to Brighton.

At the time of his death, eight months previously, Dooney was fifty-eight, and had been priest of St Patrick's Church for twelve years. He had died as the result of an overdose of sleeping

47

tablets. In the immediately preceding weeks, his manner had, by all accounts, been quite normal and he had talked with enthusiasm of a fishing holiday he had been hoping to take in Ireland. According to his doctor, and to the *post-mortem*, he had been in good health.

On the evening before he'd died, a visitor had called at his home while he was out. The housekeeper described him as 'a respectable-looking middle-aged man, stoutish, with grey hair and glasses'. He had given no name and had said he would wait. The housekeeper had shown him into the room where Father Dooney received visitors and had told the priest about him when he had come in some minutes afterwards. He had then been quite cheerful. The housekeeper had returned to her kitchen. Twenty minutes later she had heard the front door close and then Father Dooney go upstairs. He hadn't come down for dinner at the usual time. At eight she had gone up to tell him his meal was getting cold, but he had called out that he wasn't hungry. The housekeeper had been puzzled but not alarmed and had grumbled to her husband about the waste of food. Later they heard Dooney go out, which again surprised them, as it was an evening of the week he almost invariably spent in his study.

Dooney's movements while he was out were well accounted for, as he had been seen by several people. He had spent an hour in the church, just sitting quietly in one of the pews. Then he had walked the streets for another hour or so, having been noticed by one or two of his parishioners and a policeman. He was not seen to speak to anybody. He had returned home at midnight, the housekeeper and her husband, already in bed, having heard him go to the bathroom for five minutes and then straight to his bedroom.

In the morning, the housekeeper had found him lying dead on his bed, fully dressed. The sleeping tablet bottle – the pills had originally been prescribed after Dooney had had a minor operation several years previously, and he had long since stopped taking them – was found in its usual place in the bathroom, empty. The lack of any apparent reason, or of a suicide note, militated against Dooney having taken his own life; but an accident seemed equally unlikely. At the inquest an open verdict was brought in.

The visitor had never been traced.

This was the sum total of Palmer's knowledge after he and Cochran had spent a day in Brighton, talking to the local police and to those who had known Dooney best: parishioners, his curate, his housekeeper, his doctor and his friends. And he was quite convinced that Jill's guess had been right, and that Dooney had killed himself because he was being blackmailed.

'I can't think of any other explanation,' he said to Cochran on the way back to London. 'Dooney started behaving strangely immediately following the man's visit. Even if something had happened to him or he had met somebody while out walking later, it wouldn't explain his behaviour beforehand – failing to come down for dinner, going out on that evening of the week. So it must have been something that man said that drove him to it. And what could it have been, except a threat to reveal some secret he couldn't even contemplate being known about? Bear in mind his profession: he wasn't a man with a family he might hear bad news about, or a businessman who could have been informed he'd been ruined, or anything like that. And some sort of demand must have been made in return for silence – otherwise the visit doesn't make sense.'

'A demand for money?'

'I doubt it. He left £600. Nobody expects a priest to be rich. So the blackmailer wouldn't have been stupid enough to ask more than, say, a few hundred quid at the most. Or to have asked for cash on the spot. So if he *had* asked for money, Dooney could almost certainly have hushed the thing up. Now don't tell me he would rather kill himself than buy the man off – at least in the first instance. Granted he might have been driven to it later on if the pressure'd been kept up. But everything points to there just having been the one approach. So what was demanded was something Dooney could have given but wouldn't.'

'So it's the two-tier thing again, sir?'

'It looks like it.'

'Information wanted about one of his wealthy parishioners, say?'

'Well, that would be my guess. St Patrick's is a fashionable church. And R.C. priests hear things nobody else hears in the confessional. That's what I think must have made Dooney's position so intolerable: there was literally no way out – face exposure himself or break a sacred trust.'

'So I suppose the next step is to try and find out what his guilty secret was, and who could have known about it.'

'No.' Palmer spoke firmly. 'I'm letting this one drop, Gerry. Dooney didn't want anybody to know his secret – not even the police. If he had, he could have gone to the Brighton boys. And he didn't even want it known posthumously – or he would have left a note. I'm going to respect that wish.'

Cochran was silent. This to him was a new – and surprising – light on Bob Palmer. He said: 'But what about their ultimate target, sir – the rich parishioner?'

'What about him? They didn't get at him through Dooney, did they? So perhaps they never reached him at all. Probably they'd heard some rumour about him – like they did about Kendall – but obviously they didn't have all the dope they needed or they would never have gone to all the trouble of researching Dooney and pressurising him in turn.'

'They might have got it from another source since then, though, sir.'

'Of course. And we'll keep it in mind. If necessary we may come back to this business later. But only as a very last resort.'

Next, Palmer turned his attention to the case of Lady Felicity Mannering.

A little over twelve months previously, Lady Felicity had walked into West End Central Police Station and confessed to having stolen 'rather a lot of stuff – jewellery and furs and things' from various shops during the past year.

Later, in a statement, she'd said that the stolen property was in a trunk in the attic of her uncle's country house in Sussex, the house being locked up, and her uncle and aunt abroad; that they did not know the contents of the trunks, as she had simply asked them to look after it for her as she was short of space in her London flat.

The story was true, the contents of the trunk later being valued at over £7,000.

Lady Felicity was the daughter of the Earl of Hungerford, a large landowner, and a clever and exceedingly wealthy man. So clever and wealthy was he, in fact, that when the police had started to visit the shops from which Felicity claimed to have stolen, they found that Lord Hungerford's men had got there first. The shop-owners, without exception, ridiculed the idea of Lady Felicity having stolen anything from them. The notion was absurd . . . The goods had been taken on approval . . . Lady Felicity had been granted extended credit . . . They had been on loan . . . Her Ladyship was a most valued customer and the earrings had been a free gift . . . Lady Felicity had purchased the stole and they had inadvertently omitted to send her an account . . .

Lord Hungerford's solicitor provided the police with medical reports from three eminent psychiatrists, stating that their patient was suffering from acute nervous tension, coupled with a severe guilt complex, and at the time of signing the statement had not been responsible for her actions; and that she had agreed to enter immediately upon an extensive course of treatment, which they considered to be absolutely vital for her welfare.

How much it all cost Lord Hungerford was never known, but the result was that no charges were brought, nothing found its way into the papers, and Lady Felicity received a bottle of tranquillisers from her doctor and went on with her life as before.

Palmer had got together all the details of the affair from police records and from discussions with various colleagues, and it was with a feeling of expectant interest that, two days after his return from Brighton, he found himself ringing the doorbell of Lady Felicity's Chelsea flat.

He had discarded his usual dark lounge suit and white shirt in favour of a leather jacket and roll-necked sweater. There was no reply to his first ring, nor to his second, but after the third, a longer and more persistent one, the door was flung open and Lady Felicity Mannering said: 'If it's not a matter of life or death I hope your arms fall off.'

She was an ungainly-looking girl, with pale skin, good features, somewhat bleary blue eyes, black hair, dull and unkempt, and a sulky mouth. It was noon but she was wearing a heavy dressing-gown, wore no make-up, and had plainly just got out of bed. She looked as though under the dressing-gown she might have quite a good figure.

Palmer said: 'It could be a matter of life or death.'

'Whose?'

'Can I come in?'

'No. Come back at a civilised hour.' She started to shut the door.

Palmer said: 'It's the fuzz.'

She paused, looking puzzled. 'What? Where?'

'Here. Me.'

Her eyes widened. 'You're a cop?'

'Of a sort.'

'What do you want?'

'Are you alone?'

'What's that to you?'

'If you are, I'd like to come in.'

'I bet you would.'

'Don't flatter yourself. But I think you can help . . .'

'Forget it. I don't know anything about anybody.'

'I think you can help somebody who's in a nasty jam.'

'Who?'

'Can I come in?'

She hesitated, then gave a sigh and stood aside. Palmer went in. She closed the front door and went past him into the main room. Palmer followed her. It was expensively furnished and quite filthy, littered with empty bottles and erupting ash trays, and smelling of stale alcohol and stale tobacco.

Felicity threw herself down into a big easy chair and stared up at Palmer.

'Name?'

'Palmer. Inspector.' He held out his warrant card.

'Make it quick, Palmer Inspector.'

'There's a nasty gang of blackmailers around. Some of the victims have been silly, others haven't even been that. The crooks have been responsible for at least two deaths, including a suicide. I believe a lot of people are having their lives made a misery. I want to close this operation down. And I think you can tell me something about it.'

She reached across for a cigarette in a box on the table. Palmer bent over, picked up a lighter, and lit it for her. She inhaled deeply, coughed horribly, and said: 'You don't think *I'm* a blackmailer, do you?'

'No. But I think you may have been an intended victim.'

'Why do you think that?'

'Because there's no other reason I can think of for you to have

52

suddenly gone to the station like you did and owned up about those thefts.'

She started to interrupt, but he wouldn't give way. 'Now that's all over. I'm not interested in it. I don't personally care if you've got another dozen stolen necklaces in your bedroom. And I don't care how much pot you smoke, or how many traffic rules you've broken. I just want your help. I need it.'

'Sit down.' When he'd done so: 'What do you want to know?'

'First, who was it?'

'Nobody I'd ever seen before.'

'Man or woman?'

'Woman. Well, a girl.'

'How did she approach you?'

'On the top of a bus. We aristocrats like to see how the proles live now and then, you know. She just came up and asked if I was Felicity Mannering.'

'What was she like?'

'Perfectly ghastly. Oh, I dare say you'd think she was all right.'

'You mean she was a respectable type – educated?'

'If you like to put it like that. I thought for a moment she might be some fearful bitch I'd been at school with.'

'Could you describe her?'

She shook her head. 'Nondescript. Ordinary features, mousy hair, middling height, middling figure, drab clothes. That's all I could say. But I'd know her again.'

'And you said you *were* Felicity Mannering. What then?'

'She sat down and said she knew about the trunk that was in my uncle's house and what was in it.'

'And?'

'You don't want the exact words of the conversation, I suppose? They weren't very edifying. Anyway, I can't remember. The general sense was that she was going to you if I didn't co-operate.'

'And what did the co-operation consist of?'

'She – she wanted to know something. About somebody else.'

Palmer drew in his breath. Again! He thought quickly, then said quietly: 'Your father?'

She hesitated, then nodded.

'What did she want to know about him?'

'That wasn't specified.'

'What else did she say?'

'That they wouldn't ask for anything I couldn't give, and that once I'd provided them with what they wanted they'd never come back again. She said her friends were watching my uncle's house, and that if I or anybody else went near it to try to break in and get the trunk, they'd report a burglary and have the police there in no time.'

Felicity paused, took another drag at her cigarette, coughed again, then went on: 'It was damn clever, really. Any time up to about a week previously I could have 'phoned my uncle and told him to dump it somewhere. But at that time I couldn't possibly do anything. He'd asked me about it before he and my aunt went abroad, and I'd told him I wouldn't be wanting it for at least three months.'

'So the crooks could have known about it for some time – and just waited for the right moment?'

'That's how I figured it.'

'What did you say?'

'I told her I'd have to think it over, and to come here in the evening. I got her thinking I was scared. Actually, I decided almost straight away that the only thing to do was to go and give myself up. So when she came I was ready for her.'

'What did you do?'

'I asked her in and then I started kicking her.'

Palmer stared. 'You did what?'

'I started kicking her. I'd put on a pair of shoes with very hard, square toe-caps. I waited until she was in the middle of the room and then I let her have it.' She spoke dreamily. 'Do you know, I must have got in fifteen or twenty really good hacks before she managed to get out. I started on her ankles and worked my way up. Her legs must have been quite a sight for the next couple of weeks. I've never seen anyone so surprised. I don't think she'd ever been kicked before. You should have heard her screaming. Have you ever kicked a really repulsive person, Palmer Inspector? It's a strangely satisfying experience.'

Palmer laughed. It was the first laugh he'd had out of these investigations, and he laughed long and loud. Then Felicity laughed, too. And suddenly she looked quite attractive and very much younger.

Palmer said: 'Congratulations. I'd like to have seen it.' Then, more seriously, he added: 'And then you went straight to West End Central?'

She nodded. 'The rest is history.'

'You heard nothing else from them?'

'No. I yelled to her as she was trying to get out that I was going to the cops, so I didn't expect they'd try anything else.'

'You're the second person I know to have successfully spiked their guns by the same sort of idea.'

'We'd better form a club.'

'I don't think you'd get on.' Then he asked her who else had known about the trunk and its contents.

She shrugged. 'Could be anybody.'

He was surprised. 'You told lots of people?'

'No, I didn't *think* I'd told anybody. But who knows what you blurt out when you're – well, not at your best.'

'You couldn't name anyone in particular you told?'

'No.'

'But you might have mentioned it unwittingly to a number of people and not recollect it afterwards?'

'You put these things so well.'

'How many?'

'Dozens, I expect.'

Palmer muttered under his breath.

'Sorry,' she said.

Palmer asked her a few more questions, obtained a promise that she would go to the Yard and look at some photographs, then got up to leave. She took him to the front door. He was about to go out when, on an impulse, he stopped, shut the door again, and turned round to her.

'Why did you steal those things?'

She looked at him coolly. 'Investment.'

'You mean to sell later on?'

'Yes. Father had been getting more and more up-tight about my "way of life", as he called it. At last he cut off my allowance. I had a little money of my own but it was rapidly diminishing, so I thought I'd start making some preparations for the rainy day.'

'How do you manage now – for money?'

She looked at him strangely. 'Why do you ask?'

'Think I'm being nosy?'

She said thoughtfully: 'No, I don't think so. You really want to know, don't you?'

He nodded.

'Well, surprising as it may seem, you see before you a changed woman, reconciled to her papa and preparing to take her rightful place in established society and the Tory Party.'

She saw him glance towards the big room and looked amused. 'Don't mind all that. This had to be a gradual process. I've been off drugs for a couple of months. I'm now going to try to cut down on the booze. Last night was a kind of final fling. I'm sort of changing down through the gears. You should have seen me three or four months ago.'

'I'm glad,' Palmer said. 'How did it happen?'

She grinned, an unexpectedly child-like grin. 'It's too corny to be true. Love, Inspector. Of all people, I had to fall for a guy in the Foreign Office. A future ambassador, probably. He's not so much square as cubic – the works: Travellers' Club, Royal Yacht Squadron, Church of England. Happiest at the Savoy, Covent Garden, and Lord's. The funny thing is he fell for me, too. Difficult to say which of us was the more annoyed about it.' She paused. 'I don't know why I'm telling you all this. But I expect people do, don't they? Tell you things, I mean.'

He nodded. 'Mostly.'

'Must be useful. In your job.'

'Yes,' said Palmer. 'It is.'

Schoolgirls were one of the few sections of humanity among whom Bob Palmer did not feel quite at ease. And at the moment, it seemed to him that they were swarming around him in thousands. He wished he could have brought Cochran with him. But informality was going to be the essence of this part of the enquiry. And a second policeman, he felt, somehow always seemed to make a visit more of an official occasion.

He stared round him at the weathered grey stones and the Virginia creeper of Greenhill School. The mind did not easily associate one of the most exclusive girls' schools in the country with blackmail and suicide. But suicide there undoubtedly had been. Had there been blackmail as well?

Palmer waylaid one of the less fearsome-looking girls and asked to be directed to the headmistress.

'I was extremely surprised to receive your telephone call, Inspector Palmer. I cannot understand why you wish to raise this matter again *now*. It's more than twelve months since Miss Harper died.'

Miss Elizabeth Mandeville was a large, handsome woman with silver-grey hair. She looked just like the headmistress of a girls' public school ought to look. Palmer found himself wondering irrelevantly if it was always important in this life to look right. Would Joshua Kendall, for example, be in prison now if he'd had more the look of the tycoon? He wondered if he himself looked like a prospective Assistant Commissioner.

'I don't anticipate there being any raising of the matter again officially, ma'am,' he said. 'It's simply that I'm making enquiries into recent unexplained cases of suicide. Miss Harper's is only one of a series. I'm looking for a common factor.'

'And that would be?'

'Blackmail.'

Miss Mandeville's eyebrows went slowly upwards. So they might have done had a girl used an unpleasant swear word in her presence.

'It's a long-shot, I know,' Palmer said, 'but from a reading of the reports of her death, and the inquest, there seems to have been no logical reason for her to have taken her life. She left a letter for the Coroner which was quite lucid, but which gave no word of explanation. She was healthy, had no financial worries, she was apparently very happy in her profession, and she was certainly quite sane. I've been looking, among other things, for suicides of this sort in order to try to track down a criminal organisation which specialises in blackmail. A favourite ploy of theirs is to choose a person not particularly well-off or influential, but who might be in a position to provide incriminating information about somebody else. We believe this has happened at least twice already – to a Roman Catholic priest, and to the employee of a big businessman. The priest committed suicide and the businessman's employee died of a heart attack at least partly induced by the strain. I felt that a mistress in a school such as this might well be in the same sort of position: she might know something damaging about the daughter of wealthy parents.'

Miss Mandeville said: 'It would seem to me that before a person could be subjected to that sort of persecution he or she would have to have been guilty of some wrong-doing. Are you suggesting that Miss Harper . . . ?'

'Not necessarily. An innocent person can be blackmailed.' Without mentioning names, he explained how Mrs Wetherby's illness had been used as a lever against her husband.

When he had finished, Miss Mandeville said: 'How very unpleasant.'

'And that might not have been an isolated case. Miss Harper could conceivably have been another victim. If she was, I need to know. No one else need be informed, other than a very few of my colleagues. So if you have any suspicions at all . . .'

Miss Mandeville looked at him steadily for some seconds. Then she bowed her head deliberately. 'Yes.' She gave the smallest of sighs. 'I see. I have to admit, Inspector, that there could be a basis for your suspicions.'

Palmer leaned forward. 'You have reason to think she might have been blackmailed?'

'Such a possibility never occurred to me until this moment. But I see now that Eileen could well have been vulnerable. And she did have knowledge of the kind you referred to.'

'Could you be a little more explicit?'

'As to the first point – Eileen Harper had once been married. Her husband had – had died. She took up teaching again shortly after his death and resumed her maiden name. She never attempted to conceal the fact that she was a widow, but nor did she encourage questions about her marriage. If the subject came up she always managed to give the impression that her husband had been killed in some sort of accident. She'd make it plain that it was painful to talk about it. I was the only person here to know the truth.'

'Which was?'

'Her husband was John Atkins, the Axe Murderer.'

Palmer whistled.

'Let me explain,' Miss Mandeville said. 'Eileen and I were very old friends. We started our teaching careers at the same school at the same time and we shared a flat. She didn't have many friends and she had no close family. So I suppose I knew her better than anyone. Now Eileen was a brilliant teacher. English literature was her subject and she had a remarkable gift for making it come alive.

'We shared the flat for about four years and then she obtained a post in the north. We corresponded regularly at first and then more intermittently, and in one of her letters she told me she was engaged to be married. She simply referred to her fiancé as John and said she hoped I'd meet him one day. Shortly afterwards I moved away and I lost touch with her completely. Then three years later I saw her face staring at me from a newspaper. It was, of course, a great shock to learn that the John she had mentioned was John Atkins, who had committed those terrible murders. Naturally from then on I followed the trial closely. Knowing what a retiring person she was, I was glad to see that none of the newspapers went into her background at all, mentioned that she had been a teacher, or said what her maiden name had been.'

Palmer nodded but didn't speak.

'As you know,' Miss Mandeville continued. 'Atkins was found guilty and executed. Eileen had given evidence on his behalf. I don't think she'd wanted to or that she had, by then, any real doubt as to his guilt. But she was talked into it by his Counsel. He thought she would make a good impression. He was wrong. She was attacked by the Attorney General, who claimed that she must have suspected Atkins of the second murder, yet had failed to take any action – thus being partly responsible herself for the third death. He argued that nobody in her situation could have been so naive as her behaviour made her appear, and that she must have known Atkins to be really guilty. I believe feeling was very much against her for a time – I even heard it said that she should be charged as an accessory. But nobody knew Eileen as I did. She *was* a naive person. She trusted people far too readily, and I could well believe she would accept the far-fetched stories her husband had told her. However, no action was taken against her, and after Atkins' conviction she managed to escape from the limelight.

'A year later I received a letter from her. She asked if she could come and see me. I had just been fortunate enough to be appointed headmistress here at a comparatively early age, and she had read about it in some professional journal. When she came she begged me to give her a position here. She hadn't worked since the trial and was getting very short of money. She'd reverted to her maiden name and had managed to break all connections with her married life. She was really terrified of anybody finding out about it. She knew that if she applied for a position at another school, she would have to say what she had been doing for the previous five years. And she simply couldn't face the prospect of telling anyone.'

'So you took her on.'

'I did. Luckily, staff appointments at Greenhill have always been left very much to the discretion of the headmistress. I knew, of course, that I was taking a risk. It was very likely that a number of parents – and probably most of the Governors – would object to the widow of a notorious criminal teaching here, particularly in view of the insinuations that had been made about her during the trial. And if certain newspapers found out, there would certainly be undesirable publicity. But I decided that there was really very little likelihood of the facts coming to light if we were both careful. I wanted to help Eileen. But also I must admit that I wanted her as a teacher. So I engaged her. I was nervous about it for some time, and Eileen herself did not really stop worrying until much later. She had a genuine horror of the past being brought to light. But eventually she settled down. She was successful and, I think, very happy. She was officially designated Assistant Headmistress four years ago.'

'And she had been here – how long?'

'It must have been – yes, seventeen years.'

'And you think she would really have been desperate to prevent her past becoming known – now, after all these years?'

'I'm sure of it. Atkins is one of those criminals like Crippen or Christie whom everybody knows of. I have no doubt at all that there are some papers which would give considerable prominence to such an item of news as his widow being a teacher at Greenhill School. Quite apart from her personal feelings, Eileen would have hated the prospect of harming the school – and causing embarrassment to me.'

'You mentioned also that Miss Harper could have supplied some damaging information about a particular person.'

'Yes. A short time before Eileen died a girl was expelled. This is a thing that happens very rarely. But when it is necessary, we try to handle it very discreetly. And in this instance, apart from the girl's parents, only Eileen and I knew the full circumstances.'

'And those were?'

'That I am not prepared to say. The girl's activities were not illegal, and for me to tell you would serve no purpose. But I can say that her parents are well off, and they were extremely ashamed and embarrassed by what happened. I am certain they would be willing to pay a considerable sum to keep it secret.'

'Miss Harper could have provided the criminals with actual evidence? I mean of a type which would make blackmail possible?'

'Yes. There are certain papers in my safe. Eileen was the only person apart from me to have a key to that safe. She could have taken them and I would probably not even have noticed they were missing. Or, alternatively, they may simply have demanded a signed statement of the facts from Eileen herself. She *was* Assistant Headmistress.'

Palmer nodded. He said : 'May I suggest that you destroy those papers? If they were stolen, they could still be used against the girl's parents.'

The headmistress looked startled. She said : 'I'll do it before you leave.'

Palmer then asked about Eileen Harper's friends – was there anybody she might have confided in?

'I am sure that had she wished to tell anybody it would have been me. I was closer to her than anybody. Moreover, had she confided in a third person it would have necessitated her explaining why she was vulnerable, and what it was the blackmailers wanted from her. But I already knew about these things.'

'She lived on the premises, I understand.'

'Yes. She had a small suite of rooms in Meadow's. It's a house divided up into single rooms and flats for members of the teaching staff.'

'If somebody had wished to speak to her away from the school, would there have been any particular time they could have been sure of approaching her privately – was there any place she went at a set time, alone?'

Miss Mandeville considered. 'I don't think so. She didn't go out a great deal during term. Shopping, of course, or sometimes to town for a concert or a theatre – but usually with somebody, and not at regular intervals.'

Palmer said thoughtfully: 'So they would more or less have had to come here. Do you know if any strangers called on her shortly before her death?'

'I couldn't say. You'd have to ask one of the other occupants of Meadow House. Four other mistresses had rooms there at that time. They are all still with us.'

Palmer said: 'I'd like to revert to the girl who was expelled. I'm sorry, but it is very important that I should know who she was. You said her parents are wealthy. It seems highly probable that the blackmailers had set their sights on them. They might not have given up just because Miss Harper refused to co-operate. The blackmail may actually be going on now. I must try to find out. I promise you that I will not mention the school to them, or that I have any knowledge of their daughter being expelled.'

Miss Mandeville looked uncertain. Then she said: 'Very well, Mr Palmer, in the strictest confidence, the girl was Joan Stanbury. Her father is Sir Norman Stanbury. He's a civil servant, but the money comes from his wife. Lady Stanbury's family were in textiles. I understand she inherited nearly a million pounds.'

Palmer wrote down the name. 'Thank you. Now, if there's nothing more you can tell me, I'd be glad to see these ladies who were Miss Harper's neighbours.'

The women were naturally curious about Palmer's questions but he didn't enlighten them as to their purpose. The first three were able to tell him nothing of interest. But the fourth, an intelligent young woman named Brown, nodded decisively when Palmer put the question.

'Yes, she had a visitor.'

'When?'

'A day or so before she died.'

'A woman?'

'Yes.'

'Could you describe her?'

'She was about my height, medium build, about twenty-eight or thirty, I suppose. She had brown hair. Quite ordinary, small features, as far as I could tell, though I only caught a quick glimpse of her face. She was wearing a grey suit, I think.'

'How did you happen to notice her?'

'I had the rooms immediately below Harper's. I went up one evening to borrow a book. I was going up the stairs when this girl came out of Harper's door. She said something like "Don't bother to see me out", and then she came towards the top of the stairs. I thought she looked a bit annoyed to see me coming up. Anyway, she just waited on the landing until I'd got to the top. I fancied she deliberately kept her face turned away as I got level with her.'

'Did you speak?'

'I think I said "Good evening" or something. She didn't answer – just hurried on down the stairs.'

'You saw Miss Harper immediately after that?'

'Yes, for a minute or two.'

'How did she seem?'

'Well, thinking back since, I've thought she looked upset – rather pale. But I'm not sure if I consciously noticed that at the time or whether I sort of read it in afterwards.'

The girl was very honest. Palmer asked: 'Why didn't you mention this before, Miss Brown?'

'But I did – to several people – including the police. Nobody seemed very interested.'

Palmer felt a twinge of annoyance. This was a thing that should have been in the reports. He apologised, then said: 'The incident made an impression on you, didn't it?'

'Yes, it did rather.'

'Why, I wonder? Why did you remember the girl? Was it just that she tried to hide her face?'

'That – and a generally rather furtive air. And the fact that she didn't answer when I spoke. Miss Harper's manner: as I say I couldn't swear to it, but I think she *was* upset. But mostly, I suppose, it was the girl's legs. All added to the fact that Harper killed herself a couple . . .'

Palmer interrupted. 'Her legs?'

'Yes. Naturally that was what I saw most clearly about her as I went up the stairs. Of course, anywhere else I imagine she'd have worn trousers but they're not allowed here – even for visitors. It's an old tradition.'

'Forgive me, but I'm not with you. What was special about her legs?'

'Oh, didn't I mention that? Sorry. It's simply that both her legs, right up to above her knees, were covered with cuts and bruises and sticking plaster.'

5

The Stanburys proved negative. Both denied that any attempt had been made to blackmail them. And Palmer believed them. Their air of bewilderment at the mere suggestion was very convincing.

'That clears Eileen Harper,' he said to Cochran later. 'I always had in mind that she might have given the organisation what they wanted on the Stanburys and then killed herself in a fit of remorse. But now that's out.'

Cochran said: 'Sir, are you quite sure that all these cases are linked? Couldn't we have several quite independent jobs here?'

Palmer smiled. 'Think I might be getting the Master Criminal Complex, do you, Gerry? I don't think so. Look at it like this. Hemmings was blackmailed by James; the tip-off letters about James and Kendall came from the same source; we've no other explanation for Wetherby's behaviour than that he was under pressure, too, plainly from the same people, because he could give them the dirt on Kendall. Woolf, Felicity, and Eileen Harper were also victims of what you called two-tier blackmail. We've got the further tie-up between Felicity and Harper in this girl with the bruised legs. Dooney's case is almost identical with Harper's: both healthy, happy in their work, no known worries, both knowing discreditable secrets, both receiving strange visitors, both killing themselves shortly afterwards without leaving any explanation.

'Finally, there's Hurndall. I agree here the connection is a bit tenuous. This might have been an independent operator. But I doubt it. Because the m.o. is almost identical with Felicity's case: a personal approach from an apparently respectable person, details given of some past criminal activity, no specific demand made in the first instance – very unusual – and an assurance that only one demand would be made.

'So – granted that one qualification about Hurndall – every case we've looked into is linked in some way to one of the others. Convinced?'

Cochran gave a decisive nod. 'Yes, sir. I couldn't quite see the pattern before. But put like that it's pretty clear.' He thought for a few seconds, before saying: 'They're pretty formidable, sir, but they've made plenty of mistakes, too, haven't they? We already know of seven cases in which they didn't make a penny.'

'Yes, but we only got to know about them because the victims were by then all outside their reach: three dead, two having outwitted them, two – Kendall and Woolf – having called their bluff and lost. We've got to assume that such a professional outfit, with first-rate intelligence sources and a large personnel, must be having more successes than failures – otherwise they wouldn't be able to stay in business. *Ergo* – there have been and still are other victims. And we've got to find 'em.'

'But where, sir? We seem to have come to a dead end. None of the witnesses have been able to pick out a face in the rogues' gallery. What's the next move?'

'If nothing else turns up, to go over the same ground again. So far we've really only been experimenting to try to verify the original theory. Next we may have to go back to the same people and question them more closely. But there are some other angles we might try first. Lawyers, for instance. It would be a long-shot, but we might just wander round some of the more fashionable ones in the West End and the City and tip them the wink that if they should happen to get a client who's in trouble with a blackmailer, they can bring them to us – you or me personally – and guarantee them complete secrecy. Ask them to pass the message round among their colleagues.'

'And how about trying the same thing with enquiry agents, sir?'

'Yes, good idea. Do you know any?'

'One or two.'

'Right, start with them. And I'll take the lawyers.'

'Couldn't we do it on the 'phone, sir?'

'No. A personal call is always better in cases like this.'

Cochran tapped on the door of an office marked OWEN SHERWOOD INVESTIGATIONS. He was beginning to think that his idea hadn't been a very good one. This was his eighth enquiry agency of the day. At the others he had drawn a complete blank.

A woman's voice called for him to enter. He did so and found himself in a minute reception office. He showed his warrant card to a plump, cheerful-looking receptionist of about forty and asked to see Mr Sherwood. She went away, came back almost immediately, and asked him to go through to the inner office.

This was a much larger room, shabby, with several ample bookcases and with a coal fire burning in a big, old-fashioned grate. A broad-shouldered, untidy-looking man wearing an old tweed suit with leather patches on the elbows stood up as Cochran entered, held out his hand and, as Cochran took it, said: 'Prynhawn da.'

'Oh, good afternoon to you, too.'

Owen Sherwood raised his eyebrows. 'Welsh?'

'No – holiday in Snowdonia two years ago.'

'Ah.' Sherwood gave a nod. 'Beer.'

'I b-beg your pardon?'

'You're tired. You'd like a beer.'

'Well, I would, but unfortunately I'm on duty . . .'

'Nonsense, boy. I was in the force for nine years. Who's to know?' He went across to a large cupboard in the corner, rummaged inside, and emerged with a large bottle of beer, a tumbler, and a bottle opener. He put them down on the large, paper-strewn table, took his seat again, and said: 'Sit down. Help yourself.'

Cochran sat down and helped himself. 'Won't you join me?'

'Never touch it. Foul stuff. I'll be having a cup of tea in a minute.' Cochran had already noticed the five used cups on the table. 'What can I do for you?' Sherwood asked him. Cochran put down his glass and gave a brief and guarded outline of the investigation and the present purpose of his visit. Sherwood listened closely throughout.

Finally Cochran said: 'Inspector Palmer agreed with me that enquiry agents such as you . . .'

Sherwood interrupted. 'Palmer? Bob Palmer, is it?'

'Yes, sir. Do you know him?'

Sherwood nodded ruminatively. 'We used to be quite thick at one time. He doesn't like beer. Makes a bond, a thing like that. Haven't seen him lately. How is he?'

'Very well.'

'And his wife?'

'Yes, I believe so.'

'Nice girl.'

'The best.'

'Give Bob my best. Tell him I said we must get together some time.'

'I will.'

'Now about this business.' Sherwood took out a brightly-coloured packet covered with strange markings, extracted from it a thin, almost jet-black small cigar, and lit it. The smell was evil. Cochran blanched slightly and quickly lit a cigarette of his own.

Sherwood gave off a cloud of dense black smoke. 'I can't help you a lot,' he said. 'At least, I don't think so. But what I'm going to tell you may link up with something you know already. I can't say. A lady came to see me a few days ago.' He flicked back through the pages of a desk diary. 'Monday.'

'That would be the nineteenth?'

'Yes. She gave the name Miss Jean Robinson. But that was false.'

'What did she want?'

'Without actually saying so, she wanted me to get some-body worked over for her.'

'I thought you said she was a lady.'

Sherwood smiled. 'Funnily enough, I still think she was – in the old-fashioned sense. In fact, I reckon you'd have to have pretty feudal-type ideas – and have plenty of money behind you – even to think about paying to have a bloke beaten up – that is, if you were normally – quote – "respectable".'

'You know she was being blackmailed?'

'Yes. She admitted that.'

'Did she give any details?'

'No. She said she would do if I promised to help her first. All she said was that she wanted the blackmailer forced to stop bothering her. I asked how she expected me to do that, and she said she'd leave that to me – that surely there were methods, and that she'd pay very well if she was never troubled again.'

'You thought she was hinting at strong-arm stuff?'

'It was pretty obvious.'

'What did you tell her, sir?'

'That I couldn't help. And I advised her to go to her solicitor or to the police. She said something like: "I thought you might say that. But I can't. That's why I came to you." I said I was sorry, that if she liked to tell me more I'd respect her confidence and advise her, but short of that I couldn't promise anything. She just shrugged and walked out.'

'Would you know her again?'

'I doubt it. She was wearing a very full dark wig. It covered her forehead, her ears and half her jaw line. She had dark glasses on and a lot of make-up. She didn't intend to be recognised again.'

'Age?'

'Difficult to say. Mid- to late-thirties perhaps. Height about five five or six but again it's hard to be sure – she had very high heels on. Good figure, nice legs, very well-dressed. That's about it.'

Cochran was writing rapidly. He finished and looked up. 'She didn't say anything else?'

'Yes, but I can't remember what it was. I'll ring you if it comes to me.'

Cochran pocketed his notebook and stood up. 'Thanks very much. It might be useful.'

'Or it might not,' said Sherwood, also standing. 'Probably the latter. But it's the best I can do.'

He went with Cochran to the door and said good-bye. As Cochran went out to the corridor, he heard Sherwood say loudly: 'Maggie – tea!'

'Owen Sherwood, eh?' said Palmer.

'Yes, sir, he enquired after you and Mrs Palmer and asked to be remembered to you.'

'It must be two years since I saw him. Is he still smoking those appalling black things?'

'He is.' Cochran spoke feelingly.

Palmer smiled. 'They're reputed to be Bulgarian. He gets about three months' supply at a time in some back-street shop off the East India Dock Road. He says it's the only shop in London that stocks them and that he's never met anyone else who smokes them.'

'I can well believe it.'

'He's an interesting person. Fine brain. He was going to be a teacher. Did two years at the University of Wales, then packed it up, came to London, and joined the Met. He made Detective-Inspector at about twenty-eight, but a year or so later he suddenly resigned and started his own agency. I've never understood why. We used to be great buddies at one time. Jill liked him. But then I . . .' He didn't finish the sentence. He seemed thoughtful.

'About this woman, sir.'

'Sorry, Gerry, I'm not uninterested. Go on.'

'Do you want me to follow it up: see if she went to another agency, say – one of the less reputable ones?'

Palmer rubbed his chin. 'I don't know.' He saw Cochran look surprised, and went on: 'Don't get me wrong. You've done well. You've got hold of some definite data, which is more than I did with those blasted lawyers. But let's face it, there's nothing to suggest this woman's a victim of the organisation. There are still plenty of small-time men about, you know, plenty of Johnny Jameses. The fact that she thought she could get him off her back by having him done over suggests she believes she's dealing with an individual.

'Again, you talk about checking with some of the less reputable agencies. But they aren't classified as "reputable" or "disreputable". I know some first-class ones. And a few real crooks. There's every degree of honesty in between. So – where would you start checking? And do you expect them to tell you if they did work someone over for Jean Robinson?'

Cochran looked a little dejected. 'You say just forget her, then, sir?'

'Not at all. I'm just explaining why I said I didn't know what I wanted you to do. I'm really only thinking aloud. Let's sleep on it. Perhaps in the morning one of us will come up with a brainwave.'

'OK, sir, fair enough.'

Cochran went off duty. Palmer decided to spend ten minutes writing up some notes before going home himself. He had nearly finished when the telephone rang.

To his surprise, the caller was Owen Sherwood. They chatted generally for a minute or so, then Sherwood said: 'Tell you why I rang, Bob. This Robinson girl I was talking to your boy about.

I wasn't able to give him much of a description, but this might help. She had a little mannerism which I've only just remembered.'

'What's that?'

'You really ought to see it demonstrated, but she's got this habit of bending the little finger of her right hand and then holding it bent with her thumb. Her three middle fingers she keeps straight.'

As Sherwood was speaking, Palmer found himself doing it. 'Is that all?'

'Not quite. It's simply that then she gestures with the fingers in that position – little circular movements of her hand in the air: clockwise movements – that is, anti-clockwise as you look at her.'

'It sounds most odd.'

'I suppose it does. But it's not unattractive, in fact, when you see her doing it. I'm sure she's quite unconscious of it.'

'Well, thanks for letting me know. I'll bear it in mind.'

'There is one other thing.'

'Yes?'

'I told Cochran I'd ring if I remembered something else she said. I've remembered. It was along the lines of: "It's not just me. They used somebody to try to get at me. Somebody quite innocent. The sort of person who just didn't deserve that sort of thing." '

Palmer sat up with a sudden awakening of interest. Until that moment he had not really been convinced of the importance of Jean Robinson. But now it seemed that here was another instance of two-tier blackmail. And apparently another innocent victim – like Wetherby or Eileen Harper – had been involved. Keeping any note of especial excitement out of his voice, he said: 'Any other details?'

'No, that's all. Sorry I couldn't remember it before. But I didn't have much time to think when he called.'

Palmer thanked him again, said good-bye, and rang off. He sat silently for a few moments, staring in front of him. It seemed now he'd have to start looking for Jean Robinson.

But not tonight.

He yawned, stretched, got up, and went home.

71

Jill was nearly through preparing the evening meal when she heard Bob's key in the lock, and she went into the hall to greet him as usual. She was surprised when he gathered her to him and kissed her long and ardently.

'Hi,' she said breathlessly. 'What's up?'

'Nothing. I just realised I quite like you.'

'Thanks.' She gently disengaged herself.

He took her hand. 'Do you know why I like you?'

She looked at him resignedly. 'Tell me.'

'You're not a blackmailer.'

'Why, thanks. Again. I'd say that was just about the nicest compliment a girl's ever been paid.'

He laughed. 'When do we eat?'

'About fifteen minutes.'

'Fine.'

He went into the sitting-room. Jill returned to the kitchen and continued preparing the meal. Half-consciously, she heard the sound of the television coming on in the other room. She carried on her work for a further four or five minutes. Then suddenly from the other room there came a loud exclamation of surprise from Bob.

'What's up?' she called.

There was no reply, so a minute later she went to investigate. Bob was on his feet, staring at the set. Jill followed his gaze. The screen was showing a weather chart.

'What on earth's the matter?' she asked.

He didn't answer for a moment. Then he said: 'I think I've just seen somebody on there who's involved in this case I'm on.'

She looked blank. 'Oh. Don't you *know*?'

'No. I don't know the person. But I was told to look out for a particular mannerism – a trick with the hands. I've just seen it used on there.'

'Who is it – a crook?'

'No, no. At least, I don't think so.' He paused and appeared to be thinking deeply. Then: 'It's a real coincidence if I'm right. But then, there nearly always is one coincidence in a long case. Excuse me, darling, I've got to make a 'phone call.'

He went out to the hall, and she heard him lift the receiver. She gave a little shrug, followed him out, and went past him back to the kitchen.

Ten minutes later the meal was ready and she went out to the hall again to call Bob. He was still on the telephone. She was surprised, as she thought she'd heard him hanging up five minutes before.

She stopped suddenly, struck by the tone of his voice. It sounded different from usual: quieter, more gentle, persuasive – yet somehow tense.

'Well, I'm sure I can help you.

'I can't explain now but I wish you'd trust me.

'Yes, I do appreciate how you feel.

'What list?

'The Alpha List?

'No, I'm not on it – at least, I don't think so. But I know some people who are – they're letting me help them.'

Then Jill heard Bob draw his breath in sharply. When he spoke again his voice sounded strangely – artificially – calm and level.

'That's terrible. I understand how you must feel.

'No, I promise you, you've nothing to fear from me. Can I come and see you?

'Anywhere, anytime – now if you like. Have anybody you want present. I'll be alone.'

This had all been punctuated by short pauses. Now there was a longer one. Then Bob said: 'Yes, gladly. I can leave now. You'll be there all the evening?

'Then wait for me, please.

'Right. Good-bye.'

He rang off and turned round. She was shocked by the expression on his face. He gave a slight start when he saw her.

She asked: 'What was all that about?'

'You weren't supposed to hear.'

'Why not?'

'Because it could be dangerous, darling. It's an even bigger affair than I thought.'

'What's the Alpha List?'

He took her by the shoulders. 'Look, Jill, this is serious. Forget you heard that conversation. Don't mention it to anybody – anybody at all. Whatever happens. Do you understand?'

'Yes, I guess so – but . . .'

'Promise me, Jill.'

'I promise.'

He relaxed a little.

'But just tell me – what's the Alpha List?'

'I wish I knew. But I honestly don't. That's the first I've heard of it. It's something to do with this blackmail racket. That's all I know. I'm hoping to find out a little more tonight.'

'When – when are you going?'

'Now, I'm afraid.'

'But the meal's all ready.'

'I know. I'm awfully sorry. But it's fearfully important. Keep it hot for me. I shouldn't be late.'

'Listen,' she said. 'You didn't tell him what time you'd be there, did you?'

He looked blank. 'Who?'

'That man on the 'phone, stupid.'

'Oh.' He seemed to be about to say something, then changed his mind 'No. I didn't.'

'He's going to be there all the evening? And he's going to wait for you?'

'Yes.'

'Then you can at least grab a bite. It'll take about ten minutes. And you'll work better with something inside you.'

He grinned. 'OK. But make it quick.'

Jill scurried back to the kitchen.

About twelve minutes later Bob pushed away his plate, took a swig of water, and stood up. 'That was fine, darling.'

She stood up too. 'You don't know how long you'll be, I suppose?'

'No. But I'll ring you if I'm going to be too late.' He gave her a quick kiss. 'I'm going by tube, so if you should want to go out, the car'll be here.'

'I don't expect I shall.'

A minute later he had left.

Jill gave a sigh. Then she washed up, made herself some coffee, took it into the sitting-room, picked up a book, and made herself comfortable on the settee.

At eleven-thirty that evening Bob still hadn't returned, and Jill was getting anxious.

She went into the hall, opened the front door, and walked down the garden path to the road. She stared in the direction of the local tube station, which was about three hundred yards away. But there was no sign of Bob. She went slowly back indoors. She paused by the telephone in the hall, wondering whether to call Scotland Yard. But Bob had mentioned no plans to go there, and if he *was* there surely he would have called her. Besides, she hated to give the impression of a fussy wife. She decided to leave it for another quarter of an hour and went back to the sitting-room.

Then she heard the sound of a car drawing up outside. Two doors slammed, the front gate opened and closed, and two sets of footsteps sounded on the path. Jill jumped to her feet and ran into the hall. The door-bell rang.

She called out : 'Who is it?'

There was silence for a few seconds. Then : 'It's me, Jill Andy.'

She gave a little gasp. 'Oh. Andy.' She moved forward and opened the door.

Andrew Thompson was standing on the step. Behind him and a little to his right she vaguely recognised the figure of Chief Superintendent Phillips. Jill stared at them dumbly and suddenly she knew why they'd come. She felt a cold hand grip at her heart and her legs went weak.

'What's the matter? It's Bob, isn't it? Something's happened to him.'

Andrew Thompson bowed his head. He stepped into the hall and half put out his hand as if to support her. He said :

'Yes, Jill. I'm afraid – well, I'm afraid he's dead.'

6

Bob Palmer had been murdered. His body had been discovered in the darkened doorway of an office building in the heart of the City of London. He had been stabbed in the back with a narrow, long-bladed knife, and had died instantly.

Detective-Chief Superintendent Phillips took personal charge of the case. At his own request, Andrew Thompson was assigned as his chief assistant.

Jill never afterwards had any clear recollection of the ten days that followed. She passed through them in a kind of daze. The main impression left was of too many people. People were all around her all the time: friends, acquaintances, distant relatives of Bob, a man from the American Embassy; and policemen – lots of policemen, from the Commissioner downwards. And when she went out newspaper reporters, television cameras, microphones.

And all the time questions. About Bob: where he'd gone that night, what he'd said beforehand. Questions she knew she didn't – somehow couldn't – answer properly.

Because during those days she hated the police. If Bob hadn't been a policeman he wouldn't be dead. *They'd* killed him. And now they wouldn't leave her alone. Pretending they wanted to find out who'd killed him. They'd killed him themselves. She wouldn't help them. Then perhaps they'd go away. Except Andrew. She didn't want Andrew to go. For one thing he didn't ask her questions.

Her parents telephoned from the United States. They were all set to fly over and take her back with them. But she would have none of it. She didn't want them – not now. She wouldn't see them. She wasn't going home – not yet. She spoke to them quietly, almost dispassionately. But she was unyielding, repeating again and again that she didn't want them. Baffled, hurt, and trying not to show it, they'd eventually, reluctantly, agreed to stay away.

Then came the funeral, the ghastly official funeral with the guard of honour and the horses and the outriders and the uniforms with their silver buttons and the cameramen and the wreaths and the Home Secretary. And herself, somehow not a part of it. Just somebody watching a show. Angry, because even now he was dead the Metropolitan Police were still controlling Bob. Paying her all deference. Consulting her. But not really giving her a say in the arrangements. Doing it all by the book. Burying not Bob, but Detective-Inspector R. Palmer, C.I.D. With full honours.

Things were better after the funeral. Gradually the people grew less. Until at last she had the solitude she craved. Even Andrew faded into the background, seeming to know to the minute the time he was no longer needed.

Jill had the telephone disconnected. Then for nearly a week she stayed in the house, seeing nobody, not even turning on the television or radio. It worried some of her friends, who felt it was not good for her. But it was her own way, and at the end of it she returned to the normal world. She had her 'phone reconnected and the first call she made was to Andrew, asking him to stop by on the following Sunday.

Jill opened the door with an attempt at a smile. 'Hi, Andy. Come in.'

She looked and sounded almost normal, attractively dressed in bright colours, and wearing make-up. The house was clean, well-kept, and airy. The radio was on. Andrew followed her into the sitting-room.

'There's coffee made,' she said. 'Or would you rather something stronger?'

'Coffee'll be fine.'

'Won't you sit down?'

He did so and watched her as she poured the coffee. It wasn't true, he decided, that she looked quite normal – or rather she wasn't quite as he had known her before. There was a hardness about her face, around the eyes and around the mouth, that was new. It wouldn't have been easily discernible if you hadn't known her well before, but it was there. You couldn't say she looked older – just as though she had seen more things and knew more things than she had before.

She put a cup of coffee on the table in front of him and sat down opposite him with one of her own. She perched on the edge of the seat, as though she was ill at ease in a strange house.

'Well,' she asked, 'do you know yet who killed Bob?'

He was startled and must have shown it. She gave a thin smile. 'Sorry. Did that shock you?'

'No,' he said hurriedly. 'I was just surprised that you wanted to talk about it.'

'Yes. I want to talk about it. Bob is dead. He was murdered. Stabbed in the back. I'm not going to dodge saying that. No one's going to have to avoid mentioning Bob in front of me. No pretending he never existed, or that he just happens not to be present at any particular moment. Bob has been murdered. I've accepted that.'

'I think that's very wise. Brave, too.'

'You didn't answer my question. Do you know who killed him?'

Slowly he shook his head.

'No leads at all?'

'Virtually none. So far.'

'Tell me everything, will you, Andy?'

'What do you mean, "everything"?'

'All about the murder. All you know. Where Bob was found, the time he was killed, and so on. I was told before, but I didn't really take it in.'

He hesitated for a moment but didn't demur. 'He was found in the doorway of a firm of shipping brokers by a bobby on the beat at about half ten. That area is virtually deserted at that time of night, and he could have been there anything up to an hour. He was probably killed at nine o'clock, with say an hour's leeway either side. There was no blood on the ground, nor any sign of a struggle, so we think he was killed somewhere else and taken there afterwards.

'You told us he arrived home that evening at about twenty or a quarter to seven and left again about twenty-five or thirty minutes later – that is between five past and a quarter past seven. That ties up with what a ticket clerk at your local Underground tells us. He knew Bob slightly and he saw him going up to the automatic ticket machines at he thinks about seven fifteen or seven twenty. Unfortunately, he can't say which machine, so we don't know how far he was intending to go. There was a train to the West End at seven twenty-four, and the guard on it thinks he saw Bob boarding it. But he didn't notice him get off. None of the ticket collectors at any station to the terminus remembers taking his ticket. So what it amounts to is that by eight or quarter past he could have been virtually anywhere in central London.'

Jill said : 'What about motive?'

'Well, it's pretty certain to be something to do with this blackmail racket he'd been investigating. Do you know about that?'

'Not a lot. Only that he thought he was on to some kind of big gang.'

'It looks as though he was right. But according to his notes, and according to Cochran, he hadn't cracked it. What he'd been doing chiefly the last week or two was interviewing not suspects but possible blackmail victims. We've been round to see them all over again – an M.P., a school ma'am, an earl's daughter, and some others – to see if any of them had told him anything that he hadn't put in his reports. But,' he shrugged, 'so far it's been a complete blank.' He sounded tired and depressed.

Jill hesitated, licked her lips, and then asked quietly : 'What do you know about the Alpha List?'

'The what?'

'The Alpha List?'

He shook his head. 'What is it?'

'I don't know. I thought you might.'

'What is this, Jill? If it's something Bob talked about, you must tell me.'

She took a deep breath and then told him everything that had happened and all she had heard, from Bob's exclamation while watching television to his leaving the house.

When she'd finished Andrew said : 'Why on earth didn't you tell us this before?' He sounded utterly bewildered. 'Phillips asked you about that half-hour at length. I was here. You said you knew nothing at all except that Bob had made one or possibly two 'phone calls, you didn't know who to, and had gone out.'

She didn't reply for the moment. She looked at him and her lips trembled. Then she quickly stood up, moved across the room, and started straightening some magazines on the sideboard. With her back to him she said: 'I – I'm sorry. I guess the only reason is that I've been a bit crazy for the last couple of weeks.'

He got to his feet, an expression of concern on his face, and crossed to her. 'Oh, Jill, I'm sorry. Honestly I didn't mean to tick you off.'

She turned to face him. 'You've got a perfect right to get riled. I must seem like an idiot. But you see, Bob made me swear that I wouldn't say a word about it to anyone – whatever happened. I've never known him so solemn about anything. So after he went out, I made a definite effort not even to think about it, to put it right out of my mind. Then – then you came and told me he was dead. And – I don't know exactly what went on in my head then. The shock did kind of shove it all down into my unconscious or subconscious. I'd already been trying to forget it, and your news did somehow have the effect of putting it right out of my brain.

'Of course,' she walked back to her chair and sat down, 'I didn't really forget about it in the strict sense. I mean, I guess I could have told Mr Phillips everything if I'd really put my mind to it. But I *was* crazy just then. I hated him and I hated everything to do with the police except you. I blamed them for Bob's death and I didn't want to help them. And I wanted to do something more for Bob, and pretty well the last thing he told me was not to say a word to anybody about what had happened. So I didn't. Of course, it was a good excuse not to have to think about it or talk about it. It was good to be able to say I knew nothing and not feel guilty about it – because I could tell myself I was just carrying out Bob's final instructions. And then you all went away, and nobody asked me any more questions. Which was what I wanted. Anyway I don't know much about psychology but that's how I figure my mind must have worked. Frankly, the whole period's pretty hazy to me now. I wasn't normal. Was I? Be honest.'

He gave the ghost of a smile. 'You were – a little odd.'

She asked: 'Is the information any use?'

He shrugged. 'It may be. I can't say. Bob said it could be dangerous and to keep it to yourself?'

She nodded.

'Well, he knew more about it than me and he must have had a

reason. So I think you'd better keep that promise. Of course, don't take it to the extreme lengths you did last time. If you hear of me being done in before I get back to the Yard, then ring Phillips and tell him. But short of that forget it. OK?'

'OK.'

'Good. And you've told me everything now?'

'Yes.'

'Then let's talk about something else. What are your plans?'

'I'm going home, Andy.'

'To America?'

'Yes. There's nothing really to keep me here now.' She was watching him closely as she said this, and thought she might see some expression of regret. But there seemed to be no reaction at all.

He asked: 'To your parents?'

'Yes, of course.'

'Oh, I thought perhaps that in view of the way you talked them out of coming over that there – I mean, that you had something against them – that you didn't want to see them again.'

'No, nothing like that. I just didn't want them *here*, don't you see? When I get home I want to try to forget the last seven years altogether – take up my life where I left it off before I came to England. At the moment I've come to terms with Bob's death. I can talk about it. But I don't know how long I can keep that up. There's no point in trying to hang on to the past. So I'm going to wipe the slate clean. Now I haven't seen my folks in five years. They've never been to this house. So when I get home there'll be nothing to remind me of any of this at all. But just suppose they'd come over last week – stayed in this house, come to the funeral? Don't you see? To meet with them again under those conditions would mean they'd always be associated in my mind with these last ten days. They'd have shared it and be a part of it. But as it is I've kept the two sections of my life separate. I can go home and be sure there's going to be nothing to bring any of this back at all.'

'You had all that worked out from the beginning?'

'No, only since. At the time they called, I just knew instinctively that it would be best they didn't come.'

She seemed to become aware for the first time of a frown in his eyes. 'What's the matter? Don't you approve?'

'I've got no right to approve or disapprove. You must do what you want. It just wouldn't be my way, that's all. Because I don't think it can work. However much you plan to wipe out this part of your life and take up where you left off in the States I don't think you'll be able to. I don't reckon life can be divided up into watertight compartments like that. I hope I'm wrong. I hope you succeed in completely forgetting Bob and everything about England if that's what you want. I just doubt if you'll be able to.'

He stopped and lit a cigarette; they were both silent for half a minute. 'But it's none of my business,' he added. 'Don't take any notice of me. Do it your own way. When are you hoping to leave?'

'Within a week I hope. I've seen a lawyer and he's taking over everything – the sale of the house and furniture and the car and giving Bob's things to charity, and dealing with the probate court and the insurance company and anything else that comes up. I've given in my notice at the library, so all I've really got to do is pack my personal things, say good-bye to a few people, and go.'

'I shall miss you,' he said softly.

Ten minutes later Andrew left. Jill took him to the door. He said: 'I'll see you again before you leave?'

'Sure. And, Andy, I'd like to know if anything comes of what I told you.'

'We're not supposed to talk about our cases, you know.'

'Now don't be so darn pompous,' she said. 'I've a right to know, don't I? Think I'd blab it around?'

'Well, perhaps we can stretch a point.'

'You'd better.'

Nine days later, on a Tuesday afternoon, Jill sat alone in the sitting-room of her house, waiting for Andrew. She had not seen him since his Sunday visit of the previous week, but she'd called him that morning and he had agreed to stop by about three.

Her preparations to leave had taken a little longer than she had hoped, but now this was to be her last full day in England. The house seemed strangely bare. Her personal possessions had, but for the clothes she had on, a coat, and a few immediate necessities, been sent on to the United States.

A terrible sense of oppression, almost of doom, was hanging over Jill at that moment. She could not understand it, because all she really wanted now was to get away. But she felt like death as she sat there waiting for Andrew, and it was a relief when she heard a car pull up outside.

A minute later Andrew was sitting opposite her again.

'Well?' she asked.

He pursed his lips. 'Nothing, I'm afraid.'

She felt her face showing surprise. 'But the 'phone calls, the man on television . . .'

He looked embarrassed. 'Sorry,' he said.

'What do you mean "sorry"? There must be something to tell.'

'Nothing came of it, Jill. Just leave it at that, will you?'

'No, I won't. I want to know what's been happening.'

'I can't tell you.'

'But why not? You're still on the case, aren't you?'

'Of course.'

'Did you follow up what I told you yourself?'

'Not personally. I passed it on to Phillips. He put me on to – to another angle. But the 'phone calls and the television were a dead end. They led nowhere. Leave it at that – please. Don't push it.'

'What about the Alpha List?'

He looked wretched. 'Please, Jill. I can't tell you anything else. I said more than I should have last time.'

She was shocked. 'Listen, Andy. You've known me over six years – right?'

He nodded, looking unhappy.

'During that time you and Bob must have discussed hundreds of cases in front of me – some of them highly confidential. You both knew you could trust me. Do you think I've suddenly become a blabbermouth? And about *this* case among them all?'

'Don't be silly. It's nothing like that. It's just that . . .' He broke off and groped for words. 'Well, it's simply that we've been especially warned off talking about this case.'

'What do you mean "warned off"?'

'There's been a general clamp-down. Phillips had all of us who've been on the case into his office and said we had to look on our work as top secret. We're not to discuss it with our colleagues in other departments, or our wives – not even among ourselves when we're off duty. Now I shouldn't even have told you that. So don't ask me to say anything else. I'm very sorry, Jill, but there it is.'

Jill had gone white. She gasped : 'It's a cover-up!'

'What?' He looked puzzled.

'Phillips has had his instructions from above. There are a lot of wealthy and important people involved and someone's using pull to get things hushed up.'

He tried to interrupt, but she wouldn't stop. He'd never seen her like it before. Her eyes were blazing and she was shaking with anger. It was all she could do to keep coherent.

'Bob said he was on to something big. You said so, too. You said there was an M.P. involved, and an earl's daughter. There's been some big political or society scandal, and they're trying to cover it up. You're being manipulated. It's nearly three weeks now since the murder and you still haven't made an arrest, or even issued a description. Because behind the scenes somebody's pulling strings.'

It was his turn to look angry. 'That's nonsense and you know it. Don't you know the Met better than that after six years? We just don't do things like that.'

'I'm not saying the police themselves realise what's going on.'

'Do you think we're all fools?'

'No, but I don't think you're up to the politicians and the civil servants. They're expert at hushing things up. It's their job.'

'I must say you seem to have a very good opinion of us – of me personally. Just because we haven't got the killer in two weeks or so, you seem to think we're all idiots who can be given the run around by a bunch of stuffed shirts in Whitehall. What makes you think we aren't making progress, anyway? I didn't say we weren't. I just said I couldn't tell you about it.'

'Well, are you? Don't give me any details, but are you making progress?'

'Yes. Some.'

'Some! When is there going to be an arrest? Tomorrow? Next week?'

'I can't answer that.'

'Because you won't or because you don't know?'

'Both,' he snapped.

There was silence for a few seconds while they both calmed down. Then Jill said more quietly: 'I'm sorry. I got carried away.'

'That's all right. But you're wrong, Jill, honestly. Take my word for it.'

'If you say so.' She paused, then added: 'I wanted you to come round to say good-bye.'

'I know. Leaving tomorrow, you said?'

'Yes. Eleven o'clock flight from Heathrow.'

'I see. Well, have a good flight. And my regards to your folks.'

'Thanks.'

He stood up. 'I'll have to be getting back now.'

'Good-bye then, Andy. Thanks for everything. You've been a rock.'

'Good-bye, Jill. It's been an experience knowing you. I've loved coming here over the years.'

'I loved having you come. We both did. Bob thought the world of you, you know.'

'I thought the world of him. And he was crazy about you, Jill. He'd want above everything for you to be happy. I'm sure he'd say you were right to go back to America. So don't feel guilty about it. Go and be happy. Forget all this.'

He put a hand on each of her shoulders, leaned forward and kissed her on the cheek. She kissed him back and then walked with him to the gate and waved him off.

She went back indoors and sat down in the sitting-room again, lay back and looked at the ceiling. A pity they'd parted like that. Rowing and then making it up. Ending awkward and constrained. Mouthing platitudes at each other. It was her fault. She'd been cruel to him. After all, he *was* under orders. Bob himself would have obeyed an order of that sort.

But it was odd. Very odd. Hadn't they even been able to trace the man on television? Or had they traced him, and . . . ?

On an impulse, Jill got to her feet, went through the house and out to the back garden. There, in a shed just outside the kitchen door, was a pile of magazines. She found the TV programme papers that covered 22nd October, the date of Bob's death, took them back indoors, and opened the first one.

Minutes later she sat back, a strange expression in her eyes. It must have been between ten and five to seven that Bob had seen the man on television. There were three channels. And at that time one had been showing a film about Arctic exploration and another a 1940 Hollywood movie. At ten to seven both would have been about halfway through. The weather chart had come on a few moments after Bob's exclamation. Neither of the two programmes would have been interrupted in the middle for a weather forecast.

So Bob had been watching *Now*. *Now* ended up with a weather forecast. And on that channel the next programme started at seven.

Now was described as a topical magazine programme. Jill watched it from time to time and knew that much of it was given over to interviews with celebrities.

She now knew what Bob had been watching. It had been very easy to find out. She had told Andrew everything she knew – the time of Bob's exclamation, the weather chart she had seen on the screen. So nothing was surer than that the police, too, knew what programme Bob had been looking at.

And with that knowledge, surely it would have been simple for them to discover who had been appearing between ten and five to seven. It would just have been a matter of going to the studios and asking the people in charge. They would certainly keep a record. Of course, there might have been a snag. Jill remembered that *Now* went in for off-the-cuff street interviews. The man Bob had seen might have been a nonentity just casually picked up by the camera and quite unknown to the producers.

Jill was suddenly filled with a desperate urge to know. Her heart beat a little faster and her eyes went towards the telephone. Would the television people give her the same information they'd given the police? It wouldn't hurt to ask ...

She spent a few more minutes working out her strategy, then looked up a number in the telephone directory and dialled it.

It was all surprisingly easy. Having spun an involved and she feared implausible story to the press officer about being an American journalist doing a series of articles on British television, who had lost the notes she had made for a feature on *Now* and who was flying home that day, she was told to wait. A couple of minutes later she was talking to a girl in the producer's office. The girl had obviously merely been told to give Jill all the information she required, was slightly bored and completely incurious.

She said: 'You wanted a run-down on our October 22nd edition?'

'That's right.'

'I've got the whole programme here. Shall I read it out?'

'Please.' Jill grabbed a pencil.

'We opened with Ricky Radley miming his latest disc. Then we had an interview with Olaf Andersen the Swedish rally driver; film of some street interviews – men giving their opinions of the latest Paris fashions; a film report by Mark Jennings about a poltergeist in a Manchester council house; and a discussion about Women's Lib between Diane Conway and Jessica Dalton. OK?'

Jill was scribbling furiously. 'Just one thing. Have you got the exact times those items started and finished?'

'Yes. Six seventeen Ricky; six twenty-two Olaf; six twenty-nine fashion interviews; six thirty-four poltergeist; six forty-four Conway and Dalton; six fifty-six weather; six fifty-eight fade out.'

Jill stared at the scrawled notes in front of her. 'Let me get this straight: from six forty-four until the end it was just the two women talking?'

'That's right.'

'Nobody else appeared?'

'Dick Murray was the interviewer but he didn't get a chance to say much.'

'Nobody else at all came on before the weather?'

'Only Phil Holmes, the compère. Dick would have handed back to him, he'd have wound up, read the forecast, and said goodnight.'

'And there was no film or anything – to illustrate the discussion?'

'Not according to what it says here.'

'Was there a studio audience?'

'We never have an audience on *Now*.'

'Oh, sorry. Tell me again – who were those women?'

The girl gave a slight sigh. 'Jessica Dalton is the militant American Women's Lib leader. You know, breaks up beauty contests, gatecrashes men's clubs. *You* ought to know of her.'

'Er, yes, of course,' Jill lied. 'It was the other one I didn't quite catch.'

'Diane Conway? She's an actress. Or was. Very popular here some years back. Then she got married and retired. Still comes on television occasionally – champion of traditional values sort of thing – marriage, motherhood, religion, femininity. You know. They had a real set-to.'

'Was it live?'

'Oh, let me see. Ah. No, it wasn't. Oh, I remember now. We recorded it in the afternoon. Jessica only had a few hours in London. She was passing through on her way home. She had to catch a plane at six. She'd left the country before the show had started.'

Jill said: 'You've been very helpful. Just one other thing. You said Diane Conway was married. You don't happen to know who to, do you?'

'Oh, it's somebody in the Government, I think. I'll see if anybody knows.' The line went quiet for a few seconds. Then she came back. 'Yes, she's really Mrs David Romford. Her husband's a junior minister at the Foreign Office, or something.'

It had been a woman Bob had seen.

Only four people had appeared on the screen at the time when Bob had been watching. Two of them were well-known television personalities, the third an American who'd been in the country only a few hours and had left before the programme had begun. That left only the minister's wife.

Jill drew a deep breath. It fitted. A woman who'd be vulnerable to blackmail, whose husband was in a position to pull strings.

Why had Bob let her think it was a man? She had assumed it, and he hadn't corrected her. Why?

'Simply,' she said aloud, 'because if I'd known it was a woman I'd have wanted to know who. And he didn't want to have to refuse to tell me. But nor did he want me to know a thing more than was really necessary – for my own good.'

It had taken her less than fifteen minutes to identify the person Bob had gone out to see. The police must have done so just as easily. So Phillips knew Bob had gone to see Mrs David Romford. Had he interviewed her? And perhaps cleared her? If so, why had Andrew and the others been told not to talk? Had Phillips been ordered to lay off her? If that was the case, he wasn't really to blame. What else could he have done?

And what could she do? It would be no good telling Andrew what she had discovered. He would be trammelled by the same instructions as Phillips. If he was convinced of Diane Conway's involvement, he would certainly ignore orders. But this might jeopardise his career. And she couldn't ask that.

Jill started looking through the telephone directories. But no number was entered for either Diane Conway or Mr and Mrs David Romford.

Thinking deeply, Jill went to the kitchen to make some coffee. The unnaturally tidy and bare appearance of the room brought her up short as she suddenly remembered that the next day she was supposed to be leaving for good. She sat down again hurriedly and stared blankly in front of her.

She couldn't go. Not now. Not until she'd got to the bottom of things. She owed Bob that at least.

And having made the decision she felt a tremendous sense of relief. She tried to figure out why. But all she knew was that she felt she had a clear conscience again. She didn't feel guilty.

Guilty! With a shock she really took in Andrew's words for the first time. 'Don't feel guilty about it.' He must have felt she was wrong, must have felt she *would* feel guilty. Or he would never have said that. And she must, all the time, have been subconsciously feeling it herself. That explained the sense of oppression hanging over her.

Well, that was finished. She was going to stay. But she wouldn't tell anybody. Particularly Andrew. He would only try to stop her. He would say she was taking a risk. When he found he couldn't stop her he would hang around and try to look after her. And she didn't want Andrew near her. Not now. She'd been relying on him too much. It had to stop. Or she might find herself not going back to the States after all.

She brewed some coffee, and sat down to drink it and make some concrete plans.

She would leave the house tomorrow, as arranged, and let it be assumed she had flown home. But instead of going to the airport she would go to an hotel. Quickly, before anything else occurred to make her change her mind, she went back to the hall and cabled to her parents:

Delaying departure for short time. Leaving house tomorrow for hotel. No cause for alarm. Do not attempt contact me yet. Will write with address soon. Love, Jill.

But after she'd got to the hotel: what then? She badly needed help. Someone who knew how to make the sort of enquiries she had in mind. Someone who was his own master and not under the jurisdiction of Scotland Yard.

A private detective.

7

'Jill! *Croeso!*'

'Hullo, Owen.'

Sherwood stood up and came forward with his hands out as Maggie showed Jill into his office the following day. He looked straight into her eyes as she held out her own right hand and he took it in both of his.

'How are you, Owen?'

'Very well. Jill – I don't know what to say. I would have written, of course, if I hadn't seen "no letters" in the paper. But I can't *say* anything. Take it all as said, will you?'

'Of course.'

The telephone rang. He gave a sigh. 'Sorry,' he said and answered it. A shrill female voice started to speak at the other end. Sherwood made a face to Jill and waved her towards a chair. She shook her head and started to wander round the room.

Grey distempered walls, bare but for a couple of calendars; a floor of rough boards, the centre covered by a good quality carpet; a large coal fire burning in an old-fashioned black-leaded grate; an enormous old deep leather settee; a television set; a tape recorder; a filing cabinet; and books, several hundred of them crammed into three bulging bookcases; a wooden table that served Sherwood as a desk, covered with letters, bills, newspapers, sheafs of typescript, five ash-trays full of black stubs, six empty and dirty tea cups, the telephone, and a loudly ticking alarm clock. And Sherwood himself sitting at the table in an old sports coat with leather-patched elbows, a heavy woollen cardigan, and corduroy trousers.

Sherwood rang off. Jill crossed to the table and sat down facing him. He smiled. 'Have a cup of tea?'

She shook her head.

'Sure?'

'Quite sure, thanks.'

'There's no coffee, I'm afraid.'

'It's all right, really. I don't want anything.'

91

He raised his voice to yell: 'Maggie! *No* tea for Mrs Palmer.' In a normal voice: 'Right. Now, at long last, what can I do for you?'

'Would you take me on as a client, Owen?'

'Certainly.'

'Don't you want to know the assignment first?'

'No.'

'That's very nice. I don't know what your fees are . . .'

'Nothing in your case.'

'Then we can forget about it.' She made to get up.

'Oh, all right. I'll charge you a fee if it'll make you happier. What do you want done?'

'Do you know Mrs David Romford?'

'Know of. Wasn't she the actress – Diane something or other?'

'Conway.'

'That's it. What about her?'

'I want you to find out if Bob called on her the night he was killed. If he did, I want proof of it.'

He slowly reached for a small black cigar and lit it. 'Tell me more.'

'I think you'd better hear the whole story.'

'I think I'd better.'

The door opened and Maggie came in carrying a cup of tea, put it on the table in front of Sherwood, and went out again without speaking. Jill started her story. She told him everything – from Bob's recognition of a trick with the hands used by somebody on television, to her own telephone call to the studios the previous day. He remained silent throughout, listening intently, sipping his tea and puffing at his cigar.

When she'd finished, he carefully stubbed out his cigar. 'Your assumption is, I take it, that the woman on television was a victim of the blackmailers; that Bob telephoned her and persuaded her to talk to him; but that somehow *they* found out and killed him before he could report what *he* had found out about her.'

Jill gave a satisfied nod. 'That's it exactly.'

He stared pensively down at his desk for a few seconds. 'This Alpha List – got any ideas about that?'

'I wondered if it might be a list of blackmail victims, drawn up by these crooks. She is or was on it apparently, and Bob told her he knew other people who were, too. I think that was a shot in the dark on his part. He guessed that the other victims he'd been in touch with were on it too.'

'Tell me: why do you think Bob was so adamant about your not telling anyone what you'd heard?'

'I guess he didn't want me involved. He was on to something that it could be dangerous to get mixed up in.'

'I'm sure you're right: he certainly wanted you kept out of it. But really, if what you'd heard could have been dangerous, the safest thing for you would have been to spread it around as much as you possibly could.'

'What are you getting at?'

'Simply that I think when he made you give that promise he was thinking *chiefly* of keeping faith with Diane Conway – assuming it *was* her he was speaking to. He needed the co-operation of someone like her. Therefore she had to be made to trust him. So he had to protect her – from both the villains and possibly the police. The criminals weren't to find out she'd been talking to him. And the police weren't officially to be notified of whatever it was she'd done that made her vulnerable to blackmail. Bob personally was willing to overlook it – it can't have been anything too terrible, obviously – but he couldn't guarantee his bosses would agree to this. Hence his insistence that *nobody* was to know about her. Perhaps, too, he didn't know how much you'd actually heard. He could have thought you knew who he was talking to.'

'Then why didn't he ask me?'

Sherwood smiled. 'Would you have really liked that?'

Jill's face cleared. 'You mean I might have thought he didn't trust me if he'd started cross-questioning me?'

'You know the answer to that better than I. But wasn't it preferable to say nothing and just extract a promise that you wouldn't talk about it?'

'So I was wrong to tell Andy after all?'

'I didn't say that. Bob didn't know then he was going to be killed. I don't think you had any choice. And, as things have turned out, it doesn't seem to have mattered. Diane Conway appears to be still in the clear as far as the police are concerned.

'But the point I'm trying to make is this: Diane Conway would be the type terribly vulnerable to blackmail. Bob needed her. And a police officer willing to cover up for her and help her out of a jam would have been a godsend to her. It just doesn't seem she could have any motive for being involved with his death. He was on her side.'

'I'm not saying she actually killed him,' Jill said doggedly. 'But she must be involved somehow. Nobody knew Bob was going to see her that night except she herself. Bob himself didn't know until fifteen minutes before he left the house. So at the very least she must have tipped off the killer. Perhaps inadvertently. Perhaps against her will. But either way she knows something. She must do. There's just nobody else.'

'You did say you thought Bob rang someone else as well.'

'That was *before* he rang her. He didn't know then he was going to see her.'

'Any ideas who it might have been?'

She shook her head. 'He could simply have got a wrong number. Or perhaps she's got two addresses and he called the wrong one first.'

Sherwood picked up his cup, looked into it, saw that it was empty, and put it down again.

'It has occurred to you that the police might already have investigated Diane and cleared her?'

'Yes, it occurred to me. But why wouldn't they say so?'

He shrugged. 'They might have their reasons.'

'Nonsense. All Mr Phillips had to do was call me and tip me the wink that they'd traced her and positively cleared her, but that for political reasons they wanted her name kept out of things. I'd have been satisfied then, and let it drop.'

'Well, it's possible they're still investigating her – that they're *not* satisfied about her yet.'

'Again – why not say so? I mean, they don't know *I've* discovered her identity. So it couldn't do any harm to tell me the truth. No. There must be something fishy going on. Either that or Phillips and his men never traced her at all – which would mean they were so incompetent they need all the help we can give them anyway. You've got to admit it, don't you?'

Very slowly, Sherwood nodded. 'I don't go right along with you. The Yard moves in a mysterious way its wonders to perform sometimes. But certainly in this case things are not all as they seem.'

'And there are questions that need to be answered?'

'Yes.'

'Then just find the answer to one of them for me: if Bob saw the Conway woman that evening. Will you do that?'

'I'll try.'

'How long will it take?'

'I don't know. I'll ring you.'

'I'm staying here,' she said, and handed him a hotel card. 'And don't forget I've left England. You haven't seen me.'

'I understand.'

'Thanks.' She stood up. 'And now I guess I've kept you quite long enough.'

'No, no.' He spoke rather absently as he rose too. He took her to the door. 'I'll be in touch,' he said. 'As soon as possible.'

It was almost exactly twenty-four hours later that Jill received a 'phone call from Sherwood. 'Can you come round?' he asked, 'or would you rather I came to the hotel?'

'Stay there,' she said. 'I'll be right with you.'

Thirty minutes later she was again sitting opposite him. 'Well?'

He drummed with his fingers on the desk. He said deliberately: 'Question One: did Diane Conway kill Bob? Answer: to the best of my knowledge, no. Question Two: did she cause him to be killed? Answer: with same reservation, no. Question Three: did he call on her the night he was killed? Answer: yes. Question Four: does she know who did kill him? Answer: I believe she does.'

Jill couldn't take all this in at once. She stared at him stupidly for about ten seconds. Then a sense of pure pride triumphed momentarily over every other emotion. 'I was right then. It *was* her Bob saw on television – and telephoned.'

'Yes. And it was an excellent piece of detective work. I congratulate you.'

'I ought to be congratulating you,' she said. 'How on earth did you find out all that so quickly?'

He smiled. 'The conventional answer is: "I have my methods." '

'Professional secret, is it? Well, I think it's terrific.'

'Thanks.'

There was a pause.

95

'Well, go on,' she said.

'With what?'

'The rest of the story.'

'I'm sorry, I thought you understood. I can't tell you how I...'

'I don't mean that. I mean exactly *what* you found out.'

'I already have.'

'But there must be more to it than that! I mean, what proof do you have?'

'None at all. Not of the sort that would stand up in court.'

'Can you get proof?'

He shook his head.

'But you are sure of your facts?'

'Pretty sure.'

'So – where do we go from here?'

'Well, where you go is up to you. I can't really go anywhere from here. I've carried out your commission, and that's it.'

'But this is plumb crazy! You say you know Bob called on her before he was killed, and she knows who the murderer is. And you figure on just leaving it at that.'

'Listen, *cariad*,' he said. 'I've had to take a lot of things on trust during the last twenty-four hours. Also, I've had to make a solemn promise that I would not reveal my source. If I hadn't, I would have got nothing. I must keep faith. It's not as if I knew the name of Bob's killer, or that my informant does either. I've given this a lot of thought and I know of no way I can get proof of Diane Conway's involvement, or – as things stand at present – of the identity of the killer. I'm not really equipped for murder investigation, you know. I'm no Philip Marlowe. So what would you have me do? If you wish, I'll go to the police and tell them exactly what I've told you. But do you really want me to do that?'

'You know I don't. But what am I going to do?'

'Go back to the States and leave it to the pros.'

She started to protest, but he raised his hand and went on: 'Now I know you suspect that a corrupt British Establishment is shielding Bob's murderer. I don't. I do believe that one or two people in important positions are trying to cover things up and perhaps trying to interfere with the Yard. But I'm quite convinced the truth will out eventually. So I would say go home, let me keep a watching brief here for you, and wait and see. If I'm wrong and the affair isn't cleared up in a few weeks, then I've got a very good journalist friend who just loves scandals and who'd be positively delighted to blow the whole case wide open. So go home. No one will think any the worse of you.' He took a cigar from a box on his desk, leaned back, and lit it, keeping one eye fixed on Jill the while.

'Thanks, Owen.' Jill stood up. She looked pale and her voice shook a little. 'I appreciate all you've done and all you've said. I'm sure it's good advice. I – I don't know yet if I'm going to take it. I'll just have to think it over.'

'Yes, you do that,' he said, standing up and walking with her to the door. 'Sleep on it. You needn't decide anything in a hurry.'

Jill had never known greater loneliness, even in the few days immediately following Bob's funeral, than she did for the rest of that day and night. She stayed in her hotel room, having a couple of snacks sent up. She wrote a brief letter to her parents. But most of the time she just lay on her bed and thought. She felt in desperate need of somebody to talk to. Just to tell of her problem would have been a help. But there was no one she could turn to. Andrew and Owen had both tried to help in their different ways, but both, basically, had failed her. Both had kept things back, inhibited by the ethics and instincts of their craft. Both had been kind, but over-protective. And neither had been willing to go all the way with her.

She tried not to blame them. In cold logic she could see both their points of view. And yet . . . They were both professional detectives. They'd both been friends of Bob. Yet Andrew was willing virtually to ignore the data she'd given him, to leave it all to Phillips and just accept that it had been worthless. Or if he didn't deep down believe that, he still was not prepared to do anything about it.

And Owen, who had vital information, was content just to sit back and let things slide 'for a few weeks'. By which time the killer might have left the country.

They'd failed her. And there was nobody else she could turn to. So she would have to see it through on her own.

Jill couldn't sleep that night. But when morning came she

knew what she was going to do. She got out of bed and went straight to the telephone.

A woman's voice answered.

Jill asked: 'Is Gerry Cochran there, please?'

'Who's speaking?'

'Mrs Pa . . . er, Jill.'

'Hang on.'

There was a clatter as the receiver was put down, some voices off, then Cochran's voice, puzzled. 'Hullo?'

'Gerald?'

'Yes.'

'This is Mrs Palmer.'

'Good lord!' He sounded quite staggered. 'Where are you, Mrs Palmer?'

'In London.'

'Gosh, I'd thought you'd gone back to the S-States.'

'Most people think that. And I want them to go on thinking it. Listen, Gerald, I want to see you urgently.'

'See me? Why?'

'I'll explain when I see you.'

'Oh yes, of course. S-sorry, Mrs Palmer.'

'How soon can you make it?'

'Well, I don't know. I've got to be at the Yard by nine today.'

'How do you travel?'

'Tube.'

'Well, today you're going by taxi, at my expense – part of the way, at least. If you're agreeable, I'll get one and pick you up somewhere along your route. Then we can talk in the cab. Now, what's the best place?'

'Where are you now?'

She told him, he thought for a few minutes, then gave her instructions.

'Right,' she said. 'Oh, and Gerald – that lady I spoke to: who was she?'

'My mother.'

'Can she keep a secret?'

'Sure.'

'That's OK, then. I won't ask you to spin her any tale. But I don't want it spread around that I'm in town.'

'Don't worry. Mum's used to keeping my secrets.'

Jill leaned out of the taxi window and waved. Gerald Cochran came running across the road, dodging the traffic, and got in the back of the taxi beside her. Jill tapped on the glass partition and the driver started off. Cochran was panting somewhat.

'Sorry, Gerry. Did I give you a rush?'

'A bit. But it's all right.'

'I expect this all seems pretty crazy to you,' she said. 'What happened was that it was only this morning I decided I had to speak with you. I didn't want to contact you at the Yard or wait till this evening when you came off. So this was the only way I could think of. I was sorry to call so early.'

He grinned. 'My mother was fascinated. Who was my new girl friend? Why hadn't I mentioned you before; and she thought you started to say you were "Mrs" something or other, so was I carrying on with a married woman?'

'I'm sorry about the cloak and dagger stuff. It's simply that I told everybody I was going home and I don't want anybody to know I'm still here – and that includes the Metropolitan Police.'

He nodded. 'Nobody will hear anything about you from me. What was it you wanted to see me about?'

Jill said: 'I think you worked pretty well exclusively with Bob during the last few weeks of his life, didn't you?'

He nodded, opened his mouth, closed it again, went rather red, and eventually said: 'I wanted to say s-something, Mrs Palmer, about Inspector Palmer, I mean, but there never seemed to be a chance and you didn't want letters s-so I never got round to it. B-but I don't reckon anyone in the force, even Mr Thompson, thought more of him or has missed him more. I learnt a tremendous amount from him. It was a terrible thing – terrible.' He turned his head away and looked out of the window.

'He thought a lot of you, too,' she said gently.

'Did he really?' He turned to face her again.

'Yes. He said you worked like a beaver, were quick to learn, and he was sure you were going to do well. I know there was nobody he liked having better for his assistant. And I think you must know more than anybody about that last investigation.'

'Yes, I reckon I do. Of course, I've passed on everything I know to Mr Phillips.'

'You were definitely on to something big, were you? Bob didn't talk about it much.'

'No doubt about it. I think we – well, Mr Palmer, that is – would have cracked it, too.'

'What's happened to the enquiry since – has it been dropped?'

'Not exactly. It's sort of been absorbed into the . . .' He hesitated.

'The murder enquiry?'

'Yes. They're not looking for the blackmailers so much *as* blackmailers now. But Mr Phillips has had all Mr Palmer's notes – and mine too – and he's been going back over the ground Mr Palmer and I covered, trying to get a lead there. Presumably when he finds the murderer he'll have found the blackmailers automatically. I'd like to think I was going to be there.'

'I expect you will be.'

He shook his head. 'I'm not on the case now.'

'You're not?' Jill stared at him.

'No, I've been transferred to different duties altogether. I've been pretty fed up about it, actually. There's nothing I wanted more than to help get the man who killed Mr Palmer. Instead, I've been put on to assisting Superintendent Baldwin and Sergeant Harris on a blasted charity swindle.' He sounded bitter.

'Perhaps – perhaps they felt you might have been a bit too emotionally involved, having known Bob so well.'

'Nobody could have known him better than Mr Thompson, and he's in on the case up to his neck.'

There seemed no reply to this. Jill said : 'I know how you must feel. *I* feel I ought to be helping in some way, too. In fact, I think I may be able to.'

Cochran was immediately interested. 'Oh? How?'

'I'd need your help.'

'Anything, of course.'

'Don't be in too much of a hurry to agree. What I'm asking you to do is to break police regulations. Would you do that, if I promised you no one would ever know – and nobody would be harmed?'

'Well, I s-suppose so. I mean, I might. I'd have to know . . .'

'All I want is some information. You and Bob were trying principally to track down people – wealthy people – who might have been victims of this gang, weren't you?'

He nodded. 'Except that they weren't all wealthy. Some were just in a position to supply dirt on those who were.'

'Did you have much success?'

'We were pretty sure we knew of six or seven people who'd been got at in various ways by the same bunch.'

'Would you tell me their names and addresses?'

He hesitated. 'Could you tell me why, Mrs Palmer?'

'I want to go and see them. Just to talk. I think there might be some among them who'd say things to me they wouldn't say to a policeman. And I've got a question or two to ask that Mr Phillips won't have asked.'

Cochran said: 'I want to help. But if they ask how you got hold of their names, what will you say?'

'That I found some of Bob's notes among his papers at home – private notes made for his own reference, that I've since destroyed them, and nobody knows anything about them. I don't normally tell lies like that, but this is a good cause. And it would be quite impossible to disprove. So how about it? I'll be very discreet. I promise.'

Cochran was looking a little unhappy, but he nodded. 'I don't suppose it can do much harm. Have you got a notebook?'

Jill said: 'Geoffrey Hurndall. Lady Felicity Mannering. Marion Kendall. And Mrs Percy Wetherby. Is that all? You said six or seven.'

'Two of the other victims are dead.'

'So is Wetherby. And he was the victim, you said, not his wife.'

'Yes, but she may well know more than she's admitted. The other two didn't leave any families, and their friends couldn't tell you much. One was a schoolmistress.' He gave her a run-down on the Greenhill affair, then went on: 'The other was a Catholic priest in Brighton.'

'Father Dooney!' Jill exclaimed. 'So I was right.'

'How did you know about him?'

She explained, and he told her what they'd found out.

Then she said: 'I heard some talk, too, about an M.P.'

'He wasn't blackmailed by the same crowd but by a petty crook working on his own. We think our bunch had had their sights on the M.P. and thought the little guy was poaching on their preserves, so kindly provided us with evidence against him. But the M.P. himself couldn't tell you anything: the organisation didn't have any dealings with him.'

'What about the little crook?' Jill began.

'No, Mrs Palmer,' he said firmly. 'For one thing he's in prison, for another you wouldn't get anything out of him, and for a third I'm not giving you any data that's going to lead you into those sorts of circles. You be content with what you've got. None of those people are really criminal types, and I doubt if you could come to any harm from just talking to them. But I'm not going to let you get mixed up in the underworld.'

'You're as bad as Bob. OK, we'll leave it at that. And thanks very much. I do appreciate it.'

There was a sudden rather awkward silence. Cochran looked apprehensive, as if he'd just realised how much he'd put himself in Jill's power. Jill hesitated, wondering whether it would be wise to ask one further question. At last she took the plunge.

'I told your bosses about a 'phone call Bob made that evening before he went out. And about somebody he thought he'd seen connected with the case on television. Do you know if anything came of it?'

She asked really only to see his reaction and to find out if there had been any gossip about her information among the lower ranks. She couldn't say any more: to say she'd already been told her information had led nowhere would be to let Andrew down.

'I haven't heard anything about it, Mrs Palmer,' he said. 'I could ask around if you like.'

'No, don't do that. They're probably limiting it to those who are actually working on the case. If you mention it, you might be asked how you knew about it, and that could be awkward. I'll hear soon enough if it did lead to anything. It was probably a dead end. Forget it.'

'As you like. There are always dozens of tantalising little clues in a case like this that've all got to be followed up. Most of them up blind alleys.'

Jill nodded. She was eyeing Cochran thoughtfully. He was intelligent, knew more about Bob's last investigation than anyone, and was obviously dedicated to getting at the truth.

So why had he been taken off the case?

8

Geoffrey Hurndall's eyes were appreciative. They travelled slowly from Jill's hair to her ankles and back again as she was shown into his office.

Cochran had given her a piece of advice about dealing with Hurndall. 'Play on your femininity,' he had said. 'Flatter him. And be rather helpless.' She could sense now that it was good advice. And she would have no difficulty in following the last part at least. She *felt* helpless. And very embarrassed. What she was doing must, she knew, be virtually without precedent. Jill, whose whole background was one of the utmost conventionality, did not enjoy doing things that were without precedent. Moreover, she had had very little to do with men like Hurndall, and she didn't quite know how to approach him. However, she had Cochran's advice.

With something of an effort she looked straight into his eyes. 'It's real good of you to see me, sir. I know how very, very busy you must be. I sure appreciate it.'

'No, no, not at all. Great pleasure, I assure you. Do sit down, Mrs Palmer.'

He indicated a low, contemporary-style office chair. Jill gingerly sat down, showing rather a lot of leg. She gave her skirt a couple of token tugs downwards.

'A drink, Mrs Palmer?'

'Oh no, really, thank you . . .'

'Oh, come, come, it'll do you good. Help you to keep your pecker up.' He crossed to a small cabinet. 'What'll it be?'

'Well, er . . .'

'I know. Don't tell me. Cream sherry, eh? Nice and sweet.'

He poured some into a glass, came across to her, bent low over her, and put it in her hand.

'You're very kind,' Jill said softly. She cast her eyes demurely downwards.

Really, she thought, I don't think I'm doing this too badly.

Hurndall poured himself a drink of some sort and then sat down in front of her, quite close.

'Now, Mrs Palmer, just what can I do for you?'

Jill took a deep breath. 'I don't quite know where to start. But – my husband called on you about six weeks ago, I believe.'

'He did. Very nice feller. Sympathetic. Not like some cops you meet. I was very sorry to read about what happened. My, er, my sympathies.'

'Thank you. Has anybody else from the police been to see you since the murder?'

'Yes. Two Scotland Yard johnnies. Phillips was one and Thomas – Tom – something . . .'

'Thompson.'

'That's right. And I must say I didn't take too kindly to 'em at all. Bombarded me with questions for about half an hour. Went all over my road accident again. Nasty they were about it, too. Not sympathetic. Not like your husband. Why do you ask, Mrs Palmer?'

'Well, you see, Mr Hurndall, I was going through my late husband's papers a few days ago and I came across some private notes he'd made about the case he'd been investigating before he died. These weren't his official reports, you understand, and there was more guesswork in them, more of his impressions. I shouldn't have read them, perhaps, but I did. Afterwards I destroyed them. I thought it only fair. They were very frank about quite a lot of people he'd been seeing over the past weeks.'

Hurndall looked a trifle alarmed. 'Er – did he mention me?'

'Why, yes, Mr Hurndall, but not very much. Simply that you hadn't been able to help him a great deal. He added that you seemed a very honest, decent man who'd had a raw deal.'

Hurndall seemed to relax. 'Oh, that was very nice of him. But I still don't see why you've come to me. Though,' he beamed toothily at her, 'charmed, of course.'

Jill said: 'I'll try to explain. A lot of people seem to have told Bob things in confidence – things that I don't imagine he'd put in his official reports. Now he was on the track of some professional blackmailers. There are a number of things in the notes which I think might be important clues – just odd words, names, addresses, things like that. He'd only been writing for his own reference so naturally it's a bit disjointed in places, and I can't honestly understand much of it. But if it could be correctly interpreted I really think it could be valuable. But I didn't think it would be fair to show it to the police. So I decided to go round to one or two of the people whose names were there and who, from Bob's comments, are obviously not suspect, and see if they could throw any light on any of it. I thought I'd start with you, just read out some of these words and names, and if they mean anything to you and you can assure me they have no possible connection with Bob's killers, then I can cross them off the list. Then perhaps I can go and do the same with one or two other people who the notes make clear are OK. Eventually I might be able to eliminate all the innocent ones and go to the police with just one or two names they should look into more closely. That way the innocent wouldn't have their private affairs reported to the police, yet the police would be given all the relevant information.'

'I see.' Hurndall nodded slowly. 'Well, that's OK by me, Mrs Palmer. Fire away. Tell me some of these names and things.'

'Thank you,' said Jill, feeling now a lot more confident, as Hurndall had apparently accepted her story. She took out a notebook. In it she had written a number of meaningless words and names she had made up at random. She started to read these out: 'Seagull. Gregory Howard. The Brown book. Pedro Corelli. Three Angels. Mary Cunningham.' Then, watching his face very closely, she said: 'The Alpha List.'

There was not a flicker of reaction – any more than there had been for her made-up words. She went on with a few more of these, then said: 'Diane Conway.'

'Hang on,' said Hurndall. 'I know that name. Actress, isn't she?'

'I don't know.'

'Yes. Quite big a few years back.'

'You never met her personally?'

'No. Is she mixed up in this business?'

Jill shrugged. 'You tell me. Have you heard her name come up?'

'Not until now.'

'What about Mrs Romford?'

He looked blank. 'There's a David Romford has some sort of government job. That's all I know of Romfords.'

Jill read out a few more red herring words, then closed the book.

'That the lot?' Hurndall asked.

She nodded.

'Wasn't much help, was I?'

Jill leaned forward. 'Mr Hurndall, is there anything at all you know that you failed to mention to my husband or to the other policemen? No matter how trivial. I promise you if there is I'll keep it to myself. I know there are some things one doesn't like to tell the police. But I'm not the police. I'm just a woman who's been left a widow because her husband was trying to help innocent, upright people like yourself who'd been preyed upon by these vampires.' She reached timidly forward and put her hand on his. 'Do please help me.' There were tears in her eyes.

Hurndall stood up suddenly and turned away. The back of his neck reddened and he coughed. Jill jumped to her feet, too, ran round him and stared eagerly into his face. 'There *is* something, isn't there? Oh, do tell me. Please!'

Hurndall's moustache twitched. 'Ah,' he said. 'Oh. Well, one small thing, perhaps.'

'What? Please tell me.'

He pulled away from her, crossed the room, and poured himself another drink. He said: 'This is in strict confidence, mind.'

'I promise.'

'OK, then. How much do you know about my case?'

'Very little. Just that you were involved in some sort of road accident.'

'Well, it's a matter of public record. I didn't report it. The details aren't important. But the point is that I told your husband nobody else had known about it. That wasn't quite true. I had told one person.'

'Who was that?'

'A – a young lady. We were very good friends, if you follow me – this was back in the spring. I said something one day about how any kind of shunt shook you up. Then she more or less wormed the whole story out of me.'

'What was her name?'

'She called herself Joyce Summers.'

'You mean that wasn't her real name?'

'I don't know. She – she disappeared. She had a flat in town. I went there one day and found she'd gone. Left no forwarding address. Nobody knew anything about her. I've never seen her since.'

'And this was before the blackmail?'

Hurndall drained his glass. For a moment his face looked vicious. 'About three or four weeks.'

'I see,' Jill said slowly. 'It certainly looks suspicious.'

'I know, don't rub it in. And I know I should have told your husband. But I didn't want to look too much of a fool and I tried to believe it was just a coincidence. I didn't want to believe it of her. Then there was my wife. If I'd told the cops and they'd traced Joyce and prosecuted they could have subpoenaed me to give evidence. It would have all come out.'

'I – I understand how you felt,' Jill said.

'Of course, when I saw your husband there was no question of murder involved. And I reckoned it was my business if I didn't want Joyce caught. It was me she'd done the dirty on. I admit that after your husband was killed I should have told those other two all about it. But they riled me. And I didn't like being browbeaten and more or less told I'm a crook and a liar.'

'Could you give me a description of her?'

'I can do better than that.'

He walked across to a wall safe, opened it, rummaged inside and took out a postcard-size unmounted photograph, came back, and handed it to Jill. 'That's her.'

The picture was of a girl in her mid-twenties with black hair and heavy make-up. It was not a posed portrait but had been taken out of doors. It was a full-face, the girl's mouth was slightly open, her eyes staring with little expression slightly to the right of the camera.

Hurndall said: 'I took that myself. Telephoto lens. She didn't know. I was going to show it to her the day I found she'd disappeared.'

'Can I keep this? I'd like to show it around. I won't say *where* I got it.'

He hesitated, then said: 'Yes, you can have it. If you can trace her, good luck to you. And if she blabs about me it'll be just too bad. This business has got to be cleared up, I can see that. Though it'll probably mean the end of my marriage.'

'Why not tell your wife all about it, Mr Hurndall? Before she hears some other way.'

'Well.' Hurndall flung himself down into a chair. 'Might be wise, I suppose. Take a bit of doing, though.'

'Think how good you'll feel after – however she takes it. Nothing hanging over you.'

He brightened a little. 'That's true. Be rather like the way I got out of the other trouble: went and owned up, you know.'

Jill put the photograph in her handbag. 'Thank you, Mr Hurndall. You've been very helpful.'

He clambered to his feet. 'You off? Oh. Well, glad to have been of service. Best of luck. And if you catch up with her slap her face for me, will you?'

9

Lady Felicity Mannering was feeling good. For once in her some-what turbulent life things seemed to be working out. She'd been continuing her 'changing down through the gears' until now, as she said to herself and anybody else who cared to listen, 'I'm definitely down to second. Only one to go.' The wedding date had been fixed, St Margaret's, Westminster booked, Claridge's alerted. It was all delightfully square. Her fiancé, Charles, had taken another rung up the Foreign Office ladder towards his ambassadorial target, and everything was set fair.

Someone who hadn't seen Felicity for three or four months would have noticed a big difference in her. Her eyes had more sparkle, her skin more colour, and her hair more life. Her lips turned up more and she looked generally fresher. There was an improvement even since the time that Bob Palmer had seen her, a little more than three weeks before.

Felicity was whistling as she slammed the front door of her flat behind her and ran down the steps to her car at about eight o'clock on the evening of Friday, 13th of November. The car, a sober, dark blue Austin saloon, was new, a reconciliation present from her father. Charles had not approved of her old, psy-chedelically painted Land Rover.

Her mind elsewhere, Felicity put the key in the lock of the car and turned it. She tried to open the door. But it would not move. Coming down to earth, she looked momentarily puzzled. Then she realised that the door must have been unlocked all the time and what she had just done was to lock it. She turned the key back again, opened the door, and got in. She started the en-gine, switched on the lights and, rather gingerly, as she still wasn't completely at home in it, edged the Austin out into the centre of the road and accelerated gradually away.

Then she felt it. Something cold and hard against the back of her neck. Felicity drew in her breath in a strangled wheeze, and the car swerved. From low in the back of the car she heard a loud whisper: 'Careful, careful!'

Felicity recovered herself with an effort. 'You fool!' she gasped. 'You might have killed us.'

'*You* might have been killed,' whispered the voice calmly. 'I don't think I would have come to much harm down here.'

'Oh, thanks very much.' Felicity was really angry. 'Who is it? Reggie, I suppose.' She braked and pulled into the side of the road. 'I can't think of anybody else who'd play such an absolutely idiotic joke.' She stopped the car and started to turn round. Then she felt an agonising blow on her shoulder. She gasped with pain.

'This is no joke,' whispered the voice. 'And I'm not Reggie. This is deadly serious. Don't turn round. Drive on. This is a gun.'

For a second a gloved hand was passed over Felicity's throbbing shoulder and a small automatic was shaken in front of her eyes. Then it was withdrawn and she felt the pressure again on the back of her neck.

'Now,' came the whisper again, 'drive on. I don't want to shoot you but I will if I have to. So do what you're told.'

Felicity felt herself go cold all over. It wasn't a joke. It was real. Her first thought was: it's like a bad movie. Then the gun was jabbed harder against her neck. Hardly knowing what she was doing, she drove on.

After thirty seconds she got her breath back. 'Look,' she said, 'I don't know what you want with me but I ought to warn you I was on my way to meet my fiancé. We're going to the opera . . .'

'Naughty,' the whisperer interrupted. 'Charles is away. Brussels. Official talks. You were simply on your way to a little informal party at a girl friend's. You told her you might not be able to make it and not to be surprised if you didn't turn up. So nobody's going to start worrying about you for a very long time yet.'

Felicity said nothing.

'I chose this occasion very carefully,' said the voice. 'We've got the whole night ahead of us. Turn left here.'

The drive went on for over an hour. Felicity was forced to go right out of London, then off the main road and into the country, along narrow, twisting lanes, and at last off public roads altogether, slowly along a rutted cart track sloping downwards through a wood. Suddenly, car headlamps flashed thirty yards ahead.

'Flash your lights once.'

Past arguing by now, Felicity did so.

The other lights came on again and stayed on.

'Pull up in front of that car.'

Again Felicity obeyed.

'Right. Turn off the engine and get out.'

Terribly frightened by now, Felicity got out. She was dazzled by the lights of the other car, but she appeared to be in a clearing about forty yards wide. She stood blinking as she heard the rear door of her car open and close. The gun was poked into her back again. In the gloom behind the headlamps she could dimly see two large figures.

The voice behind her whispered: 'Lean against the side of your car. Put your hands out along the roof and stay there.'

Felicity did as she was told. She heard the whisperer go across to the two men by the other car, and there was a muttered conversation. Then the engine of the other car started up, it backed and seemed to move round in a circle until it was facing the side of the Austin, its lights now shining straight on to her back. The engine stopped, and for a few seconds there was a silence which was broken only by an icy east wind shifting and rattling the branches of the trees. Felicity, who was wearing a winter-weight coat, nevertheless found herself starting to shiver uncontrollably.

'Turn round.'

Felicity did so, putting up her hand to shield her eyes from the light. The three were standing around her in a semi-circle. The two big men from the other car each wore stocking-masks, and it was impossible to see their features. Her captor, the whisperer, whom she now saw for the first time, was shorter and was standing between the other two, wearing a dark-coloured anorak with the hood up. The face under the hood was deathly white and – Felicity gave an hysterical sob – without nose or mouth. A second later she realised that what she was looking at was another mask – simply a piece of white cloth with two eye-holes cut in it. In the left hand the whisperer still held the gun, in the right something long and thin.

Together, the three took a step towards her. Felicity shrank back against the car, the door handle digging into the small of her back. The whisperer spoke again:

'Felicity Mannering, you have been brought here to be punished. Your punishment will be to be beaten until you can't stand up, and then beaten some more, and more again, until we are tired.'

The right arm was raised, and Felicity saw that the long thin thing was a riding whip.

She stared at it in undiluted horror for a full five seconds. Then she made a sudden desperate dash to her right. It was hopeless. One of the big men caught her before she'd moved six feet. She struggled and kicked like a mad thing, but within a few seconds the two of them had her firmly, one by each arm. Felicity started to shout as she continued to kick and struggle.

'Take her coat off.'

The two men manhandled her out of her coat, tearing it badly, and threw it on to the ground. Under it she was wearing only a light silk cocktail dress, cut low at the back. But now she didn't feel cold.

'Turn her round. Put her up against the car and hold her arms out.'

Felicity was forced into position, her face turned sideways and pressed against the curved edge of the car's roof.

'Right.' The voice was gloating. 'In a moment I will tell you what you are being punished for. But so you will properly be able to anticipate what lies ahead here is a taste to go on with.'

There was a nerve-destroying pause, a swishing sound, and the riding whip landed with a crack on her bare shoulder blades. Felicity's body arched in anguish, but she didn't scream, only intensified her yelling. Again the whip was raised and brought slashing down, again a searing pain shot across her back. And this time Felicity could not keep back a scream.

'That's just an aperitif,' said the voice, 'to give you something to think about while we get your clothes off. Hold her tight. I'm going to cut through this dress with a razor. She'll get a few extra gashes if she keeps jumping about. But they'll hardly notice by the time we've finished.'

Felicity felt gloved hands fumbling at the back of her dress, and she felt cold metal against her skin. 'Now, as to why you are being punished . . .'

The voice broke off. Then, so fast that she couldn't properly take it all in, Felicity was conscious of a lot of things happening in quick succession. She saw a bright jerking light away to her left. She heard the sound of a car horn repeatedly blown, a shout of alarm from one of her captors, an urgent 'Scarper' from another, and – incredibly – a police whistle. She felt her arms released, and the Austin apparently starting to float straight upwards.

As she sank to the ground, she was just aware of a confused jumble of sounds: running footsteps, slamming doors, racing engines – all around her, some departing, others approaching. Then she blacked out.

Felicity came round to a dim light, a swaying motion, and a vaguely familiar chugging sound. She lay still for some seconds, then realised that her head was on somebody's shoulder, and that this somebody's arm was round her.

Suddenly the clearing in the wood and all that happened there came flooding back. Terror engulfed her and she started to struggle. Her back came in hard contact with something and it ramped with pain.

'Hey, steady,' said a soft voice, 'you're safe now. Take it easy.' Somebody was trying to push her gently down, but she forced the restraining arms away and sat up.

She was half lying, half sitting on the back seat of a London taxi. Her coat had been put over her to act as a rug, and the person she had been leaning against, who apparently had been trying to keep Felicity's back away from the seat, was a girl – a nice-looking, auburn-haired girl, a few years older than herself.

Felicity stared at her, then said: 'They – they kidnapped me – with a g-gun – hit me – made me drive for miles – b-beat me with a riding whip – tore my clothes.' She broke off and burst into tears, sinking her head on to the other's shoulder. The girl smoothed her hair. 'I know. I saw it all. That's right. You cry. It's the best thing you can do.'

So for some minutes Felicity cried. Then she stopped and sat up, feeling rather foolish. 'I'm sorry.'

'What for?'

'Being such a drip.' She groped for her coat, reached for a

handkerchief in the pocket, blew her nose hard and said: 'I heard a police whistle.'

The girl smiled, opened a handbag on the seat beside her, and took out a whistle on a chain. 'That was me. My husband gave it to me years ago. I've carried it ever since. This was the first time I've ever blown it for real. They don't use them much now, but I guess it's a kind of reflex action with characters like that to take to hills when they hear one.'

Felicity was looking at her blankly. 'Do you mean it was just *you* frightened them off?'

'Me and the cab-driver.' She motioned towards the burly figure sitting up impassively in front of them. 'He was great. I figure he would have taken the whole bunch on single-handed.'

'But how was it you were there? Who are you?'

'My name's Jill Palmer. How I came to be there's rather a long story. Can it wait till we get you home? I told the driver to take us both back to your apartment. I hope that was all right. I didn't think you'd want to bother with police stations yet – though I had to fight with the cabby over that. He was all for stopping at the nearest nick.'

Felicity said: 'You know where I live?'

'Yes. I was on my way to see you earlier this evening.'

'Why?'

'My husband was Bob Palmer – Inspector Palmer.'

Felicity's hand went to her mouth. 'Oh, gosh! The detective who was...'

'Murdered,' said Jill.

'He came to see me.'

'I know. That's what I wanted to talk to you about.'

'My place was crawling with – with police for ages after it happened.'

'Yes, I expect it was.'

Felicity hesitated, then asked: 'Do you know about me – I mean, why he came to see me in the first place?'

'Not in any detail. Bob didn't tell me about you, if that's what you mean.'

'Why did you want to see me?'

'Let's leave that for now, shall we? I'd like to talk to you properly when we get to your place, if I may.'

'You can talk till Christmas, if you like, after tonight. It was

114

a miracle. You saved my life.' She was silent, then said: 'My car.'

'I locked it. I took your purse out first. Here it is. The car key's inside. The car'll be quite safe there until you can fetch it.'

They didn't talk much after that. The taxi stopped outside Felicity's flat, and the girls got out. Jill assured the driver he would be called as a witness if it was necessary, Felicity forced a five-pound tip on him, and he drove off protesting. The girls went indoors.

Felicity walked straight over to a drinks table, filled two spirit glasses to the brim with colourless liquid, came back and handed one to Jill.

'What is it?'

'Vodka. Don't you like it?'

'I've never tasted it. But I'm sure I can't drink all that.'

'Try. Like this.' She tossed hers down. 'Whew. That's better.'

Jill took a tentative sip. 'Nice,' she said. She drank some more. 'But that's enough for me.' She put the glass down. 'Let me have a look at your back.'

'Oh, there's no need for that...'

'Don't be stupid. Sit down.'

Felicity sat down, and Jill removed the coat from her shoulders. She drew in her breath sharply.

'Is it bad?' Felicity asked.

'There's been some bleeding. And there are two very nasty weals about twelve inches long. And there's a big black bruise higher up by the side of your neck.'

'Yes, that's where the devil slugged me in the car – with a gun, I think.'

'Where's your medicine chest?'

'Haven't got one. Anything I do have in that line is scattered in various corners of the bathroom.'

'Where's the bathroom?'

'Through there. But look, there's no need for you...'

'Just shut up, will you, and stay there.'

She went through the door Felicity had indicated. Felicity called after her: 'You sure you don't want this vodka?'

'Quite sure, thanks.'

Felicity picked up Jill's glass and sipped from it slowly. Jill came back with a bowl of warm water, some lint, and sticking plaster. She bathed the wounds and covered them with long pieces of lint held in place by strips of plaster.

'Perhaps you ought to get a doctor to look at it. But I don't think I'd bother if the pain's not too bad. The marks should disappear in a few days.'

'They stung pretty bad when you touched them but it's bearable. Thanks.'

'I think you'd be wise to cover yourself – keep warm.'

'You're probably right. I'll go and change.' She went to her bedroom, took off her dress and put on a heavy warm dressing-gown.

When she came back, Jill said: 'You will go to the police, I suppose.'

'Not likely.'

'No?'

'Too damned embarrassing. Think I want it in the papers that I was dragged off into the country and walloped like a school kid? Father haring down from the country, Charles dashing back from his talks in Brussels, both having fits. No thank you!'

'Well, I won't try to persuade you. I'll be rather glad myself not to have to give a statement to the police just now.'

'That's settled, then. Hungry?'

'I am rather.'

'Scrambled eggs suit?'

'Well, thanks, sounds lovely, but you can't . . .'

'Why not? I had worse beatings up than this at the genteel school for aristocratic young ladies I attended – and played hockey half an hour later. That's what made me what I am today – utterly depraved.'

Twenty minutes later Felicity put her tray on the floor, sat back in a big armchair, kicked off her shoes and tucked her legs up under her. Jill, who was pouring coffee, handed her a cup. Felicity took it, lit a cigarette, waited until Jill was sitting down also and said: 'Right. First things first. How did you come to follow me this evening?'

'I was on my way to see you. I'd called here earlier as well, and one of your neighbours said you were out. But he pointed to your car and said you couldn't have gone far or you'd have taken it with you or garaged it. I was coming along the street in a taxi the second time and we got held up by a van turning. Then I saw your front door open and somebody come out. I thought it was probably you but I couldn't be sure. I was watching you closely to see where you went and then I looked to see if the car was still where it had been. It was, and I clearly saw someone move in the back. Then they seemed to get down on to the floor. I thought it was odd. Then you went to the car, got in and drove off, just as the van got out of our way. I told the driver to follow you. I was keen to see you as soon as I could anyway, so I wanted to know where you were going. But also I was a bit uneasy about what I'd seen. You see, I knew you'd had some sort of trouble with the men who killed my husband.

'I couldn't have seen anything if I hadn't been watching closely. There was only the street lighting. Next I saw a silhouette rise up in the back. My driver saw it, too. Then your car swerved. A few seconds later you pulled up. We stopped thirty yards behind. I was going to get out and run up to you, but then it looked as if the figure in the back hit you, and you drove on again. We stayed with you.

'We nearly lost you when you turned down that track, but I just got a glimpse of your tail light. We followed a little way with the lights off. Your car seemed to stop, so I got out and went ahead on foot. I got quite close and then I saw those guys with stockings on their heads and the other one pointing a gun at you, and I knew you were in real trouble. So I hared it back to the cab and told the driver to coast down with his lights off. We could see quite well in the lights of that other car. Then those two big toughs grabbed you and that other one started hitting you and it was obvious we couldn't hang around any longer. The driver started his engine and switched on his lights and began tooting his horn, and I leaned out of the window blowing my whistle. And that was just about it. They melted. I felt like John Wayne leading in the 7th Cavalry.'

'You couldn't have been more effective if you had been. I can only say thanks. I'd have been a pretty bloody mess by now if you hadn't shown up – and I use that word literally.'

'Did you see anybody else – apart from those three who went off in the car?' Jill asked her.

'No. Why?'

'I'm sure I got a glimpse of another figure lurking about in the trees – after they'd taken off, when we were getting you into the cab.'

'Just a tramp, perhaps?'

'Maybe. Anyway, now it's your turn. Who were those guys? What did they want?'

'I haven't a clue who they were. Just hired thugs, I imagine.'

'But hired by whom?'

'Her, of course.'

'*Her?*'

'My charming little friend with the riding whip.' She saw that Jill was staring at her, a look of astonishment on her face. She stared back, not understanding Jill's expression. Then her face cleared. 'Of course! You must have thought that was a man.'

'It wasn't a woman!' Jill's voice was incredulous.

'A girl. A very respectable, quietly-spoken girl of the type who might call on you collecting for the Red Cross.'

'But who is she? Why did she do it?'

'As to why I should guess it was just revenge. But I don't know. *Who* she is I don't know either – though I have had dealings with her before.'

'Tell me. Please.'

'She tried to blackmail me. And I kicked her. A lot. Very hard.'

Jill's face was a study. Felicity laughed. 'I'll tell you the whole story.'

And she did. When she'd finished, Jill said: 'And you think all this was just to get her own back?'

Felicity lit a second cigarette from the stub of the first. 'I should imagine so. I can't think of any other reason. She told me I was being punished.'

'You're quite sure it *was* her tonight, are you?'

'Oh yes. She tried to disguise her sex by speaking in a whisper. But I knew, all right. Not a doubt.'

Jill's handbag was beside her. She opened it, took out the photograph Hurndall had given her and passed it to Felicity. 'Is that her, by any chance?'

'Good lord! You can't mean it.' Felicity grabbed the picture and stared at it.

Jill waited a few seconds. 'Well?'

'I don't know,' Felicity said slowly. 'It could be. If it is, she's tarted herself up a lot and she's wearing a lot more make-up. And she's got a wig on. It's like her. That's all I can really say. Who is this, anyway?'

Jill said: 'Do you mind if I have some more coffee?' She got up, poured herself another cup and sat down again. 'I think it's my turn to tell the whole story. I've felt the need of an ally for some time and I think I can trust you.'

'I'm a thief, you know. An ex-junkie, a lush, and pretty corrupt all round.'

'I don't think you're corrupt.'

'Well, perhaps I'm not as corrupt as I was. As *you* might say, "Corruptionwise I have de-escalated".'

'I most certainly wouldn't. But I still think I can trust you.'

Felicity smiled. 'Thanks. Actually, you can. So shoot.'

The only things Jill kept back were Cochran's name, and the other names he had given her. Felicity listened attentively, chain-smoking throughout. At the end, she stared at Jill silently for several seconds, then leaned forward, stubbed out her cigarette, and laughed. 'Fantastic,' she said.

'What do you think?' Jill asked.

'I agree with you. There's something nasty in the woodshed. I think you've done wonders to uncover all you have done.'

'And you know now why I was coming to see you.'

Felicity nodded. 'And the answers are as follows. I've never heard of the Alpha List, and if I'm on it it's news to me. I know Diane Romford slightly. Charles, my fiancé, comes under her husband at the F.O., and we went to a dinner party there a few months ago. But I certainly don't know of any connection between her and a gang of blackmailers.'

'What's she like?'

'We've never really moved in the same circles, but she's sort of queen in the circle I'm going to have to move in after I marry Charles. She seems almost too perfect – very attractive, super clothes, and always about two months ahead of everybody else with new fashions. She's quite charming and never seems to put a foot wrong in anything she does. Being an actress, of course, has made it all easier for her. The part of the flawless Mrs Romford is just her biggest and best part so far. From what they say she's very ambitious and determined David's going to get to the top. She made a packet from films, but gave it up quite happily when she got married, by all accounts. She was extremely nice to me, and I'd be delighted if she was mixed up in this business. But that's pure cat. I can't stand anybody quite as good as she is. And I think she's highly suspicious and quite definitely a master lady criminal.'

Jill smiled absently. 'What about David Romford?'

Felicity shrugged. 'I've no real views on him. He's pleasant, quiet, rather intense. Negative sort of chap. But he must have something, I suppose. He's out of the country at the moment, incidentally – official talks.'

'Oh? Same ones as your fiancé?'

'No, funnily enough – Far East. It's been quite a tour – he's been gone about a month. I don't know what it's about. Exports, or something equally sordid, I expect.'

'So,' Jill said thoughtfully, 'she's had plenty of time to get into trouble. When's he coming home, do you know?'

Felicity shook her head.

Jill said : 'Lady Felicity, is there anything...'

'Drop the Lady bit for Pete's sake. Just Felicity'll do.'

'OK. Thanks. Is there anything you didn't tell Bob that day which might help me now? It's important.'

'Oh dear,' Felicity said, 'I hoped you weren't going to ask me that.'

'That means there is?'

'Two things, I'm afraid. I told him two lies. I didn't think it was important at the time, but then, of course, I had to repeat them to the other cops who came here. You won't tell them, will you?'

'No, of course not.'

'Well. In the first place I told your husband that the woman was after information about my father. Or, rather, he assumed it was my father, and I let him think so. It wasn't. It was Charles. But I couldn't have Charles mixed up in it, do you see? He's got to be so terribly careful.'

'What did they want to know about him?'

Felicity didn't answer for a few seconds. Then she gave a quick little shake of her shoulders. 'Oh well, you've trusted me with so much, I suppose I've got to trust you. A good few years ago Charles did something stupid. He joined the Communist Party. He was never a Red. But he wanted to find out more about them and he thought that was the best way to do it. He must have been pretty naive in those days. But at least he had the sense to use a false name. And it only lasted a few months. But you can imagine it could scupper his career if it ever came out he'd been a Party member. That little – little – that girl I kicked knew about it, or at least a part of it. How I don't know. Certainly not from me, although Charles did tell me all about it before we ever got engaged. The point is that she knew all the details except the two most important – the name he'd used and the branch he'd joined. And that's what it was all about.'

'I shouldn't think that could have been very important from Bob's point of view,' Jill said reflectively. 'I mean, it couldn't have misled him at all. Whoever they were after ultimately – your father or Charles – doesn't seem relevant, because they didn't get to either of them, after all. They only got as far as you. It was the attempt to blackmail you I think Bob was interested in. Because that really did happen.'

'Yes, but I didn't tell him the strict truth about that either.'

'Own up,' said Jill.

'Mind you, that's not quite as bad as it sounds. What happened was that your husband asked me who might have known about the trunk in my uncle's house with all the loot in it. I told him there were dozens and that I couldn't put a name to anyone in particular. Well, that wasn't true. There probably were quite a number of people who knew about it. But in my own mind I've no real doubt who it was blabbed.'

'Who?'

'A man called Philip Harrington. I can't tell you much about him. He's an accountant and he lives in Hampstead.'

'Why are you sure it was him?'

'Well, that's it. That's why I said the lie's not quite so bad as it sounds. I mean, I've got no evidence of any kind – nothing that a policeman would call evidence. Philip was just one of a gang I used to go round with. We were never lovers or anything. The only reason I've got for feeling sure it was him is simply a look in his eyes one day.'

'You'd be surprised,' Jill told her, 'how often Bob would get a lead from a look in someone's eyes. Did you never tackle this man about it?'

'No. I mean, how could I? He'd just laugh. And he'd put it round that I was making crazy accusations about him. I never see him nowadays, anyway – or any of that crowd.'

Jill didn't answer. She was deep in thought. Felicity watched her face for a few seconds, then said: 'Look, am I in on this? You said you wanted an ally. I'd love to help.'

'I don't quite see what you could do.'

'Haven't you got to see those other people – the millionaire's wife and the old widow and the priest's friends and the school-mistress? Let me take on one or two of them. You may not believe it, but I can be very discreet.'

'Are you sure you want to get involved?'

'Involved! Aren't I involved already? Not content with trying to blackmail me, nearly getting me jailed and trying to ruin Charles, they then kidnap me, drag me off into a wood and start belting me with a riding whip. Don't I owe them something?'

'I guess you do. I'd like to have you around, I really would. Let me think over how you can help and come and see you again tomorrow, can I?' She stood up. 'I'd better get back to my hotel now. It's late.'

'Stay here.'

'What – overnight?'

'Why not? There's an empty room with a reasonable bed and clean sheets.'

'Why, thanks a lot.' Jill was touched. 'It's very nice of you. But all my things are at the hotel.'

'I do happen to have soap and towels and I can lend you a nightdress, if you want one – I don't usually bother myself. The only thing you'd have to do without would be a toothbrush – and can't you manage without cleaning your teeth one night?'

'Yes, of course, it's not that . . .'

'Do you have a particular love for your hotel?'

'No, it's kind've grim, actually.'

'Then that's settled. In fact, there's no need why you should go back there at all except to fetch your things tomorrow. Move in here permanently till all this is cleared up. Would you like that? Do say if you couldn't stand my company all that time. I won't be offended.'

'Oh, that's not it,' Jill said hurriedly. 'It'd be great. But are you sure you want a stranger cluttering up the place . . . ?'

'I don't feel you're a stranger,' Felicity interrupted. 'And I'll be glad of the company. Charles will be away for a week. I've broken with all my old crowd. Normally I'd be pretty much on my own and I might fall back into bad habits. You'll be able to help keep me on the straight and narrow.'

'Don't count on me being too good at that. But it's a wonderful invitation. I love your apartment. And I'll be very glad of your help. Thank you very much.'

'That's fixed, then. And tomorrow the Daring Girl Detectives go into action . . .' She broke off. 'Sorry. I shouldn't joke about it. It's damn serious, really, isn't it?'

'Yes,' said Jill. 'It's damn serious.'

Half an hour later Jill was just snuggling down into bed in Felicity's spare room when there came a tap on the door and Felicity pushed her head in. 'Which would you say would be the more painful: a hard kick on the shin from a solid toe-cap, or a swipe across the back from a riding whip?'

'Heavens, I don't know. About the same, I should think.'

'Yes, I would, too. And that means I'm still about ten to one up on her. A happy thought on which to retire. Good night.'

10

The next morning Jill went back to her hotel to collect her things, while Felicity telephoned their taxi-driver of the previous day and arranged for him to take her out to collect her car. This was necessary because they suddenly discovered that neither of them had any idea how to get there.

Jill arrived back with her luggage at about ten o'clock while Felicity was still out. She let herself in with Felicity's spare key, put her things away, and then went straight out again to call on Mrs Wetherby. By eleven-thirty she was back the second time, to find Felicity home and making coffee. They sat down to talk.

Jill said: 'That was a waste of time. She knows nothing about her husband or Jo – or his boss, the millionaire, or the Alpha List or Diane Conway.'

Felicity said: 'Look, if I'm going to be any use to you at all, I really must know who all these people are. I've already guessed the millionaire is Joshua Kendall, so why not tell me about the others? You know so many of my guilty secrets, about my lying to the police, and all about Charles and the Communist Party that I'm hardly likely to risk getting your back up by gossiping about your secrets, am I?'

Jill gave a nod. 'All right, then. Everything except the name of the fellow who gave me the names. He doesn't exist – I got them all from Bob's private notes. Check?'

'Check.'

Jill gave her all the names. Felicity then said: 'So you're left with Marion Kendall, Father Dooney, and Greenhill School?'

'I don't know if it's worth bothering about Father Dooney,' Jill said thoughtfully. 'When you can talk to a person who was actually blackmailed himself, or to a relative, there's always a chance he'll tell you something new – something that was kept back from the police. But if it's just friends or colleagues – well, they're not likely to have anything *to* keep back.'

'You could say the same about the people at the school, though, couldn't you?'

Jill nodded. 'I don't think I'm going there, either.'

'Let me go, Jill. Let me borrow that photograph and show it to the teacher who saw the visitor. What's her name . . . ?'

'Brown. If she does identify her, is it going to get us anywhere?'

'Maybe not from your point of view, but this is a personal thing between her and me. I'm getting more and more certain the girl in your photo is my girl. If I can tie her in with the school business as well, then it'll be another step towards catching up with her.'

'OK, if that's what you want. And I'll tell you something else you can do while you're there.'

'What's that?'

'Find out the name of the girl from the very wealthy family who was expelled. Her parents were one of the gang's next targets apparently. It might be interesting to know who they are.'

'Right. I'd better not say "expelled", though. I'll say "left the school suddenly".'

'Yes, that'll be better. When will you go?'

'Today, if possible. Let's see exactly where it is.'

She fetched a road map and soon located Greenhill School. 'Oh, I can get there in two hours. If I leave now I can have lunch on the way, be there by mid-afternoon and back by six comfortably.'

'Hadn't you better call first and make sure Brown is there today and can see you? It is Saturday.'

'Oh, she'll see Lady Felicity Mannering, all right – particularly as I shall say it's a private matter of great urgency. They're all snobs in these places. But it might be as well to check she's not down with foot and mouth or taking a party of brats climbing Everest or something.'

Five minutes later she'd fixed an appointment with Miss Brown for three o'clock that afternoon.

'What about you?' she asked Jill before she left.

'I'm stuck with Mrs Kendall. I fancy she may be the most tricky of all.'

It was four o'clock exactly when Jill rang Marion Kendall's front door-bell. Her heart was beating fast, but not so fast as when she'd called on Hurndall. This sort of thing was getting easier.

The door was opened almost immediately by a lean, tired-looking woman of about forty.

'Mrs Kendall? I'm Jill Palmer. I called you earlier.'

'Well, you're punctual, anyway. Come in.'

'Thank you.' Jill went past her and stood waiting in the hall while Marion Kendall closed the door.

'In here.' Mrs Kendall opened a door on the right of the hall, and Jill walked in. It was like an old-fashioned dentist's waiting-room – clean, cold, tidy, and utterly impersonal. 'Sit down,' Marion Kendall said, indicating a high-backed, hard-looking brown leather chair. Jill sat down. Marion Kendall sat down in another identical chair opposite her across a small highly polished table, saying, rather surprisingly as she did so: 'I sent the girl out.' It occurred to Jill that the other woman was embarrassed at having answered the door herself.

Jill said: 'It's good of you to see me, Mrs Kendall.'

'I didn't quite understand what you were on about. You said you're Inspector Palmer's widow?'

'Yes.'

'I was shocked to read of his death, of course.' She spoke flatly and slowly, enunciating her words clearly, 'and you have my deepest sympathy. But you'll excuse me if I say that I didn't feel very well-disposed towards your husband. Frankly, he behaved badly to me – tried to trick me into talking about Joshua's affairs, and let me think he hadn't seen Joshua when in fact he'd just come from him.'

'I'm sorry you feel like that,' Jill said. 'I know that there would be only one thought in Bob's mind – to round up this gang of blackmailers he was after. That's why he was killed. He was very sorry for the people who'd been persecuted by these crooks and he wanted to help them. And he believed you'd been suffering at their hands. That's why he behaved like he did. It was for your own good.'

'You said on the telephone you'd found notes of his in which we were mentioned?'

'Yes. I've destroyed them now. But I can tell you what they

said almost word for word, I think. Shall I?'

Marion Kendall nodded.

' "I feel sorry for the Kendalls. They've suffered, I think – particularly Mrs Kendall. I should guess they were decent people who'd been driven desperate. Whatever trouble the Kendalls are in the blame can be laid fairly and squarely on the shoulders of these gangsters." Apart from that it was just more or less verbatim notes of the conversations he had with you and Mr Kendall.'

'He really said that?' Marion Kendall sounded genuinely surprised.

'Isn't that what he more or less said to you himself?'

'Well. Something like that, I suppose.'

'But you didn't believe him, is that it, Mrs Kendall?'

Marion Kendall shrugged. 'I did at the time. But after, when I heard what had happened at the prison and how angry Mr Cadwallader – our solicitor – was, well, then . . .'

'But you didn't tell him the truth, did you? About the blackmail, I mean.'

Marion Kendall's eyes widened, she hesitated and seemed to be torn between two desires.

'It's all right,' Jill said. 'There are no witnesses and I'm not connected with the police. I don't feel too well-disposed towards the police myself, actually. All I'm interested in is seeing the men who killed my husband behind bars. They're the same men who caused you so much misery. If there's anything at all you can tell me that you didn't tell the police, it might lead to your getting your own back. So please tell me the truth. I give you my word I won't tell the police you've talked to me. You *were* blackmailed, weren't you?'

Marion Kendall's eyes dropped. Then, without looking at Jill, she slowly nodded her head twice. Jill said nothing. Marion Kendall looked up. 'Your husband knew it quite well. Perhaps I should have told him everything there and then, as he wanted.'

'It must have been awful for you,' Jill said softly.

And at that, without warning, all the emotions which must have been pent up within Marion Kendall for months seemed to be uncorked. 'Awful?' The word came out as a kind of squawk. 'It was a nightmare! Josh was nearly driven crazy. We had everything. Everything! Josh worked his way up from nowhere and we had it made – two houses, a yacht, Rolls-Royces, posh friends. And then it started.'

She was speaking louder and faster now and enunciating less distinctly. Her voice was not so well modulated, her accent coarser. 'Your husband thought I'd suffered, did he? I'll say I suffered – knowing that any moment they might hand those papers over to the police, knowing we might be arrested. And worst of all knowing that Josh could get right out of trouble, could get those ruddy papers back if he'd just co-operate with them.'

'He didn't consider paying?'

'Pay! They didn't want money.'

Jill stared at her blankly. 'What did they want, then?'

'They wanted industrial secrets. Those are the words Josh used to me. Don't ask me what they mean. I don't know. But Josh has got control of dozens of different firms – chemicals, engineering – anything you like to name. He's not a scientist himself. He doesn't know what his bright boys are doing all the time. But he could have found out! He could have got hold of the formulas or the blueprints or whatever you call the things that these people wanted. If he'd really wanted to. There'd have been nobody who could have really stopped him. He owned the companies!'

She was flushed. She took two or three deep breaths and went on : 'It wouldn't have cost us a penny personally. Not a penny. Josh could have got them the plans they wanted and they'd have given him the papers back and everything would have been all right. But not him! He said it would be letting the firms down – all the workers and the shareholders. And the country. The country! I ask you! Do you know how much he offered them for the papers? A hundred thousand pounds. They turned it down.'

Jill whistled silently. 'Heavens! How much could those secrets have been worth to them, then?'

'I don't know. Millions I expect.'

'Who were these people? These blackmailers.'

'I don't know. I never had anything to do with them. It was just one man, I think, Josh dealt with. But he didn't tell me anything about him – simply that he had these papers and what he wanted in return for them.'

'Does the Alpha List mean anything to you?'

'The what?'

Jill repeated it. Marion Kendall shook her head.

'Diane Conway?'

'The actress? What's she got to do with it?'

'I don't know. I thought you might. She's Mrs David Romford in private life.'

'So what? What is all this?'

Jill told her the same story she had told Geoffrey Hurndall, only this time casting Mrs Kendall in the rôle of the innocent victim who could be trusted. 'So you see why I wanted your help,' she finished. 'Now, is there anything else at all you can tell me? Please say if there is. You can deny every word of it afterwards, if you like.'

'Josh only told me what I've told you. If you want to know my personal suspicions, for which I haven't an atom of proof . . .'

'Yes, I do.' Jill spoke eagerly. 'I said anything.'

'Well, to my way of thinking, all our troubles started when Josh hired Metropolitan Promotions.'

'Who are they?'

'They're a public relations firm. About a year ago Josh put them in charge of all advertising and P.R. work for the whole group. Somebody suggested to him that the whole thing needed co-ordinating and that he wanted somebody to deal with the press and TV and the Government, and generally look after the group's image – and his own.'

'And you think Metropolitan Promotions weren't straight?'

'The firm itself may have been. But the man who handled our account wasn't. I'd stake my life on that. His name's Maurice Parkstone and he's as sly as they come. We had to have quite a lot to do with him socially. He more or less arranged some of our parties for us. During one of them I found him eavesdropping outside a room where Josh had taken an old friend to have a private talk. He had a good excuse, of course. He was very glib. Then again, Miss Rowlands, Josh's secretary, told me that he called at the office one day when Josh had gone out for a few minutes. She told him to wait in Joshua's private office and when she went in a few minutes later he was bending over the desk. There were some papers there that Josh had left – nothing important, as it happened, though they might have looked important at a quick glance. He straightened up quickly and said he was looking for an ash-tray. But Miss Rowlands said he put something into his pocket, and it looked like a small camera. There were other little things, too, not as definite as those, but all adding up.'

'What did Mr Kendall say about it?'

'Oh, he wouldn't hear a word against Maurice. Said Miss Rowlands and I were imagining things. And everybody else liked him, too. It was only her and me didn't trust him. But she'd back me up if you asked her.'

Jill heard the front door slam, and two seconds later Felicity lunged into the sitting-room. Jill jumped to her feet. 'Well?' They both said this together, then :

'You first,' said Jill.

Felicity threw off her coat and flopped down on to the settee. 'Quite satisfactory, on the whole. I saw Brown. Nice girl. Not really a snob, after all. I showed her the photograph. And she's pretty sure it is the same girl. She can't be positive, of course, and it's not a clincher. But it is a pointer in the right direction.'

'Great. What about the girl who was expelled?'

'Ah yes. Nasty bit of work, according to Brown. Name of Joan Stanbury. Mother's people were Lancashire cotton tycoons. Lady Stanbury's loaded.'

'Is there a Lord Stanbury?'

'No. A Sir Norman. Not fabulously rich in his own right, but not exactly on the bread line either. I popped into a library on the way home and looked him up in *Who's Who*. He's in the Ministry of Defence – an Assistant Under Secretary of State. There's nothing special about the Stanburys, I should say and – hey, what's the matter?'

For Jill had frozen in mid-movement and plainly wasn't hearing. Felicity repeated her question. 'Wait a minute,' Jill said. Her voice sounded strained.

'Had a vision?' Felicity asked.

Jill turned to her, a strange, half-excited, half-frightened expression on her face. 'I think I've just found the answer to a lot of things. It never occurred to me before. But it must be right. Everything fits.'

'I'm sure it does, darling, like a glove. But could I judge for myself, d'you think?'

Jill said: 'Tell me: your Charles – is he wealthy?'

'Charles? Lord, no. He's got his salary, that's all. But what's that got to do . . . ?'

'His family aren't rich?'

'Far from it. His father's a vicar.'

Jill banged her hand on the table in exasperation. 'I ought to have seen it long ago! It didn't make sense otherwise – not with *you* broke as well and estranged from your father. While I thought they were after the Earl it made sense. But the idea of a gang of ordinary professional crooks going to all that trouble to blackmail you just to get at Charles when neither of you had any money . . .'

'But I assure you they did.' Felicity sounded indignant.

'Yes, but listen: what's Charles's job exactly?'

'He's Assistant to a Head of Department in the Foreign Office.'

'Which department?'

'NATO Department – oh!' Felicity's hand went up to her mouth and she stared at Jill speechlessly.

'Exactly. And Sir Norman Stanbury's a big bug in the Ministry of Defence; Diane Conway's husband's a Government Minister; Geoffrey Hurndall's company make airplane parts; and Kendall was actually told he had to hand over scientific papers: Mrs Kendall calmly handed me that on a plate, and still I didn't see it. I thought the crooks were just hoping to sell Kendall's plans to another firm.'

'Then – then they're not after money at all . . . ?'

'Of course not. The whole thing's some sort of espionage racket. It's secrets they're after. We were misled by so many of the people involved being well off. But that was just incidental.'

'Do you think Bob realised that?'

'Not until the very end, when he made that last 'phone call. That's when he said it was a bigger affair than he'd thought.'

'And do you think the police are on to it yet?'

'How do I know? And if they are, how far will they be allowed to go?'

'It explains why your friend had to be so secretive, and why they said the lead you gave them was no use. The case has probably been taken out of their hands, except just nominally. Most likely M.I.5 or somebody are handling it. I'll bet it's all under the Official Secrets Act. There *has* been a cover-up, not for the reason you thought but because that's just the way these security people work.'

'Well, they're not making Bob's murder an Official Secret,' Jill said grimly. 'They're not going to swop the killer for some crumby student who's been arrested for smuggling pot behind the Iron Curtain, or something. I'll see to that.'

'How?' Felicity asked simply.

'I don't know. I can't think what to do. Somebody ought to be told what we've found out. I've got the names of two men who are probably implicated – your Philip Harrington, and another one Marion Kendall gave me' – she briefly recounted Marion Kendall's suspicions – 'I've got that girl's photograph and evidence she was involved with you and the Harper woman as well as Hurndall. I've got Marion Kendall's admission that her husband was blackmailed for industrial secrets. All put together that must be valuable data if it could be fitted into the overall pattern. *I* can't do that. It ought to be given to the police. But if I gave it to them, how could I be sure they wouldn't just thank me politely and file it all away? Besides, I've made all sorts of promises about keeping things secret! I can't just go back on them all.' She flung herself down on to the settee.

'Well, if you're including me among these promises, forget it. You can use everything I've told you in any way you like – except about Charles and the Communist Party, of course.'

'That's nice of you. Thanks.'

'Now never mind about the other promises for the moment. Come back to it later if necessary. You might be able to get round it in some way. If you can, who's going to get the information? That's the first thing. Now how about that chap at Scotland Yard who gave you our names?'

Jill shook her head. 'He'd pass it on to Phillips. He'd have to. It wouldn't be fair to expect anything else. And if Phillips is under orders from the Secret Service it's all just going to be sat on.'

'You don't know that for a fact.'

'I'd have a bet on it. But even if I'm wrong, there's another point: I don't fancy anyone in authority is going to take me very seriously if I don't give all the details – where I got the girl's photo, how I know about Kendall's blackmail. They're going to insist on my telling them. It'd all be too vague otherwise.'

'Oh, but surely if you went to somebody you know – like your husband's friend – what's his name? – Andrew? – well, surely he wouldn't press you too much. He'd take it on trust, wouldn't he?'

'Probably. But I'm not going near Andrew until I can present him with Diane Conway and prove Bob called on her that night and that she knows something about his death.'

'Frankly, I think that's just pride.'

'Maybe. I can't help it.'

Felicity shrugged. 'Then what about that private detective?'

'Owen? I don't think he wants to be involved.'

They were both silent for a few seconds. Then Felicity said slowly: 'Then you've got to have another go at getting Diane tied in, haven't you? And as you've seen everybody else connected with the case, there's only one person left.'

'Diane herself.'

'You've thought of that, then?'

'Of course. From the first moment the TV people gave me her name. But – well, quite honestly I didn't have the guts at first. So I asked Owen to look into it. But he couldn't get any proof, and I thought how much better it would be if I could go see her armed with some definite evidence that she was implicated. I hoped I could get something from you or one of the others to tie her in. But it didn't work out. So I guess I'll just have to try a bit of bluff.'

'How do you mean?'

'The only chance is to scare her into talking. If I can do that, I can then call Andrew and just fade out. So I've got to convince her I know more than I do – and that I've got proof.'

'And how will you do that?'

'Tell her straight out I know Bob called on her that night and that she knows who killed him. Threaten her with the press if she doesn't talk. I'll call her in the morning first thing.'

'Aren't you scared?'

'Scared stiff,' said Jill.

133

11

The next morning Felicity came into the sitting-room to find Jill sitting at the table, writing. 'What's that?' she asked.

'I was thinking about what you said last night and I realised it might be a good idea to make some contingency plans.' She stopped writing, glanced over the paper and handed it to Felicity.

Jill had written: 'The enclosed photograph is of a girl who about seven or eight months ago was going under the name of Joyce Summers, but who later left her address and disappeared. She was almost certainly involved in the blackmail of Lady Felicity Mannering (as Lady Felicity herself will confirm), of the late Miss Eileen Harper of Greenhill School, and of at least one other person. She may well have information concerning the death of my husband, Detective-Inspector Robert Palmer.

'I can state that the blackmail of Lady Felicity was motivated by a wish to gain information concerning a member of the Foreign Office; and that an attempt was made to obtain industrial and scientific secrets from Mr Joshua Kendall. In addition, I have reason to believe that the following are also implicated in the series of crimes investigated by my husband immediately prior to his death:

'Philip Harrington, an accountant, of Hampstead, London;

'Maurice Parkstone, a Public Relations executive with Metropolitan Promotions.'

Jill watched Felicity read it. She said: 'I haven't broken any confidences. I don't say *who* I got Joyce Summers' photo from, or the source of what I know about Kendall. That's all I promised not to reveal.'

Felicity looked up. 'What are you going to do with this?'

'If anything happens to me, I want you to . . .'

Felicity went pale. 'You really do think you're going to be murdered.'

'No,' Jill said firmly. 'I don't. But I might be knocked down by a truck on the way back. Now listen: if anything happens to me, I want you to take this to the Yard and give it to Andrew, Detective-Inspector Andrew Thompson, personally. If for any reason you can't see him, give it to Detective-Constable Gerald Cochran. But nobody else. Understand?'

'Write the names on the envelope, will you?'

'I've said as little as I can. Just the bare facts as I know them. Do you think it's all right?'

'You haven't said anything about Diane Conway.'

'For two reasons. Firstly because I haven't yet got the evidence. And as Bob did make certain promises to her, I'll give her the benefit of the doubt until I'm a hundred per cent positive. Secondly, because if someone high up *is* trying to keep her out of things I don't want to put her name down on a document like this. If the wrong people got hold of it, it might mean the whole statement would be suppressed just to protect her. I'd rather rely on word of mouth for passing on all about her. That's your job, too.'

'How?'

'Take Andrew to see Owen Sherwood. Tell Owen that I want him to repeat to Andrew everything I said about Diane Conway. And also what Owen himself found out about her for me. Do you follow?'

Felicity nodded.

'After you've done that just forget it and leave them to sort it out.'

Felicity handed back the paper and Jill folded it and put it in an envelope.

'Thanks for not mentioning Charles,' Felicity said.

'If Andrew looks into it he won't have much bother guessing who the member of the Foreign Office is. But it might be better for your image if you tell him the actual name yourself – if you want to. Can I have that photo now, please?'

Felicity fetched it and Jill put it in the envelope with the letter. She sealed the envelope and wrote Andrew's and Cochran's ranks and full names on it. She stood up. 'Now I'll call Diane Conway.'

'Do you want me to go out?'

'Heavens, no. Stand by me and give me moral support. You said you have her number?'

'In that little book by the 'phone. Under R for Romford, I think.'

Jill found the number, lifted the telephone receiver and dialled. Felicity put her head close up by Jill's to listen.

A male voice answered.

'Er – could you tell me, please – that is – is . . .' Jill cursed herself silently for this show of nervousness, coughed, and said loudly : 'I'd like to speak to Mrs Romford, please.'

'Who's calling, please?'

'My name is Miss Forbes but that won't mean anything to her. Tell her I'm calling with reference to the Alpha List.'

'I beg your pardon, miss?'

'Alpha. A.L.P.H.A. The Alpha List.'

'The Alpha List? Miss Forbes?'

'That's it.'

'Hold on, please. I'll see if she's in.'

There was the clattering sound of the receiver being put down. Jill covered the mouthpiece. 'Gone to see if she's in.'

'I know. I can hear. She is in, of course. He'd have said otherwise. And don't yell so.'

'Was I? Shh.' There came some sounds from the other end of the line. Jill snatched her hand away from the mouthpiece.

There was a pause. Then a woman's voice said : 'H-hullo? Who is that?'

'That's her.' Felicity whispered.

'Is this Mrs Romford?' Jill asked.

'Speaking.'

'My name is Jill Forbes, Mrs Romford. We haven't met. I wanted to talk with you about the Alpha List.'

'I—I don't know what you mean. What are you talking about?' The voice was low and slightly husky.

'You know quite well what the Alpha List is.' Jill was gaining confidence. 'You mentioned it on the telephone a few weeks ago to a Scotland Yard detective. That same evening he called on you. I have cast-iron proof of this. Then he was murdered.'

There was dead silence at the other end. Then : 'What do you want?'

'Just to see and talk with you. If you didn't kill Inspector Palmer yourself, you have nothing to fear from me.'

'I really don't know what this is all about.' The voice was now completely self-possessed, rather bored, slightly arrogant, and very English. 'It sounds sheer nonsense. However, as you are so keen to see me, I can probably spare half an hour.'

'Today.'

'Possibly. I'll have to consult my diary. Hold on.' There was silence again.

'She's good, you know,' Felicity whispered.

'Hullo?' came the voice. 'I could see you at three o'clock.'

'That's satisfactory. But I hope you don't have any important appointment at three-thirty. Our business may take a little longer than half an hour.'

('Good for you,' Felicity hissed.)

Diane Conway said: 'That would be a nuisance, but I dare say I could manage it.'

'Very well. I'll be there at three.'

'Not here.'

'Say where, then. It's no odds to me where we meet.'

'Then how about this? My husband and I hope to be moving house soon, and I've made arrangements to look over a couple of empty ones. I can get the key to one of them this morning and meet you there. That would be quite private.'

Felicity gripped Jill's shoulder and shook her head violently, mouthing 'No.'

'As you wish,' Jill said. 'Privacy's not important to me, but I can see your point of view. What's the address?'

Felicity threw her arms up in a gesture of incredulous despair and turned away.

'I'm not quite sure of the exact address. I can get it quite quickly. Can I ring you back? What's your number?'

'Don't bother. I'll call you again in half an hour.' Jill rang off. 'Whew!'

Felicity turned on her fiercely. 'You little ass! What did you want to agree to that for? An empty house! It's too dangerous.'

'Listen. When I call back I'll tell her I've got a friend who's listened to the whole conversation and knows everything. Besides, Owen said she didn't kill Bob or have him killed. She's not going to harm me.'

'But somebody killed Bob after *he'd* arranged to meet her.'

'After Bob had assured her *he* wouldn't tell anybody where he was going. That's the difference. And he wasn't on his guard. Now stop worrying. I can take care of myself.'

'All right.' Felicity sounded resigned. 'It's your life. But that was all lies about having made arrangements to look over empty houses, you know. I bet now she's looking madly through the property ads for an empty house in a quiet part – and either a private seller or an estate agent open on Sundays. She might have a problem finding one in half an hour.'

Jill gave a shrug. 'I'll let her worry about that. She can have all the morning to fix it if she wants. As long as she sees me today.'

The road had a languorous air. The houses were large Victorian villas – solid, ugly, inconvenient, set well back, and mostly surrounded by evergreen. Many of them bore For Sale boards. Half a century before they had been homes for the moderately rich. But they had outlived their function and were dying. In three, five years they would all have gone the inevitable way and be divided into apartments and 'maisonettes'. Life – a different sort of life – would return. But not yet. For the time being the road hung in a sort of limbo between two social orders.

The atmosphere was oppressive as Jill walked along the road. It was an overcast day, mild for November, quite still. Nowhere was there sign of life. Diane Conway had chosen well.

Eventually Jill stopped by a wrought-iron gate, pushed it open and started up a weed-speckled gravel path. She found herself treading gingerly, trying to make her footsteps silent. Then she pulled herself together, squared her shoulders, stuck her chin in the air and marched briskly on to the front door. It was just three o'clock.

It was just three o'clock when the front door-bell rang. Felicity went to answer it. On the step stood a tall, thin young man.

'Er, Lady Felicity Mannering?'

'Yes.'

'I—I wonder if you can help me. I'm looking for a lady by the name of Mrs Jill Palmer. May I ask if you've s-seen her lately?'

'Who wants her?'

'Oh, my name's Cochran, Gerald Cochran. I'm with the C.I.D. at Scotland Yard. Here's my warrant card.' He stuck it under her nose. 'B-but this isn't an official call. I'm off duty at the moment. I wanted to see her on a private matter. I know she was intending to call on you some time and I wondered if she had done so yet.'

Felicity hesitated. Then : 'You'd better come in.'

In the sitting-room she said : 'You're the fourth sleuth who's been here in as many weeks. Palmer, Phillips, Thompson and now you.'

'I'm very small fry compared with them. I was Inspector Palmer's assistant on the blackmail case he was investigating before he was killed.'

'And it must have been you who gave Mrs Palmer my name, and Mrs Kendall's, Miss Harper's and the others.'

Cochran stared, shocked. 'She told you that?'

'No. She very strictly refrained from telling me. It was just a guess – based on something she said in another context. I'm the only one who even knows she got her information from someone at Scotland Yard. And you needn't fear I'm going to blab it about – because she also knows a lot of horrible things about me : including the fact that I lied to the police.'

'I see. Is – is Mrs Palmer here?'

She shook her head.

'Do you know where I might find her?'

'Sit down.'

Cochran sat down. Felicity said : 'She's been staying with me for the past two days. She called to see me, and happened to arrive at a time when she was able to get me out of a sticky situation. We got to talking and seemed to hit it off. I asked her to stay on. And she's more or less taken me into her confidence. She went out this morning to see somebody who may have information. She should be meeting them about now. I'm not allowed to say who. And I can't say where. All I know is that it's an empty house somewhere in London – she wouldn't tell me the actual address.'

'What time did she leave?'

'About eleven-thirty.' Felicity sat down.

'Early, wasn't it, if the appointment was for about now.'

'I thought so. But she said she had some shopping to do first.'

'And is she coming back here after?'

'Yes. She said I could call the police if she wasn't here by six.'

Cochran looked startled. 'Did she think she might be in danger?'

139

'I don't know. She said it jokingly. It was me who was worried, really. But she did say that if anything happened to her I was to get in touch with Gerald Cochran or Andrew Thompson. That's how I guessed it was you'd given her my name, incidentally. Only the chap who'd done that would have thought to come here to look for her. Why did you want to see her?'

'Just to find out how she's getting on – if she's discovered anything.'

Felicity gazed at him without saying anything for a few seconds. Then: 'Do you want to catch the murderer very much?'

He raised his eyebrows. 'What do you think?'

'You tell me.'

'Of course I do. Not that I'm likely to get the chance.'

'Why is it so important to you?'

He paused before saying quietly: 'I've been in the C.I.D. two years. I learnt more in a few weeks from Mr Palmer than all the rest of the time put together. And he'd always listen to your ideas and let you try them out yourself. I owed him a lot. And then I know Mrs Palmer. And as you know her, too, that should answer your question.'

'Tell me: suppose you learned – this is purely hypothetical – that there were people in high places who weren't keen for the murderer to be caught.' Felicity was speaking deliberately. 'That they were trying to suppress information. Leaning on your bosses. Covering up. How would you react?'

He stared at her in astonishment. 'Is that what Mrs Palmer thinks?'

'Never mind what she thinks. Just tell me how you'd take it.'

'I'd be hopping mad,' he said simply.

'Yes, that's what I thought.'

'Why do you ask? Has Mrs Palmer discovered something that made her think that might be happening?'

'I—I can't tell you.' Felicity stood up suddenly.

'Look, Lady Felicity, this could be important.' Cochran got to his feet, too.

'I don't know what to do. I must think.'

'She told you to get in touch with me or Mr Thompson if anything happened to her – is that right? What did you have to tell us?'

'Nothing. I had to give you something.'

'Well, why wait? If it's something important every second may matter. What's the point in delaying?'

'It was a sort of last resort. She's been hoping to get some sort of proof. She's written out a sort of statement of what she knows. Just so that it won't be wasted if anything goes wrong. But she doesn't want you to have it yet.'

'Why?'

'In case nothing's done about it. In case it's suppressed.'

'Do you – does she – honestly think we'd suppress important evidence about Mr Palmer's murder?'

'Not you personally. But it might be taken out of your hands.'

He ran his hand through his hair. 'Do you know what's in that letter?'

'Yes.'

'Is it new information?'

'I think so. Some of it, anyway.'

'Then I beg you to let me have it. I promise you that nobody will suppress it – even if I've got to give it to the Sunday papers. Even if it costs me my job. Do you believe me?'

Felicity nodded.

'Well then?'

'I'm not going to *give* it to you,' she said after a few seconds. 'But yours *is* one of the names on the envelope. If you saw it lying on the table, there wouldn't be anything wrong in your taking it, would there?'

'None at all.'

'One condition. I'm not going to be questioned about it. You're not to open it here. Take it back to Scotland Yard first.'

'You've got a bargain.'

Felicity opened a drawer, took out Jill's letter, and laid it on the table. 'I'm now going into another room. Can you see yourself out?'

'Of course.'

'Then I'll say good-bye. It's been nice meeting you.'

There was a bell-push set into the door and a big brass ornamental knocker. Jill pressed the bell. Nothing happened. She caught hold of the knocker and banged hard three times. The sound echoed through the empty house. There was silence for some seconds, then Jill heard footsteps briskly approaching the door. It was opened quickly, and Jill had her first sight of Diane Conway.

She's beautiful, was Jill's first thought. Diane Conway was tall, slim and stately. She had black hair, exquisitely coiffured, pale creamy skin, bright red, very full lips and large, innocent-looking blue eyes. She was wearing a long mink coat, and she stood looking down at Jill, a very slight expression of contempt in her eyes, one gloved hand on the knob of the door, the other resting in the pocket of her coat. She didn't move and didn't speak.

Jill's next thought was that Diane Conway wasn't really beautiful at all. Her features were quite commonplace when analysed. Everything striking about her was artificial. Yet she looked so cool, so much at home, and so superior in her consciousness of beauty, money and position that it was difficult for Jill not to think of herself as applying for a housemaid's job.

Jill half opened her mouth to speak, then she thought: I've got the upper hand. I demanded this meeting and she agreed to it like a lamb. I won't speak first.

At last Diane Conway spoke. 'Miss Forbes?'

Jill nodded. 'Mrs Romford?'

'Come in.'

Jill went in, casting quick glances around her. The interior was in fair condition and there was little dust. Diane Conway closed the door and turned to face her.

Jill asked: 'Where do we talk?'

'There's only one room with any sort of seat. Upstairs.'

She walked to the stairs and started up. Jill followed. The two sets of footsteps clattered on the bare boards. Four or five doors led off the first-floor landing, one of them open. Diane Conway went towards this. Jill continued to follow her, glancing towards the other doors as she did so. She had an urge to check that each room was empty; but what good would it do to know now if one wasn't? It was too late to withdraw. And she still wanted to hear Diane Conway's story.

The room the other woman entered was a large, airy bedroom. It had a big marble fireplace and a large bay window, with a window seat running round it. Diane Conway crossed to the window and sat down on one end of the seat. 'The next door house is empty, too. So we're not overlooked in here.'

Jill shrugged. 'I don't care who sees us. I've got nothing to hide.' She sat down on the opposite end of the seat, facing Diane Conway across the six feet of bay. She put her bag on the seat beside her, conscious of the other's eyes on her constantly. Jill stared back, and as she did so the actress ran her tongue hastily round her lips. It was such a spontaneous, unsophisticated action, almost child-like, that it surprised Jill. It *showed* that Diane Conway was scared. Jill felt her own control of the situation increasing every second.

'Well?' It was as if Diane Conway tried to sound bored and impatient, but to Jill she sounded only self-pitying and edgy. 'What do you want? Who are you?'

Jill let her wait before saying : 'I'm Jill Palmer. Inspector Bob Palmer was my husband.'

Diane Conway drew her breath in; not sharply, as in surprise, but slowly and out again equally slowly, almost like a symptom of relief.

'So that's who you are. And I thought . . . I'm sorry.'

'For what?'

'Well, for – for treating you so suspiciously – as though I thought you were a criminal, or something.'

'It doesn't matter how you speak to me, as long as you tell the truth.'

'About what?'

'You know very well – the night my husband was killed. I know he called you and then went to see you, so don't try to deny it.'

'Suppose I say you're talking sheer nonsense? That I'd never heard of your husband until I read about his murder in the papers – let alone spoke to him or had him call on me?'

'I'd say you were a liar. I know he called you on the 'phone. And I know he visited your house.'

'You *know*? How can you *know* that?'

'I know about the 'phone call because I was there when he made it. I know he went to your house because I've got a very reliable eye-witness who saw him go in and who'll swear to it in court if necessary.' Jill uttered this blatant lie coolly and unhesitatingly.

Diane Conway's shoulders seemed to sag. 'All right.'

'You admit he called at your house?' Jill's heart was beating fast.

'Yes.'

'And you talked with him?'

'No, I never saw him.'

'What do you mean?'

'I was upstairs in my bedroom when he arrived. Somebody else let him in. And – and – I'm sorry – he was killed in my drawing-room and they took his – his body away.'

Jill stopped breathing. She sat quite still, closed her eyes, and tried not to think. Then she looked straight at Diane Conway, and said in a low, steady voice : 'Who was it?'

'I don't know.'

'Don't lie to me! Of course you know!'

'I don't! I didn't see his face. I've never seen it. He covers it up. A sort of mask.'

The exact words used did not escape Jill. 'He's been there more than once?'

'No. But I've met him in – in another place.'

'And you've never seen his face?'

'Never.'

'He's been blackmailing you, has he?'

Diane Conway nodded.

'And you told him that night Bob was coming to see you?' Fierce, cold anger was rising in Jill. 'You knew Bob wanted to help you and you deliberately told this man about it.'

'No! I wanted your husband to help me. Can't you understand?' As she spoke, she made a circle in the air with her right hand; her thumb held the little finger bent; the other three were straight.

Jill thought : that's it, that's the mannerism.

'I was waiting for him. I didn't know he was a policeman. He was just someone who'd promised to help me when I was at the end of my tether. Why should I want him killed? He was my only hope. And then the – the other man arrived. He knew I was waiting for a policeman. He was angry. He hit me. And he made me go upstairs and wait.'

'You knew what he was going to do. You went upstairs and let Bob walk into a trap.'

'No! I didn't know he was a killer. I swear it. I thought he'd

144

bluff it out somehow – send your husband away. And then afterwards he called me down and told me what he'd done. He'd had a couple of other men waiting outside in a van, and they'd come in and taken the body away. And he said – I'm sorry to tell you this – but they'd carried your husband's body all over the ground floor of the house and they'd dabbed his fingerprints everywhere. And put smears of his blood in different places.'

Jill felt a great wave of sickness start to engulf her. She stood up quickly and walked across the room, leaned up against the big marble mantelpiece and rested her brow on it.

She only dimly heard Diane Conway saying: 'I'm sorry,' in a low voice. Then she straightened up and turned round.

'Go on.'

'He said I'd never succeed in finding all the traces and getting rid of them, but the police experts could find them, and if they were tipped-off anonymously they'd go over every inch of the house, and they'd only have to find one print . . . He said he'd tip off the police, about the business he'd been blackmailing me for and make sure they found out I'd been blackmailed. Your husband had been investigating blackmail and looking for people who had something to hide. I'd already got rid of the servants with various pretexts that they must have thought were odd, and all put together it would look certain I'd killed him. He said no court in the country'd let me off against that evidence.'

'And how do I know that's not what did happen? Bob knew you'd been blackmailed, and when he got to your house you told him why. But you didn't know he was a policeman then. He wasn't interested in what it was you'd done, but you didn't believe that, and when he told you who he was you thought he'd been playing you along and was sure to arrest you. So you panicked and stabbed him in the back.'

'No, no, it wasn't like that.' She sounded frantic. 'I've told you the truth.'

'Have you, Mrs Romford?'

'Yes, I swear it.'

'Detective-Inspector Palmer, my husband, was killed in your house?'

'Yes, yes, I've told you. But not by me.'

'By a man who's been blackmailing you?'

'Yes.'

145

'Thank you. Now look.'

Diane Conway fixed tearful eyes on her. Jill walked back to the window, picked up her handbag, and took out a tiny tape recorder. A microphone hung from it. Jill unplugged this and held up the recorder. Diane Conway's eyes widened and one hand went up to her mouth in horror. Jill moved a knob to reverse the tape. 'Neat, isn't it? I only bought it this morning. I haven't seen one quite so small before.' She turned the knob back again. 'That should be far enough. Let's see what we've got.' She pressed a switch. The voice of Diane Conway blared out: '. . . as though I thought you were a criminal, or something.' Jill let their whole conversation play back, then switched off, removed the cassette and dropped it in her bag. She put the recorder on the seat between them. 'No tape and no mike plugged in. So now you can talk quite freely.'

'How – how do I know you haven't got another one in there?'

'Do you want to search my purse?'

Diane Conway shook her head sulkily.

'Now, listen to me,' Jill said. 'I don't want to do the dirty on you. It seems to me you're in real bad trouble. Bob wanted to help you. He promised you that if you trusted him you had nothing to fear. I don't know if you did trust him, but if you did I want his promise kept. And I'm willing to give you the benefit of the doubt – on one condition. If you've told me the truth so far, I think you've behaved like a coward and a fool, but I won't hold that against you. Provided you tell me the full truth now, I promise I won't rat on you. You can walk out of here taking this tape with you – if you can convince me you're not hiding anything. That's a solemn promise. I'll even do my best to help you. But you must tell me everything. So far you haven't. You've only told me part of the story. I want it all. If you lie to me, or hide anything, I'll see that every paper in the country gets a copy of this tape. Now talk.' Jill sat down. She was shaking.

Diane Conway sniffed. She seemed on the verge of tears. She reached into her bag. Jill tensed, but she only took out a handkerchief and dabbed at her nose and eyes. She said: 'All right. I'll trust you. Heaven help you if you let me down. What is it you want to know?'

'Everything you can tell me about this man – his build, age, voice, clothes – the lot. I want to know what you've done that makes him able to blackmail you. What it is he wants from you. What the Alpha List is. What you said to my husband on the 'phone that bowled him over so. And how this man knew Bob was going to call on you that night.'

'It's a long story.'

'I've got all the time in the world,' said Jill.

12

Diane Conway said: 'I married David nearly ten years ago and I gave up my career almost immediately afterwards. David wanted it. For two years or so I was very happy. But then I started to get bored. Not with my marriage – far from it. That was good. And I still love David. But the trouble was he was eaten up with politics. I tried to take an interest in them, but I never felt really at home in his world. I missed my work terribly. He'd have all-night sittings, or go off visiting his constituency at weekends. I could have gone with him but I was just no good at anything like that in those days, so I just used to be left on my own.

'I suppose a bored wife always looks for consolation in one of three things. Well, I wasn't interested in other men and I don't drink. But I'd always been a bit of a gambler and I started going in for it more and more. It was a hackneyed sort of situation, only complicated in my case by the fact that I was the wife of an M.P., and that this was before the Gaming Act. In other words, a lot of my fun was illegal. Perhaps that added to the excitement. You can guess what's coming, of course. I won't go into all the details, but eventually I found myself in debt to various club-owners to the tune of £10,000.'

Diane Conway took out a lighter and a packet of cigarettes. She lit one, inhaled deeply, looked at Jill out of her big, watery, pale blue eyes again, and continued.

'I was desperate. I couldn't tell David. Besides, though he could have probably raised the money, he only had his salary and TV or journalistic fees sometimes.

'Then he got his first Government post. He was made a junior minister at the Treasury. He didn't suspect there was anything wrong with me – he was too wrapped up in his work, and I'm too good an actress. He was – well, still is, I've got to say it, crazy about me. From the very beginning he trusted me implicitly and he told me all sorts of things I was sure he oughtn't to be telling me. Not that it mattered, because it would never have occurred to me to talk to anybody about it. He was like a clam too, as far as anybody else was concerned. It was just me he had this blind spot about.

'Then just when I was at my wits' end I met someone at a party. I knew nothing about him except that he was supposed to be an up and coming man in the City. He wangled an introduction to me and kept me talking. I didn't like him much and I thought he was getting round to making a pass. But he wasn't. I don't know if he knew I had money troubles, but he suddenly said: "Budget coming up next month, then."

'I said: "I believe so."

' "I expect your hubby's pretty busy then, isn't he?"

'I said: "Yes, very."

' "Responsible position he's got. In possession of a lot of valuable information. Some people would give a lot to know what he knows." And he gave a little wink and moved away. That was all.

'The awful thing was that I never really hesitated. I rang him up the next day and arranged a meeting. We didn't have any difficulty in understanding each other. The outcome was that he agreed to pay me £20,000 for certain advance information about the Budget.

'Quite casually, a bit at a time, I pumped David over the next week or so. Of course, he didn't know all the tax changes and things that were coming up, but eventually I did get what I wanted. I don't even remember exactly what it was now – changes in the import duty on some kind of chemical, I think.

'I only just found out in time. I knew this man had to have the information before the Stock Exchange closed the next day. I tried to get hold of him that night, but he was out of town. I realised he must have given up hope of my getting what he wanted. He wasn't at his office the next morning either, but they told me was going to be at some important luncheon at the Savoy. I 'phoned the Savoy twice. The first time he hadn't arrived. I left a message for him to ring me, but he didn't get it. The next time I called he was making a speech and couldn't come to the 'phone. I was frantic. I knew there were only a few hours to go, and that if he didn't get the information I wouldn't get my twenty thousand. I was terrified he'd leave the luncheon and go out somewhere for the afternoon and never get my message.

So that's when I did the idiotic thing. I wrote him a note and sent it round to the Savoy by special messenger. Even then it might have been all right if I'd typed it and just said "Telephone me" and put my initials, or something like that. But no. I didn't want him to be in any doubt as to who the letter was from or what it was I had for him. So I wrote: "Please 'phone me as soon as possible. I have the information you wanted about next month's event." I used a letter-card, I wrote it in longhand, I signed it, and I addressed it to him care of the Something Luncheon, Savoy Hotel.

'Everything worked out. He made a killing and I got my twenty thousand. In cash. I paid off my debts and banked the rest. Everything was fine again. I gave up gambling and a few months later I told David I didn't want to be told any more confidential Government information – in case I was careless and something slipped out, I said. He agreed and he's never told me anything since.

'I didn't worry much at first about what I'd done. My only feeling was one of relief at being out of trouble. And it wasn't as if I'd harmed anybody – except perhaps a few foreign banks. But later on I did start to feel guilty. I became more used to being a politician's wife. I got in the circle more, made some friends among David's colleagues and their wives. I got to understand the code. There'd be gossip sometimes about old political scandals and leaks, and I'd feel terrible. It got so that I had to tell somebody about it. I'm a Catholic, you know, and eventually I went and told my priest. When he was convinced I was truly penitent he advised me not to say anything. He said this could only harm David, whose only error had been in trusting me too fully, and wouldn't do anybody any good. He suggested that I might feel better if I could start paying some of the twenty thousand to charity.

'Well, by then we were much better off financially. David's salary had increased, he did well from journalism when the Party was in Opposition, and he got some directorships, too. And they'd started to show my old movies on television, and I got a fee every time. They were quite popular, and as a result I began to get TV work occasionally – not acting, but talk shows, panel games, that sort of thing.

'I took my priest's advice, and so far I've been able to give about five thousand pounds to various charities. I felt much happier and until about nine months ago everything was great. But what I didn't know was that that rat had kept my letter all those years.'

Jill stirred. 'You mean the letter you sent to him at the Savoy?'

'Yes.'

'Well, was it all that incriminating?'

'What do you think? It's a matter of record that he bought or sold those shares or whatever it was at the eleventh hour. There was a lot of talk about it at the time. Suppose a letter comes to light to him from the wife of a Treasury minister, written the actual day he made the deal – in March – promising him information about an important event the next month – April, the month of the Budget.'

'But could anybody tell when the letter had been written?'

'I wrote it on a letter-card, remember. With those the message is written on one side, folded in, the card is sealed, and the address is written on the outside. So when it's opened the address is on the back of the letter. And anybody could check up when that particular luncheon was held at the Savoy. Bear in mind, too, that it's on the books in my bank that a couple of days after he had made that deal I paid in over £9,000 cash, when previously I'd been in the red. Oh yes, the letter-card would have been damning, all right. But it's worse than that. He'd also signed a statement admitting that he paid me £20,000 for the information. And added to the letter that would just about seal my coffin.'

Jill stared at her without speaking. She was thinking. She thought – but only thought, so far – that the story was true. She asked: 'What's this man's name?'

Diane Conway dropped her cigarette on to the floor and ground it fiercely into the floorboards with a high heel. 'Joshua Kendall,' she said.

Cochran kept his word. He went to the Yard with the envelope unopened and enquired for Thompson. But he, too, was off duty. Cochran went to the canteen and sat down in a quiet corner. He opened the envelope. He first took out the photograph. As he stared at it a strange expression came into his eyes. He looked up and stared blankly ahead of him, his brow furrowed. He looked down at the picture again for several seconds. Then he gave an irritated shake of his head, put the picture down, and opened the statement. He read it through rapidly. He'd got nearly to the end when he suddenly seemed to freeze. Then he bent his head and closed his eyes. After ten seconds he opened them and stared at the photograph again. An expression of intense excitement spread over his face. He jumped to his feet and rushed out.

'Joshua Kendall?' Jill stared at Diane Conway incredulously.

'Yes. It was me gave him his first big boost. He never looked back after that – until six weeks ago.'

'Is that how they got on to you – through him?'

She nodded. 'I was shown a photocopy of the letter I'd sent him. They've got the original. They could only have got it from him. He must have kept it as a sort of insurance.'

'Go on. What happened nine months ago?'

'That's just about the nastiest part of the whole business. It was about six years back that I confessed to my priest. Shortly afterwards we moved to town and I didn't see him again. Then back in February I had a letter from him. He said he was writing to warn me. He'd just had a visitor – a man who'd been making threats. He knew about something Father Dooney had done years ago – something he'd always been terribly ashamed of . . .'

Jill caught her breath. 'Father Dooney!'

'Yes. Why?'

'Bob – my husband – knew he'd been mixed up with the blackmailers. It doesn't matter. Go on.'

'It must have been a tremendous shock to Dooney,' Diane Conway said. 'Before he had a chance to recover his wits, the man said that he'd keep the secret on the condition Father Dooney told him exactly what he knew about Kendall and me. And he was so shaken that instead of denying he knew anything, he said he couldn't possibly talk about it. The man said he'd give him until the next day to make up his mind. He'd been gone about an hour when Father Dooney wrote to me. He told me he wanted me to know that he hadn't given away any details and he wouldn't do. But he had to warn me that this man did know definitely now that there had been *some* secret between Kendall and me. And he asked my forgiveness for letting it slip out.'

Diane Conway turned her head away and looked out of the window. 'As soon as I got the letter I tried to 'phone him. They told me he was dead.'

Her mouth had gone tight. There were a dozen little wrinkles round her eyes. She blinked rapidly four or five times. Jill just waited for her to continue.

'I learned later that he'd killed himself. I suppose I should have gone to the police, but I couldn't have added much to what they already knew. So I just kept quiet. I worried about who the visitor could have been, and how he knew about my connection with Kendall. I was pretty frantic for a while but after a couple of months I began to think I was safe and that Father Dooney had saved me by what he'd done. I stopped worrying so much. Until about a month ago, that is.

'I found out later that these people had got an inkling of some old secret between Kendall and me. Kendall must have talked carelessly. But they had no idea of what it actually was. And as it would be a gold mine to get a hold over both of us they put a lot of work into trying to get at the truth. It was pretty well routine for them to have a go at the priest whenever they were after a Catholic. In my case it failed. But, of course, at the same time they were also probing Kendall. And in his case they did get what they were after. In fact they found out about this latest fraud of his as well. And he was willing to admit that old business if they'd keep quiet about the new racket. From his point of view the new one was by far the more serious crime. So he was quite prepared to rat on me. But it didn't work. They used what he gave them about me. And they still went on pressurising him about the new business just the same.'

She lit another cigarette. Her hands were shaking and she had to make three attempts to light it. She was the very picture of a tense, nervous woman recollecting a horrible experience that still wasn't over. But it seemed to Jill that she had heard stories told in the same way with the same mannerisms many times before. She could not help thinking that, lacking a good director, Diane Conway was giving a rather hackneyed performance. It would have been easy, nevertheless, for Jill to have got caught up in the story, to let herself believe it. But she fought this.

'Go on,' she said. 'Or have you forgotten your lines?' Her

voice sounded harsh. Diane Conway cast her a quick, appraising glance out of the top of her eyes as she at last got her cigarette alight. When she spoke next her voice was flatter, less charged with emotion.

'They had what they wanted on me. But they didn't approach me straight away. They left that until last month – the fifteenth to be precise, the day after David went abroad.

'Now I've got to explain something about that. Otherwise nothing will make sense.

'David has gone overseas on a special mission as the personal representative of the Prime Minister. If that sounds a bit pretentious, I'm sorry. It happens to be true. He went to the United States first and saw the President. Since then he's visited about six countries altogether – including, I think, China. I don't know what it's all about. But it's very hush-hush and frightfully important. I haven't had any letters from David direct – they've all been sent on from the F.O. and none of them has been headed. What I know or think, I've pieced together from odd phrases in them, plus things he said before he left. It's easily the most important thing he's ever had to do, and he did say that if he pulled it off – whatever "it" is – he'd be world famous. Apparently, there won't be any immediate statement of what it was all about – there'll be a lot more talks at a lower level first. But in six months or a year the P.M. may make a pretty sensational announcement – if everything goes well. And David will get a lot of the credit. There'll be no limit to where it could lead him – probably to Number Ten himself in five or six years' time. So now you know the sort of stakes that are being played for.'

'I'm not interested in the stakes,' Jill said. 'Frankly at the moment I don't give a hoot for prime ministers or presidents or chairmen or anybody else. My husband was murdered. And I'm going to know by whom. That's all I care about. So stop name-dropping and get back to what concerns me.'

Diane Conway bit her lip and took a deep breath. 'The day after David left, just over four weeks ago, a photocopy of my letter to Kendall came in the post. Nothing else. Just that alone in the envelope. Well, you can imagine . . .'

'From now on all your emotions can be taken as read. Stick to the facts.'

'All right, damn you, you're going to get the facts. Just shut up and listen.' She gulped, closed her eyes for a second, and said: 'Two hours after the letter arrived I had a 'phone call. I was instructed to go to a certain hotel that afternoon and ask for Mr Masters. I went. It was a shabby, dirty little place. There was a man waiting for me in Mr Masters' room. He had a kind of white hood thing over his head, with holes cut for the eyes – like the Ku Klux Klan. He also had gloves and he only spoke in a whisper.'

Jill caught her breath. 'You sure it was a *man*?'

Diane Conway shot her a surprised glance. 'I'm sure. Quite sure. Why?'

'It doesn't matter. Go on.'

'In short, he said that when David got home I had to find out everything about his trip and pass it on to Masters' association, as he called it. If I didn't, he'd send copies of my letter to Kendall, and Kendall's statement, to the press.'

'But could you get the information from your husband – just like that?'

'Yes,' Diane Conway said simply. 'And I'm the only person in the world who could. Things haven't changed. I'm still his blind spot.'

Her voice broke. For the first time Jill found herself believing what she was hearing – and feeling sympathy. But she didn't show it.

Diane Conway blew her nose. 'There was no way out. Masters said it was no good my running away, or even thinking of killing myself. If they didn't get the information, no matter for what reason, they'd carry out their threat. If I went to the police and got Masters arrested, somebody else would take over from him. He told me to go away and think things over. Three days later, on the Sunday, I had instructions to go to the hotel again, in the evening. This time Masters told me that he wanted – well, wanted me. It seemed he'd taken quite a fancy to me. David was away and he knew I was in no position to refuse him.'

She stood up suddenly and took two or three steps into the centre of the room. She spoke with her back to Jill. 'It was horrible. That dingy, smelly little room. I'd never been unfaithful to David before. And Masters never once took off that loathsome hood. I was revolted. I – I suppose I could have said no. There would have been nothing he could have done really if I'd just walked out. He only had the one hold over me – evidence of my deal with Kendall – and he had to keep that lever to use when David got home. But I was frightened of antagonising him. And I did have some notion that if I – if I was nice to him I could perhaps – well, appeal to his better nature, talk him out of the whole thing. I tried to be as pleasing as I could and afterwards I thought I might have partly succeeded, that he might be softening. He let me go eventually and told me to come again on the Wednesday.'

She turned round, went back to her seat and sat down, still with her eyes away from Jill. 'I went home and I was physically sick. The next day I was more or less insane. I thought I just couldn't face going to him again. I had all sorts of crazy ideas for getting him beaten up or something and perhaps frightening him off. I'd more or less recovered by Wednesday, that was the 21st, and I managed to steel myself to go to him once more. He had a bottle of whisky there and he was drinking a lot. I flattered him, pretended my marriage was on the verge of breaking up. I let him think I was falling for him. I asked him all about himself, what he did for a living, and so on. And then he told me all about his gang – his association.'

'Tell me about that.'

'About the association, you mean? What do you want to know?'

'Everything. Who's behind it, for a start?'

'A foreign government, according to Masters. He didn't say which one, but of course I can guess. They finance it completely – pay all the expenses and give Masters and his buddies fat salaries. So the victims can never afford to buy them off.'

'And they don't extort money at all – only secrets?'

'That's right.'

'Always political and scientific stuff?'

'Ultimately. Of course, they pressurise other people to try to get at the ones who've actually got the strategic information. Like Father Dooney. All *he* knew was something damaging about me. They couldn't get directly at me at that time. So they tried to force it out of him. They use that technique a lot – solicitors and clients, doctors and patients, servants and employers, people like that. Masters said it didn't work with Dooney and me, but it was usually very effective.'

'And what's the Alpha List?'

'All their victims or prospective victims are entered on one of the Lists: those who actually have access to strategic information themselves, on the Alpha, Beta, Gamma Lists, and so on, according to the value of their information; and the people like Father Dooney, who can provide data about the Alphas and Betas and the rest, on the Gnostic Lists.'

'The what?'

'Gnostic Lists. Meaning knowledge. They've coined these words Alpha-gnostic, Beta-gnostic, and so on. For instance, Father Dooney knew certain secrets of mine. I'm an Alpha. So he was an Alpha-gnostic. Then again, all the Lists are sub-divided into Potential, Active, or Ex-: those they're still trying to get dirt on; those they've actually started putting the squeeze on; and those whom they've used once and who mustn't be approached again. So at the moment I'm an Active Alpha. Later, when I've given them what they want I'll become an Ex-Alpha and be safe from them in the future.'

'Why will you be safe?'

'Because nobody must be pushed too far. That's one of their golden rules. He said the average blackmailer goes wrong in asking for too much and driving his victim to despair – so that eventually he goes to the police. He said another rule was that bargains must be kept. I said they hadn't kept their bargain with Kendall – they'd still blackmailed him even after he'd squealed on me. So how could I trust them? But Masters insisted Kendall had *offered* them the dirt on me. They'd demanded something quite different from him. Besides, Kendall was an Alpha, not an Alpha-gnostic. So they looked on what he gave them as a sort of bonus.'

'Why did he tell you all this?'

Diane Conway shrugged. 'Just showing off – letting me know how big he was. Men often seem to want to do that with me. And he knew I couldn't talk. That's all of it, too, that's all he told me. But you can imagine when I saw the scope of it all I realised the futility of pleading with him. He'd only been playing with me, anyway – pretending to believe what I'd said about divorcing David. He told me it had been a good act. So then I told him exactly what I thought of him and got out. The next day was Thursday. I recorded a television show in the after-noon . . .'

'How come – if you felt so bad?'

'Do you think I wanted to? But in my position you've got to keep up appearances. Actually, I did the whole thing in a kind of daze. I remember practically nothing about it. Funny. Every-body I met afterwards said I'd never been so good.

'Anyway, we recorded it in the afternoon, and then in the evening I stayed in to watch the transmission – just to do some-thing to try to take my mind off the other thing for a few min-utes. Just after it finished your husband 'phoned me. He said he wanted to help me. I wasn't sure I believed him – but what had I got to lose? I agreed to let him come over. You know what happened then.'

Diane Conway looked straight into Jill's eyes, her gaze steady. 'That's it. The full story. What are you going to do about it?'

13

'Sir, c-could I see you at once, please?' The voice on the line was breathless.

Detective-Chief Superintendent Phillips frowned. 'Who is that?'

'S-sorry, sir. Cochran.'

'What's it about, Cochran? I'm very busy.'

'About Mr Palmer. And the blackmail, sir. I've got a lead.'

Phillips stiffened. 'What sort of lead?'

'A photograph, sir. And some names. I – I think I may know who's responsible. And for the b-blackmail. Everything.'

'Where are you?'

'Criminal Records, sir.'

'Come to my office straight away.'

Cochran arrived in minutes.

'Now, what is all this?' Phillips asked.

Cochran was pale with excitement. 'Sir, I've b-been given two names – men who I'm told are probably implicated in the blackmail. I've checked up on them. One's got form. And there's a connection between them. Then there's this photograph, sir.'

He took it from his pocket and passed it across. 'I'm informed, sir, that this is the girl who called on Lady Felicity and Miss Harper. Apparently, she was involved with one of the other victims, too. She called herself Joyce Summers then. And she's linked with the two men in the same way.'

'What way, Cochran? You're not making sense, lad. Where did you get all this?'

'From Mrs Palmer, sir.'

Phillips stared. 'Mrs Palmer? From America?'

'No, sir. She didn't go to America. She's still in London. She's been making some enquiries of her own.

'She's been doing *what*?'

'Just talking, sir. To the people Inspector Palmer and I interviewed in the couple of weeks before he was killed. Apparently they told her things. She wrote out a statement, sir, mentioning those two names. She enclosed that photo with it . . .'

'Stop.' Phillips held his hand up. 'First – who are these men?'

'Philip Harrington, sir. An accountant. And Maurice Parkstone. We know him. He did eighteen months for false pretences ten years ago.'

'And Mrs Palmer's managed to get evidence against them?'

'I don't know about evidence, sir. At least, she doesn't mention evidence. I imagine they're just names that have been given to her as suspiciously involved in some way.'

'Have you got this statement on you?'

'Yes, sir.'

Cochran took it from his pocket and handed it to Phillips, who read it through. His eyebrows went up. 'She's twigged the espionage angle.'

'You knew about that, sir?'

Phillips didn't look up. 'Don't ask too many questions, Cochran.'

'S-sorry, sir.'

'How the devil did she find out about Kendall and the Mannering girl and Harper and the others?' Phillips muttered. 'Palmer didn't tell her, surely.'

Cochran flushed. 'She – she said something about finding some private notes he'd made – a sort of diary.'

Phillips pounced. ' "Said"? You've seen her?'

'I ran into her a couple of days ago, sir.'

'You knew what she was doing and didn't tell me?'

'She made me promise not to tell anyone at all, sir. She didn't want people to know she was still in the country.'

Phillips looked angry. 'Didn't you realise she might be putting herself in danger? Apart from getting in our hair. You had no right to keep a thing like that to yourself.'

Cochran looked stubborn. 'With respect, sir, I don't think I did wrong. She was only going to talk to people – ordinary people, not criminal types. You'd already finished with them. I didn't consider she could come to any harm or interfere with your enquiries. And she's an ordinary civilian with a right to go where she wants and see who she likes – apart from being Mr Palmer's widow. I didn't think I could refuse when she asked me to respect her confidence, particularly after what she's been through. Frankly, sir, I'd do the same again.'

Phillips stared at him, grim-faced. Then: 'Well, maybe you're right,' he said unexpectedly. 'But I'd like to have known all the same.'

Cochran gave a silent sigh of relief.

'Now,' Phillips said, 'you say you've found some connection between these two men and the girl? What is it?'

This was the moment Cochran had been waiting for. 'Gordon Hemmings, sir,' he said.

'I don't know what I'm going to do,' Jill said. 'I must think.'

'You do believe me, don't you?'

Jill stared at her. Then: 'Yes,' she said.

Diane Conway closed her eyes. 'Thank you.'

'I believe you provisionally. Your story hangs together. I think it's probably true. But I could easily be convinced it wasn't.'

'But you'll keep your promise, won't you? You won't go to the papers or the police?'

'I'll keep my promise unless it's proved to me you've been lying. Now tell me one more thing: have the police or anybody like them – security men, M.I.5, what you will – have they been in touch with you at all, in any way, in any sort of connection since my husband was killed?'

Diane Conway hesitated, licked her lips again, then shook her head.

Jill eyed her keenly. 'Sure?'

'It's not the sort of thing one would be likely to make a mistake about, is it?'

Jill was silent. Diane Conway sat watching her, biting her lip. Suddenly she burst out: 'You said you might be able to help me. I don't know how you can, but if there's anything – anything at all . . .'

'I know I said that. I hadn't heard the whole story then. Frankly, now, there's only one way out I can think of. You won't like it. But you've got to tell someone who's in a position to help you. I'm not. But I know someone who might be.'

'Who?' She sounded as though she hated asking.

'He's a policeman. An Inspector at Scotland Yard.'

'You're crazy! I couldn't possibly. It'd mean going along and making a statement and . . .'

'I don't mean that. I mean talk to him unofficially. He was Bob's best friend. He's actually on the case. If I was to call him and say I could introduce him to someone who actually knows the killer, I'm sure he'd do his darndest to keep you out of things. He wouldn't be interested in what you'd done in the past. How about it? Just see him privately, without any witnesses, quite off the record.'

'I – I don't know.' She shook her head in perplexity. 'It's too dangerous. I've got to think of David's position.'

'Suppose you do nothing until he gets home? What are you going to do then?'

'I don't know! I told you, I don't know.'

'Then I'll tell you: you'll only have two choices – do what Masters wants and have the leak traced back to your husband eventually; or tell David the whole story as you told me. If you leave it any longer, that'll be your choice – one or the other. Your only chance to get out of this is somehow to clear it up before he gets home. And for that you've got to have help. And you couldn't do better than Andy.'

'Andy? Is that the Inspector?'

'Andrew Thompson. If I were in your position he'd be the man I'd want pitching for me. What's your alternative? Come on, tell me.'

'All right, you win.' The capitulation was instantaneous and unexpected. It was as if Diane Conway had suddenly run out of fight. 'I'm in your hands. When can you arrange it?'

'Perhaps now.'

'What – this afternoon?'

'Maybe. It's Sunday. He's usually home at this time when he's not on duty. I could call him and perhaps have him come over right now.'

Diane Conway looked desperately frightened. For a moment Jill thought she might go back on her decision. Then her shoulders drooped. 'All right. Might as well get it over with, I suppose.'

'Good.' Jill got to her feet and picked up her bag. 'I passed a 'phone box down the road. I'll call him from there.'

Cochran said: 'As soon as I looked at that photo I knew I'd seen the girl before. But I couldn't think where. Then I read Mrs Palmer's statement and the words "accountant" and "public relations" struck a chord. I was sure that I'd come across a connection between them once before in the case. Then it hit me. Mr Palmer had remarked casually that Hemmings was an accountant and also had an interest in a P.R. firm. Then I remembered where I'd seen this Summers girl. She was the one in the photos with Hemmings – the ones we found in Johnny James's flat.'

'Quite sure?'

'Yes, sir. Then I checked up on Parkstone and Harrington. Parkstone's with Metropolitan Promotions – of which Gordon Hemmings is a principal shareholder. And Harrington works for a firm of accountants called MacKenzie, Gilliat and Hemmings.'

Phillips' face was impassive. Deliberately he picked up his pipe, filled it and lit it. Then he said: 'Well done, lad.'

'Thank you, sir. But I didn't do much.'

'You did all you could have done. I never ask more.' He picked up Jill's statement and read it through again, then looked carefully at the photograph.

'Wonder why she doesn't say who she got this from,' he said musingly.

'I'd guess she was asked not to, sir.'

'And who among all these people she's been calling on would be most likely to have a picture of a girl and not want it known?'

Cochran thought for a second. 'Hurndall, I suppose, sir.'

'Right. Let's say she was his girl friend. And tied up with his blackmailers. And she was Hemmings' girl. And apparently a victim, along with Hemmings, of Johnny James. And mixed up in the blackmail of Lady Felicity and Eileen Harper. And Hemmings employs Harrington and Parkstone. Both of whom are tied in with the blackmail of one of the other people on Palmer's list . . .' He was silent, then tapped the photograph. 'Shown this to C.R.O.?'

'Not yet, sir. Shall I try them now?'

'No, it doesn't matter. Got Hemmings' address or number by any chance?'

'Yes, sir. I had to make a note of it at the time of that Johnny

James business.' He took a notebook from his pocket, flicked through it and handed it open to Phillips.

'Hm, not far away. Wonder if he's home now.' Phillips lifted the telephone receiver, asked for an outside line, glanced at Cochran's book again and dialled a number. They heard it ringing. Then a man's voice answered.

'Oh.' Phillips sounded strangely surprised. 'Who is that, please?'

Cochran could hear the reply: 'Hemmings here.'

'I'm sorry. I've got the wrong number.'

Phillips rang off, looked at Cochran's surprised expression and gave one of his rare smiles. 'Just checking if he was in. A call on Mr Hemmings is the next logical step but there's no need to warn him first. Like to come along?'

'Now, sir? Yes, please!'

'Right. Meet me out front in fifteen minutes. Clear off now, will you? I want to make a few more calls.'

'Yes, sir.'

Cochran left the room, and Phillips pressed the switch of the intercom on his desk. 'I want a patrol car and two uniformed constables outside in ten minutes. Get through to Superintendent Youngman of the Fraud Squad for me – I don't know where he is. Then put me through to Special Branch – senior duty officer. And try to raise Inspector Thompson at his home.'

He rang off and sat thinking. No observer would have been aware of it, but there were stirrings within him to which such a phlegmatic and case-hardened man was unused. He felt expectant, perturbed, tense, even slightly nervous. He knew that if he obeyed orders he would consult his superiors before taking such action as he was now contemplating.

But he wasn't going to.

'Andy?'

'Yes. Who's that?' The familiar voice had a puzzled tone.

'Jill.'

'Well, I'll be ... Where are you?'

'London.'

'London! What are you doing here? When did you get back?'

'I never left, Andy.'

'What?' He sounded staggered. 'But – but you said . . .'

'I know. I'm sorry, Andy. I've been looking for that woman Bob saw on television. And I've found her. Andy – Bob was killed in her house. She was there. She's talked to the killer. And she knows a lot about the blackmailers and all their organisation.'

'Jill – are you being serious?'

'Oh, Andy! Would I joke about a thing like this?'

'Of course not. Sorry. I'm not thinking straight. Go on – who is this woman?'

'I can't tell you yet. But she's in deep trouble. They've got her over a barrel. I've persuaded her to talk with you – privately and off the record – on one condition.'

'What's that?'

'That you do all you can to keep her out of things. If she's telling the truth – and I think she is – she didn't have anything to do with Bob's death and she's not mixed up in anything criminal. You've got to promise to help her and keep her secrets as far as you possibly can. Bob promised her that, so I think you can, too. I think she can help you nail Bob's murderer – and round up this gang. But only if she trusts you. So you must play along with her. Will you?'

'Well, yes, of course – if what you say's right.'

'And you mustn't report any of this until you've seen us – to Phillips or anyone else.'

There was silence.

'Promise, Andy.'

'Well, yes, all right, then. If that's what you want. I promise.'

'Are you free this afternoon?'

'I can be.'

'Can you come right now?'

'I should think so. Where?'

She gave him the address. 'Will you come by car?'

'Yes.'

'Then I'll open the gates and you can drive straight in. Don't park outside.'

'Right.'

'I'll be waiting for you.'

'I'll be as quick as I can. Now, Jill – be careful, d'you hear?'

'Don't worry about me. I can look after myself. And Andy . . .'

'What?'

'Thanks.'

As Phillips rang off, his intercom buzzed. He pressed the switch. 'Yes?'

'No reply from Mr Thompson, sir. And the car's ready.'

Phillips put Jill's statement and the photograph in his pocket, went downstairs and outside. A car was waiting for him, Cochran standing beside it, talking to the driver. He opened the door, Phillips got in, Cochran followed him, shut the door, and the car moved forward.

The two women sat silently in the big first-floor room of the empty house. Darkness was drawing in and it was getting cold. There were few signs of life in the street. Diane Conway was lighting cigarette after cigarette, dropping them on to the floor half-smoked. It was so quiet that Jill could hear the ticking of her wrist-watch. She glanced at it. It was just gone twenty to five. Andrew should arrive any minute.

There was the sound of a car engine from the street. Diane Conway stiffened. Jill turned and looked out of the window. A car had stopped in the road outside. As Jill watched, it moved slowly forward again and pulled in through the gates. It came up the drive and went out of sight the other side of the house.

Diane Conway stood up. 'Is it . . . ?'

'I couldn't see. But it must be. I'll go and let him in.'

The police car pulled up outside a pair of ornate wrought-iron gates. One of the constables got out and opened them, and the car went through and carried on along the drive. It rounded a large, beautifully kept lawn and pulled up in front of the house. Phillips heaved himself out and Cochran followed. They stood for a moment, looking about them. The house was of grey stone, solid, and squarely built. It was quite secluded, standing in about an acre of ground, surrounded by a high wall and lots of trees. Not another building, not even the road outside could be seen. Phillips was impressed. You had to pay high for this sort of privacy if you wanted to live within fifteen minutes' drive of Westminster – or at least, fifteen minutes in a police car on a Sunday afternoon.

There was no sign of life in the house. 'Come on,' said Phillips. They went up to the front door and Phillips rang the bell.

They waited.

Jill opened the front door and saw Andrew approaching. He paused momentarily as the door opened, then recognised Jill and hurried forward again and into the hall.

'Jill!' He took her by the shoulders and looked deep into her eyes.

'Hullo, Andy.' She managed a wan smile. 'It's sure good to see you.'

'Jill, I can't believe it. This is fantastic. You've really been in London all this time?'

She nodded.

'But why didn't you tell me?'

'I thought you'd try to talk me out of – of, well, making enquiries of my own.'

'You bet your life I would. But, Jill, what *is* all this? I couldn't take it in properly on the 'phone. It sounded impossible. You've really found someone who knows Bob's killer?'

'Yes. She's upstairs.'

He whistled silently. 'Who is she?'

'I'll let her tell you herself. Come on up.'

She shut the door, walked to the stairs and started up. Andrew followed her.

'What is this place?'

'Just a house that happens to be for sale. She thought it would be a good place to meet privately, so she got the key from the agent.'

'I'd say she was right.'

They reached the top and Jill turned along the landing. The

door of the big bedroom still stood open. Jill approached it, Andrew at her heels.

'It's all right,' she called out softly. 'It *is* Andrew.'

She entered the room. 'He . . .'

But what she saw inside the room caused her to break off and stop dead in her tracks.

14

The door slowly opened, and Gordon Hemmings, M.P., said: 'Yes?'

'Mr Hemmings?'

'That's right.' His eyes went past Phillips and Cochran to the car and the two uniformed men. 'Is anything wrong?'

'May we come in, sir? This may take some little time. Thank you.' Without waiting for a reply Phillips moved forward, more or less forcing the M.P. to step backwards, opening the door wider as he did so. Cochran followed closely behind.

Phillips stared around him appreciatively. 'Nice place you've got here, sir. Must have cost you a pretty penny, though.'

'Look – what is this? What do you want?' Cochran well remembered the petulant, self-important tones.

'Phillips. Detective-Chief Superintendent Phillips. C.I.D.' He held out his warrant card. 'This is Detective-Constable Cochran.'

'Mr Hemmings and I have met before, sir.'

Hemmings glanced at him sharply.

'Back in May, sir,' Cochran said. 'I was Inspector Palmer's assistant.'

Hemmings' eyes flickered. 'Oh yes, of course, that business of the photographs. Terrible thing about Palmer. Quite shocking. But why have you come to me? I don't understand.'

'We think you may be able to help us in our enquiries, sir.'

'Enquiries? What – you mean into Palmer's murder?'

'I didn't say that, sir. But yes: that – among other things.'

'But how on earth do you think I could possibly help you? I only saw Palmer a few times – over six months ago.'

'Is that so, sir? Oh well, I did say that among other things.'

'Superintendent – you must be more specific. What other things?'

'Things like blackmail, sir – and espionage.'

Hemmings gave a laugh. 'You're not suggesting I know anything about these matters? My only experience of blackmail ...'

Phillips broke in on him. 'You may find you know more than you think, sir, if you put your mind to it. Now: may we all go into the sitting-room?' And he opened a door to the left and walked through.

'Now, wait a minute. You can't just push yourself in – I mean . . .' Protesting incoherently, Hemmings hurried in after him.

Cochran followed them. Just inside the door he stopped short and drew his breath in sharply. In front of the large ornamental mantelpiece stood a girl. She was transfixed in an awkward position, as though she'd paused in mid-movement, and was staring at them, a startled expression in her eyes. She was in her twenties; had short, blonde hair swept back from her forehead, and grey eyes. She was wearing a tight-fitting off-white dress.

And Cochran knew beyond a shadow of doubt that she was the girl in the photographs.

He, too, stood still, not knowing what to do or say. He cast an urgent glance at his chief. But Phillips was smiling pleasantly at the girl.

'Good evening, madam. Sorry to burst in on you like this. I hope we didn't alarm you.'

She recovered her composure rapidly and gave a quick and charming smile.

'No, not at all.' She had a toneless, classless voice. 'What can we do for you, Mr – er . . .'

Hemmings said: 'Oh, this is Superintendent Phillips of Scotland Yard, darling. Superintendent, this is my wife.'

It was an effort for Cochran to keep back an exclamation of surprise. But Phillips was completely unmoved. 'How do you do, Mrs Hemmings.'

Hemmings said: 'Now, Mr Phillips, perhaps you'd be so good as to say exactly what it is you . . .'

'Do sit down, Superintendent,' his wife interrupted. She turned to Cochran with another smile. 'And you, of course.'

'No thank you, Mrs Hemmings,' Phillips said. 'I don't think we will sit down.' And suddenly his voice, his whole bearing, was somehow subtly, indefinably, different – harder, more formal. His hand went inside his coat and brought out the photograph. He held it out to her, face down. 'I'd like you to look at this, if you would.'

She took it, turned it over and stared at it without a trace of emotion. 'Who's this?'

'It's you, Mrs Hemmings.'

'Me?' She sounded genuinely surprised and amused. 'Oh no, I don't think...'

'I think it is, madam. You look superficially different, of course, but there are certain characteristics no trained police officer could miss.'

'Well, I can't agree with you. I've never worn my hair like that, for one thing. But even if it were me – what about it?'

'We've been given that photograph by a gentleman who says that he knew you very well earlier this year when you went under the name of Joyce Summers. Now you married Mr Hemmings only a few weeks ago but Summers wasn't your maiden name, was it, Mrs Hemmings?'

'No. It was Lucas.'

'Yes, I know. Dorothy Lucas, in full, according to a colleague of mine in the Special Branch.'

'Which just goes to show how absurd this all is.'

'Is it? I don't think so. I think if the gentleman were here now he'd make a positive identification. His story, you see, is that Joyce Summers disappeared. Shortly after that he was involved in a nasty case of blackmail. It's also been stated that this young woman' – Phillips tapped the photo – 'was responsible for the attempted blackmail of Lady Felicity Mannering and also paid a visit to Miss Eileen Harper at Greenhill School shortly before she committed suicide. Again, I'm confident we can get a firm identification of you, Mrs Hemmings, when the witnesses meet you face to face.'

Dorothy Hemmings made no reaction of any kind, just stood perfectly still holding the photograph. Phillips swung round to Gordon Hemmings.

'Sir, I believe you are a partner in a firm called MacKenzie, Gilliat and Hemmings?'

'Yes.'

'And one of your employees is a man called Philip Harrington?'

'I – I believe so.'

'I see. Well, Mr Harrington has also been mentioned to us as being involved in various attempts at blackmail. Then there's the matter of Metropolitan Promotions. You have an interest in that company?'

'I have an interest in many companies . . .'

'One of the chief executives of this company is a Mr Maurice Parkstone. Another colleague of mine in the Fraud Squad, who's been investigating the Kendall Group's affairs, tells me Mr Parkstone handled their account. And he has been named as being connected with the blackmail of Mr Kendall. Strange, isn't it, that so many people who come into contact with you and your wife sooner or later have their names cropping up in connection with cases of extortion – and all the cases which the late Inspector Palmer was investigating before his murder?'

'Superintendent!' Dorothy Hemmings' voice rasped out. 'I don't know whether we are supposed to take all this as some kind of accusation, but if so it's just about the vaguest one I've ever heard. You keep using phrases like "has been named", "has been mentioned", "it has been stated". They're meaningless! Who's doing all this "mentioning" and "stating"? What sort of proof have you got?'

Phillips just stared at her, then nodded deliberately. 'So you'd have no objection to confronting, say, Lady Felicity and seeing whether she identifies you?'

'I'd have every objection.'

Phillips and Cochran had both had their eyes on the woman and had failed to notice Hemmings edging away. Now as he spoke they turned and froze.

The M.P. was standing beside an open drawer and in his right hand was clasped a heavy automatic pistol.

Dorothy Hemmings walked rapidly across to her husband's side. Phillips swore quietly.

Cochran made to move forward.

'Stay where you are!' Hemmings snapped this out, and Cochran stopped.

'You fool, Hemmings,' Phillips said. 'Don't you realise this is as good as an admission?'

'I'm admitting nothing. Just say that if my affairs are to be investigated, I'd prefer not to be around at the time.'

'Expect your little friends behind the Iron Curtain to take you in?'

'Oh no. They're disagreeable people and it's a very disagreeable climate. A more temperate region is indicated. I've been planning it for some time.'

'South America?'

'Shut up. No more questions. Sit on the settee and put your hands on your head.'

Phillips didn't move. For seconds it seemed he might defy the M.P. Then the moment passed and he slowly did as he was told.

Hemmings said: 'Now – how many men have you got out there?'

Phillips said nothing.

'Listen,' Hemmings said. 'I don't want to hurt anybody but if I'm not told what I'm up against I'm liable to shoot anything that moves. My wife and I'll be disappearing for ever in a few minutes, so it makes no odds to me. This gun is very effectively silenced, and the house is soundproofed. If you co-operate no one will get injured, but if you don't I'll shoot you both, call in those two bobbies, put a bullet through each of them, and then go outside and do the same to any others I find hanging about. So if you value the lives of your men you'll answer me. Now: I saw two uniformed men outside. Are there any more police here?'

Reluctantly, Phillips shook his head.

'Thank you.' Hemmings moved round behind the settee and put the muzzle of the automatic against the back of Phillips' head. To his wife he said: 'Fetch your gun.'

She went to the same open drawer and took out a smaller automatic with a pearl handle. Hemmings looked at Cochran. 'You will go into the hall, open the front door and call the two men in the car. When you see them approaching the front door, turn round, come back into this room and sit down next to your boss. My wife will be right behind you all the time. Follow my instructions to the letter and everyone will be all right.' He cast a glance at his wife. 'Stay in the hall, standing by the door. When they come in tell them *he* wants them in here. Then shut the front door and follow them in. Have your gun at the ready and don't stand too close to them.'

She nodded briefly, waggled her gun at Cochran, and said: 'You heard.'

Cochran looked at Phillips, but Phillips looked straight ahead and stayed silent. Cochran walked out to the hall, the woman right behind him. Phillips heard the front door open and Cochran shout out as ordered. Then came the sound of two car doors slamming and two sets of heavy footsteps on the path. Cochran reappeared in the doorway, came across, and sat beside him. They heard Dorothy Lucas say: 'Hullo. Your Superintendent wants you in there.'

The two constables appeared in the doorway. Then they saw the situation and stopped dead. One gave an exclamation, the other took a step forward.

Phillips said sharply: 'Stay there. Do exactly what he tells you. No heroics.' Both men relaxed fractionally. Phillips said more quietly: 'Sorry about this. I had no choice.'

'But you have nothing to worry about if you do as you're told,' Hemmings said. 'We're simply going to shut you up for a while in the cellar. I don't imagine it will be too long before your headquarters start to get worried about you. Of course, my wife and I will be gone for good in about a quarter of an hour.'

Phillips said: 'Do you seriously think you can get away?'

Hemmings nodded. 'Oh, yes.'

'You see, we've been ready for this for a long time,' Dorothy Hemmings said, coming round from behind the constables but keeping her gun on them. 'The whole success of the operation depended on Gordon remaining in the clear. We knew that once there was the merest hint of suspicion it would be time to close down and disappear. So we made our preparations a long time ago. There's a vehicle garaged here that nobody knows we own. In it there's money, clothes, all the documents we'll need for moving round under false names – passports, driving licences, everything. The vehicle's registered in the name on one of the licences. We'll need about quarter of an hour to completely change our appearances. Once we've left this house you'll never trace us. We could be out of the country in an hour – or we might decide to stay on for a few weeks or months. We've got several sets of identities in different places, carefully created over long periods. So you see, you really haven't got a chance.'

'Everything's been rehearsed,' said Hemmings. 'We knew this moment had to come sooner or later. It's amazing what arrangements one can make when one has plenty of time, plenty of contacts, and virtually unlimited funds.'

They stood smiling smugly. They seemed to be enjoying themselves. To Cochran, their words and their airs of complete self-confidence were dauntingly convincing.

'Now that's enough talk,' Hemmings said. 'My wife is going to go outside and open the door to the cellar while I watch you four. She will then stand near the cellar door and call out. You will go out into the hall one at a time. As soon as you get out of my sight, you will be in hers. You will go down into the cellar, and as soon as you reach the bottom my wife will call out and the next one will go. Then you will be locked in. How long it will be before you are discovered I don't know. I should warn you that in ten minutes' time you may find the temperature rising and the far wall of the cellar getting hot. But there'll be nothing to fear, so don't panic. There's another room beyond that wall and I'll be setting the contents alight before we leave. I have several gallons of paraffin all ready. But the room is completely fireproof, and the flames will burn out without spreading or damaging anything else. And that, I think, is everything. You first, superintendent. Stand up.'

Phillips heaved himself to his feet.

'Right, my dear,' Hemmings said to his wife. 'Carry on.'

'No.'

Cochran's voice was hoarse. He stood up. He was pale but there was a gleam in his eyes that Phillips had seen in other men's. It told him things were out of his hands, that he had to keep silent. And it made his heart beat faster.

'All you've s-said's been very convincing.' Cochran tried to gulp and seemed to have difficulty in swallowing. 'Too convincing. B-because you've made me believe it.'

'Good,' said Hemmings, 'so perhaps you'll . . .'

'I believe that if we let you get out of this house, you'll escape altogether. And I'm not going to let Mr Palmer's murderer get away.' And Cochran took a step towards Hemmings.

Hemmings gripped his gun tightly and thrust it out in Cochran's direction. He shouted: 'Don't be a fool. I'll shoot. I'll kill you.'

'Yes, I expect you would. You've had some experience already, haven't you?'

Cochran moved forward again. Hemmings stepped back.

'Shoot him!' Dorothy Hemmings screamed.

'I will. I've given fair warning. Get back!' Hemmings was sweating.

Instead, Cochran eased another foot towards him.

Phillips watched them in horrified fascination, his eyes darting from one to the other. Then he glanced at Dorothy Hemmings and his heart gave a leap. She'd taken her eyes off him.

Phillips took one huge step towards her and wrenched the gun from her hand. She screeched with rage and tried to wrest it back. Phillips thrust her savagely away. She staggered against the two constables, who grabbed her and held her fast.

Phillips swung the gun round on Hemmings. The M.P. did not shift his eyes an inch from Cochran. He stopped retreating, stepped forward, and jammed his gun against Cochran's stomach.

'Drop that gun,' he yelled to Phillips. 'And let go of my wife. You've got five seconds or he's dead.'

Phillips said: 'You shoot him and I shoot you where you stand. Drop your gun, Hemmings. You haven't got a chance. There's no one backing you up now.'

Dorothy Hemmings gasped: 'Don't take any notice of him. Keep the gun!'

'Yes, keep the gun,' Cochran said calmly. 'Shoot me. See where it gets you.'

'He's right.' Somehow Phillips, too, kept his voice steady. 'You can live, Hemmings – if you choose to. But if you squeeze that trigger you're committing suicide.'

'Release my wife!'

'Don't!' Cochran yelled before the constables could move. 'Hold her!'

Phillips said: 'Life or death, Hemmings, life or death. Which is it to be?'

Nobody moved, nobody spoke. It seemed as if ages passed. It was a contest of wills between two men. And the stronger man won.

Hemmings' gun hand fell to his side.

Cochran bent forward, took the pistol from him, and stepped back. Phillips, who'd been holding his breath, let it out very slowly. And Dorothy Hemmings gave an animal-like screech of frustrated rage and malice that turned Cochran's blood cold.

Hemmings sank down on to a chair, put his head in his hands, and started to sob.

For the first time in many years Phillips did not know what orders to give. He felt drained of energy. Then he pulled himself together. 'Right, get the cuffs on them.'

The two constables brought Dorothy Hemmings forward.

Hemmings looked up, a hopeless deadness in his eyes. 'You said I killed Palmer. I didn't. I can prove it. There was a big debate in the House that night. I was there all through until one a.m. I spoke in the debate. I voted at the end.'

'So what?' Cochran said. 'You had him killed. You didn't hold the knife, but you paid the thug who did.'

Hemmings shook his head wretchedly. 'No. I had nothing to do with it. I knew nothing about it till afterwards. I swear it.' His head dropped again.

'Tell that to the jury,' Cochran said.

Phillips said to Hemmings: 'I want a look in this second cellar of yours. How do I get in?'

'Don't tell him!' Dorothy Hemmings spat it out.

He snapped at her: 'Don't be a fool! They'll find it sooner or later.' Then, to Phillips: 'In my study across the hall there's a bookcase. It's hinged. Behind it there's a door. It looks like a big safe. It's got a combination lock. Beyond it there's a trap-door in the floor and a ladder going down. At the bottom there's another door. That's got a combination lock, too. Behind it you'll find everything you want.'

'Write down the combinations.' He handed Hemmings his notebook and a pen, and with some difficulty Hemmings jotted down the two numbers.

Phillips took the notebook from him and walked to the door. 'Come on,' he said to Cochran. In the doorway he turned round. 'Don't take your eyes off them. I don't think they'll give you any more trouble, but don't bank on it.'

Phillips and Cochran stared silently round them. They were in a large underground room. It was lit by fluorescent tubes. What could be seen of the walls was of rough stone, painted white. Behind the two men was a newer-looking wall of brick and concrete, with a door in it through which they had just passed.

177

On the other side of this there was a narrow space and then the original wall of the cellar. From this space a steel ladder went straight up to the cupboard behind Hemmings' bookcase. At the far end of the cellar was another new wall, like the one behind them.

Phillips said : 'You can see what they've done. Beyond that' – he pointed to the wall at the far end – 'is the outer cellar – where they were going to shut us. You get at that down the cellar stairs normally. Originally it was all one, but they've bricked off this half and made an entrance to it through the study. This wall' – he banged the bricks behind them – 'is just an added precaution, so you'd have to know both combinations to get in. Here you're completely enclosed.' He pointed up to a ventilator grille in the corner of the ceiling. 'That's the only link with outside. Come on, let's take a look round.'

The room looked like an efficient modern office. There was a large wooden table in the middle, with several upright chairs around it. Along the walls were crammed filing cabinets and metal cupboards, each one numbered. There were three or four shelves, stacked with lever-arch files. There was a writing-desk and on it a strange cube-shaped framework of wires and wood, about a foot square, with small castors at the bottom corners. Next to the desk was a photo-copier. A film projector was set up on a stand facing a screen hanging on the opposite wall. A slide projector was beside it.

Phillips and Cochran started to open cupboards. They found half a dozen tape recorders of various sizes, six stills cameras, three cine-cameras, editing equipment for film and tape, and one shelf full of tiny microphones, amplifiers, and headphones. 'For bugging,' Phillips said grimly.

One corner of the room was partitioned off to form a small enclosure. There was a door in it, which Cochran opened. He looked inside. 'Dark room, sir.'

Phillips opened one of the filing cabinets, took out a cardboard wallet and glanced at the papers inside it. 'Files on individual victims. There are about thirty separate dossiers in this drawer alone.' He put the wallet back, closed the drawer, and moved on.

There were five large cupboards full of photographs, spools of recording tape, cine-films. Everything was numbered and in meticulous order.

Cochran moved away to the writing desk. He opened one of the drawers. Inside was a large, hard-covered, loose-leaf book. Cochran took it out, laid it on the desk and started to turn the pages. He gave a whistle. 'Come and look here, sir.'

Phillips came across. 'What is it?'

'It's a list of all their victims, I think. The first half's an index. There are hundreds of names in alphabetical order. Each one's got a capital letter by it, some Greek, some English – oh, of course, they're the ones that are the same in both. And some have got another letter or word or number as well. Then farther on' – he turned over about fifty pages – 'look, sir.'

Phillips read out the words: 'The Alpha List.'

'And later on you get the Beta, Gamma, Delta Lists, and so on, sir. All the names are listed again – but with more detail. The index at the front tells you in which list you can find any name. I reckon this is a sort of summary of the whole organisation. And just look at some of these names, sir – him, for example. I say, sir, let's see what they had on *him*.'

'No, look up somebody we already know about. Try Hurndall.'

Cochran turned back to the index and ran his finger down the H's. 'Here we are, sir: Hurndall, Geoffrey – Beta.' He located the Beta List, turned over the pages, and found Hurndall's entry. 'Yes, sir, it's all here, in a sort of shorthand: Dorothy Lucas's initials, the date Hurndall was first approached, a brief outline of his accident, the number of the filing cabinet in which his full dossier is kept, and so on. At the end it says "Comments: failure – subject confessed to police".'

'Put it back, Cochran. As you found it.'

Cochran did so. Phillips said: 'Come on, let's get back upstairs. This whole place will have to be gone through systematically. But not now. And not by us. The A.C. will have to see it. Then it'll be up to the top brass to decide what's to be done. Which'll make the fur fly, I fancy. I can see myself not being very popular in certain quarters.'

They went back up the steel ladder and into the study, Phillips locking both the doors after them. He said: 'I want you to stay here in the house for the time being. I can't risk leaving that cellar unguarded. I shouldn't imagine anybody but those two have the combinations, but we mustn't chance anything.

That's why I didn't let you get a sight of those numbers, incidentally. Not because I think you would mess around down there, but so nobody can ever accuse you of it. I'll send relief as soon as possible.'

'Right, sir.'

Before they left the study, Phillips said: 'I should have said well done, Cochran. I think you were an insubordinate young idiot just now. But well done. It won't be overlooked.'

Cochran went red. 'Couldn't let Mr Palmer's murderer just walk away, sir.'

Phillips cast him a quick glance. 'He denied knowing anything about that, you know.'

'Yes. It was a good effort, wasn't it, sir?'

Phillips nodded. 'Very good.'

15

Jill stopped dead in her tracks and stared uncomprehendingly into the big bedroom. Behind her she heard a muttered exclamation from Andrew.

For Diane Conway was standing tall and stiff in the centre of the room, her arm outstretched. Then her voice rang out, deep and vibrant, echoing through the empty corridors.

'That's him. That's the man who killed your husband.'

Her finger pointed straight at Andrew Thompson.

For seconds the words made no sense to Jill. When they sank in, she thought she must be dreaming. Either that or Diane Conway was mad.

'No,' she said, 'you don't understand. This is . . .'

'That's Masters. He's one of the leaders of the gang. He thought I wouldn't recognise him. But I'd know him anywhere! He stabbed your husband in the back.'

Jill turned to Andrew, bewildered. He looked at her and gave a shrug. 'You didn't tell me she was crazy, my sweet.'

'But she's not. At least . . .'

She stopped, a cold hand clutching at her heart. For as she looked into his eyes she suddenly knew. She gave a little choking cry and her hand went to her throat.

Thompson's face changed, grew harder. He gave a sigh and seemed to relax.

'He never passed on what you told him to Phillips.' Diane Conway hissed the words at Jill. She swung round to Thompson. 'Deny it – go on, deny it!'

He shook his head. 'She knows.' He took a step towards Jill. 'Jill, I'm sorry. I had to do it. He was practically on to us. If this little bitch had spoken to him it would have been all over. I couldn't kill her – we needed her – so it had to be him. I didn't want to kill Bob, believe me. But I had no choice. He didn't suffer. It was quick.'

Jill swayed and her legs nearly buckled. She tottered back and found herself leaning against the mantelpiece. Thompson continued to walk towards her, explaining, justifying. But there was a pounding in her head and a roaring in her ears, and she could only take in odd snatches.

'Fate, really . . . amazing that he should have actually rung *me* for help in tracing her number . . . gave me the whole story . . . managed to get there first . . . opened the door to him . . . told him there'd been trouble and I'd been sent over . . . he never suspected . . . not my fault . . . destiny, really – like Banquo and Macbeth . . .'

Strength came back to Jill's legs slowly, the pounding stopped and the roaring faded. Thompson came back into focus in front of her. She stared up at him, unblinking. He stopped talking suddenly when he saw the expression in her eyes.

'Does it show?' she asked in a quiet, quiet voice. 'Does the loathing and the contempt show in my face? It doesn't all show, you know. It couldn't. No face on earth could express what I feel about you now.'

'Shut up!'

Diane Conway gave a harsh laugh. 'Got you on the raw, hasn't she? Funny, you didn't seem to mind when *I* told you what I thought of you . . .'

Thompson whirled on her. 'You've got nothing to laugh about. You're not off the hook. On the contrary. Because you're going to suffer for this. You'll look back on the past month as a holiday besides what's coming. But first I've got her to deal with.'

Diane Conway stepped forward and grabbed his arm. 'You mustn't . . .'

'Keep out of it!' He shook her off, drew back his arm, and swung a punch at her. It caught her a glancing blow on the jaw, she staggered back, fell into the corner, and lay half dazed.

Jill screamed and made a dash to her right. But Thompson grabbed her and thrust her back against the wall, his hands gripping her shoulders. His face was close to hers.

'I never thought it would end like this, Jill. I loved you – d'you know that? If you'd given me the slightest encouragement, I'd have – everything'd've been different. After Bob was gone I hoped – that's not why I killed him, but I did hope you might turn to me. You didn't. But I would still have come running if you'd given the nod – like I have today. Even up to a few minutes ago I was trying to work out something – thinking how I might convince you everything I'd done was necessary. But now you've looked at me like that – as if I were filth – something's happened. You've killed every feeling I ever had for you – in a flash. You committed suicide with that look, Jill. Before that I don't think I could have harmed a hair of your head. But now killing you's going to be a pleasure.'

Jill screamed again and tried to push him off, but it was useless. His hands slid from her shoulders to her neck and he started to squeeze . . .

There was the clatter of shoes on the bare boards, a shout, a confused blur of struggling figures – and she was free. She gasped and coughed. Her eyes were watering and she couldn't make out what was happening. She dashed the tears from her eyes and managed to focus her sight.

Thompson was lying quite still on the floor by the window seat.

Two men, their backs to her, and who must have gone down with him, were struggling to their feet. The first to rise turned and gave her a sort of a smile.

'He hit his head on the seat. Out cold.'

It was Owen Sherwood.

Jill murmured: 'Owen . . . I don't understand. What . . .'

But she never finished the sentence. For the other man – tall, straight, and with iron-grey hair – rose, turned and came towards her, arms outstretched.

'Jill – darling.'

She gasped. 'Dad! Oh, Dad!'

She fell forward into his arms and everything went black.

It was a particularly pungent, yet familiar smell which brought her round. She opened her eyes. The first thing she saw was her father's face straight above her.

'Dad,' she whispered. 'It is you. Not a dream.'

He bent and kissed her. 'No dream, honey.'

She found she was lying full-length on the window seat, her father kneeling on the floor beside her. With an effort, she sat up and put her arms round his neck. 'I can't believe it,' she said.

'It's true. I'm here.'

He got off the floor and sat beside her, his arm around her. She leaned against him and looked at Owen Sherwood, who was standing in front of them, the small black cigar in his mouth giving off dense clouds of smoke. 'Owen,' she said shakily. 'I wondered where that smell was coming from. I should have known.'

'Best thing in the world for faints, *cariad*. Never fails.'

She gave a convulsive start as full recollection came flooding back. 'Andrew! He killed Bob. He tried to kill me.'

'Yes, yes, we know all about it. It's all on tape.'

'Where – where is he?' She cast a bewildered glance round the room. Standing by the door was another man – middle-aged and bespectacled. He gave her a reassuring smile as her glance fell on him.

'Don't worry. Quite safe.' Sherwood jerked his head towards the landing. 'There's a room at the back with barred windows. Been a nursery at some time. There are two big bolts across the door, which I fixed there this morning, just in case. He was only half-conscious when we put him in there, but he's probably come round by now.'

Jill tried hard to focus her thoughts. She felt strangely detached from all that was going on. She had to wait and think carefully before speaking, so that she'd be sure of asking the right questions.

'And Diane – Mrs Romford?' To Jill her own voice sounded flat and dull.

'I sent her home.'

'Is she all right?' It had to be OK to ask that.

'Bit of a sore jaw but otherwise fine. She played her part well.'

Some response seemed to be expected to this. What could it be? She concentrated, before saying hesitantly: 'Her part? Wasn't that story true?'

'Quite true in substance, I'm sure, though I imagine she dramatised a little.'

She stared at him, perplexed. 'I – I'm sorry. You'll have to explain.'

'Later. There's no time now.'

'But what are you doing here?'

'I suspected Thompson from the first. I set all this up just to catch him. I fixed up a tape recorder earlier. We've got every word Thompson spoke. With the help of the U.S. Air Force and the Church I've got him cold.'

'The Church?'

'Oh, sorry. Allow me to introduce the Reverend Mr Grant.'

He indicated the man by the door, who smiled and bowed his head.

'I got Mr Grant to come along as an irreproachable independent witness. I've never met him before today, and he has no connection whatever with anybody else involved in this case. I wanted somebody like him to overhear everything and take charge of the tape until the police arrive, so as to be able to testify it hadn't been tampered with. He also saw Thompson try to kill you. His evidence should be invaluable. A parson seemed ideal – though I had quite a job finding one free on a Sunday.'

'Normally I wouldn't be,' Mr Grant said. 'But today as it happens I was able to get away for a few hours. I must say it's been quite an experience.'

A word had stuck in Jill's mind. 'Owen – the police: you've called them?'

'Not yet. I wanted to tell you a few things first – and ask you a favour.'

'What's that?'

'Mrs Romford's my client. I want to get her off the hook. So when the police come, will you keep quiet about the story she told you – and not say anything about the recording *you* made?'

'Yes, of course, but . . .' She broke off, then said: 'But, surely, they'll have to know she was here – and why?'

'Yes – and that an attempt had been made to blackmail her. But if it's possible, I want the details blurred over. I'm hoping I can get Phillips to co-operate with me in getting her out of trouble, and the fact that I can hand him Bob's killer is my trump card.'

'Whatever you say, Owen. You saved my life. I'm in your hands.'

'Thanks. I'll go and 'phone now. I want to get hold of Phillips personally, if I can.'

He went out. Mr Grant murmured something about taking a turn in the garden and followed him.

Jill turned to her father. She tried to say something but all that came out was 'Oh, Dad.'

185

'I know, I know,' he said.

'I want to talk,' she said, 'but I can't. But I'd like you to. Explain as much as you can. I'll just listen.'

'Well, your mother and I were worried when we got your cable; and more so when we had your letter – the one from the hotel. We got that on Friday and decided I should fly over right away. I got here yesterday morning and went straight to the hotel. But you'd checked out and hadn't left a forwarding address. I booked in there myself. I was going to go to Scotland Yard and ask about you. But then I had a visit from Mr Sherwood. He'd been worried about you too, and he'd tried to call me at home. Your mother had told him I was in London, and where I was probably staying. He told me the whole story – or as much as he knew – and how he planned to flush Thompson. He persuaded me to keep away from you yesterday . . .'

'You couldn't have found me, anyway.'

'Oh, we could have. He knew you were staying with this Lady Mannering.'

'He did?' Jill sat up and stared at him.

'Sure. He's been keeping a pretty close watch on you, Jilly. When he told me what he planned for today, I said I'd like to be around, and he agreed I could come along in place of one of his operatives. The idea was to get Thompson's full confession on the tape, then move in. We neither of us figured he'd be in quite such a hurry to do away with you. We were only just in time.'

Jill gave a dazed shake of her head. '*Andrew*,' she said. 'I just can't believe it's Andrew we're talking about. It's so utterly impossible. *Andrew* killed Bob. *Andrew* tried to strangle me. I haven't taken it in yet. I suppose sooner or later it'll suddenly hit me. But right now I just feel any moment I'm going to wake up.'

Ten minutes later Sherwood returned. 'The police are on their way,' he called out from the stairs. He entered the room. 'I got through to Phillips. He's coming straight over. He'd just got in from making some sort of arrest, apparently.'

'Did you tell him – who . . . ?'

He nodded.

'How did he take it?'

'Who can tell what Phillips ever feels?'

Jill asked: 'What did you mean about him co-operating in getting Mrs Romford out of trouble?' She was making an effort now to get a grip on reality again.

'If Thompson's high up in this blackmailing ring, as he claims, then now there's a good chance the police'll be able to close the whole operation down. They've got Mrs Romford's letter to Kendall and his statement stashed away somewhere. I want it. I don't think in all decency Phillips can turn me down. He wouldn't have Thompson now if it hadn't been for her.'

'But suppose Andrew himself tells about her at his trial? He might – just out of spite.'

'There'd be no point. Without the papers to back it, he'd have no proof. And without proof it wouldn't do his case any good at all to drag her into it. Because then she could testify how he treated her.'

Jill picked up her handbag from the floor. 'Is there a bathroom in this place?'

'Sure,' her father said. 'I'll show you.'

She got to her feet, swayed slightly, then determinedly followed her father out to the landing. He showed her the bathroom. She looked past it, down the passage to another door beyond. 'Is – is that . . . ?'

'Yes, but he can't get out. Are you all right, Jilly?'

'Yes. A bit shaky, that's all. Go back to Owen.'

She went into the bathroom, bathed her face in cold water and drank some from her cupped hands. She dried herself with some tissues from her handbag. There was a mirror over the handbasin, and for the first time in weeks she took a long look at herself. Her face was white and she thought she looked older. And harder. She took up her bag and went out to the landing. There she stopped and stood quite still. From her left she could hear the voices of Sherwood and her father, conversing in low tones; to her right was the door with the two new bolts. She turned her head and looked at it.

It seemed a long, long time later that she found herself turning right, taking six or seven brisk paces, reaching out her hand, pulling back the bolts, and pushing the door open.

Andrew stood facing her. His face was putty-coloured, his hands hung limply at his sides. He took one, two steps towards her.

'Jill . . .' He raised both hands in supplication. 'Jill – forgive me.'

Jill stood motionless, without speaking, her face expressionless, looking straight into his eyes. He came closer, till he was at arms' length.

Without shifting her gaze from him she reached into her bag. Her hand came out, clasping a small black automatic. She raised her arm, keeping it straight.

He didn't see the gun until it was too late. He didn't try to disarm her, just ducked away to his left, throwing his hands up higher, as if trying to ward her off.

The voice came in a hoarse whisper: 'No! Jill, don't – for . . .'

The muzzle of the gun was two inches from his right temple when Jill squeezed the trigger.

Without a sound Andrew Thompson crumpled at the knees and collapsed on to the floor.

It was a matter of seconds before Sherwood and her father joined her. They stood staring mutely down at the tall, handsome man lying crumpled on the dusty bare boards. Then Sherwood pushed her gently aside and knelt down. He put his hand on Thompson's heart, looked up, and shook his head.

The gun had fallen from Jill's hand on to the floor. She looked down at it and said flatly: 'I only bought it this morning. In case Mrs Romford tried anything. There's a little place in Soho. Andrew pointed it out to me years ago. Just joking. He said if ever I decided to shoot Bob that would be the place to get a gun and no questions asked. He was right.'

They heard the clatter of running footsteps downstairs. Sherwood acted like lightning. He picked the gun up, simultaneously taking a handkerchief from his pocket. He wiped the gun, and holding it by the handkerchief in one hand, picked up Thompson's wrist with the other and pressed his fingers round it. Then he let gun and hand drop back to the floor. The dead fingers loosened and the gun slid a few inches from the hand and stopped. The whole action took not ten seconds, and by the time Grant came panting up behind them Sherwood was on his feet, his handkerchief back in his pocket.

Grant paused in the doorway. 'What . . . ?'

Sherwood stood silently aside. 'Oh no,' Grant breathed. 'Suicide.' It was half question, half statement.

Sherwood got heavily to his feet. 'My fault. I should have realised he might have a gun. I ought to have searched him. I called out on the stairs about the police coming just now. He must have heard me and realised it was all up.'

There came the sound of a car outside. 'The police,' said Sherwood. He turned. 'Now I've got to tell Phillips we haven't got a prisoner for him after all – just a corpse.'

16

Phillips said: 'It's against all the rules.'

'I know,' said Sherwood.

'It could lose me my job.'

'I know.'

'You've got no right to ask it.'

'Yes I have.'

'Well, perhaps you have. But I don't like it.'

'Look, Malcolm, you said only you and Cochran know about Hemmings' cellar so far. Let me go there now. Ring Cochran and tell him to expect me. He and I can go down together. If the set-up there is as efficient as you say, I should be able to find what I want in a couple of minutes. Then I'll scarper before the rest of your boys arrive. Nobody else'll know a thing. And I give you my word that the contents of the file don't involve any threat to state security or have any bearing on a major crime.'

Phillips said: 'Don't touch or look at anything else. Don't leave your prints about. Stay with Cochran the whole time. Don't let him know the combinations. Lock the doors yourself when you leave. Now get your pen out and take down these numbers.'

'Here you are,' said Sherwood. He held out a buff-coloured cardboard wallet.

Diane Conway grabbed it, opened it, drew out some papers.

Sherwood said: 'It's all there: your letter, Kendall's statement, spare photocopies of both, and a summary of your case from the organisation's point of view. The lot.'

She closed her eyes, took a deep breath, and let it out very slowly. She opened her eyes, smiled, and said briskly: 'Thank you very much, Mr Sherwood. Now would you wait in the drawing-room a few minutes, please. I must just go down to the basement and stoke up the boiler.'

*　　*　　*

Later she asked: 'And there was nothing else there that could implicate me?'

'No. Your name and some brief details are entered in a book. But that only proves they'd been attempting to blackmail you – not the grounds for it, or your reaction.'

'There's still that tape Mrs Palmer made. Suppose she . . . ?' Her hand swung in the air in the characteristic little gesture that had led to so much.

'I know. I didn't anticipate that, I admit. I'll have a word with her about it. Perhaps I can persuade her to destroy it. Her father won't talk, I know – or Mr Grant.'

'The police know I was involved with Thompson – and at the house where he was killed?'

'Yes. I had to tell them whose is the third voice on my tape. They'll be bound to talk to you. But you needn't tell them what the hold was Thompson had over you. Let them guess.'

'And the inquest on Thompson?'

'You'll probably be called. But I'm sure they'll let you be Mrs X.'

'I could still be recognised.'

'Could you? I didn't recognise "Jean Robinson" just a few feet from her, though I'd seen Diane Conway many times. There's no law about what sort of clothes or make-up you'd have to wear, you know. It could be an interesting challenge for you.'

Jill asked: 'Owen – why do you think he really killed Bob? Was it like he said? Or – or was it – was I something to do with it?'

'We can never know. Perhaps he didn't know himself. I shouldn't speculate, if I were you. It won't do any good.'

'I'm not sorry about what I did, you know. I don't feel guilty. In fact, since I did it I've known some sort of peace of mind for the first time since Bob died. I didn't have any hatred for Andy at the very end. It just seemed right I should do it. Meet is the old word. It was as if justice demanded it.'

'You mean that now Thompson has paid his debt – which thirty years in jail wouldn't pay?'

'I suppose that's it. Bob put great store by the concept of debt, you know, and justice and paying a fair price.'

'Life for life, eye for eye, tooth for tooth,' he said softly.

'And you don't believe in that.'

'Let's just say there was a later law that meant I wouldn't be called upon to pay all my debts. For which I am very grateful.'

'You think I was wrong?'

'I didn't say that. It's not for me to judge.'

'You covered up for me. You could have just let me take the rap. You must have thought justice had been done.'

He shook his head. 'I don't always go much for justice. What did the man say?

'Though justice be thy plea, consider this
That in the course of justice none of us
Should see salvation. We do pray for mercy.'

Jill said:

'And that same prayer doth teach us all to render
The deeds of mercy.

'A woman says it, actually. But I get the point.'

She went on: 'Well, whatever the reason you did it – thanks. *Diolch yn fawr*, Owen.'

He looked surprised and pleased. '*Peidiwch a son*, Jill. Which being freely interpreted means "You're welcome".'

She said: 'Owen – what's the position about Mrs Romford now?'

'She's made a statement to the police admitting an attempt had been made to blackmail her, that Bob had an appointment with her that night, but that he never turned up.'

Jill opened her mouth, looking angry, but he forestalled her. 'Don't be too hard on her. She had a lot to lose, you know. And she wasn't in any way to blame for Bob's death. Can either of us be sure we would have acted differently in her shoes? She's suffered a lot, Jill – I know largely from her own stupidity. But can you let her off? Can I tell her you'll destroy that tape and keep quiet about what really happened?'

Jill hesitated. He added: 'We wouldn't have got Thompson without her help, you know.'

192

'OK,' she said suddenly. 'As long as I'm not expected to clasp her to my bosom in forgiveness I'll let it ride.'

'Thank you.'

'Where do the *police* think Bob was killed?'

'They say they don't know. Phillips could make a pretty good guess, I daresay, but in view of Mrs Romford's statement, officially they'll have to assume he was hi-jacked on his way to her house.'

'Couldn't they get evidence if they examined the house?'

'Have you ever tried to get a warrant to search a government minister's house on no grounds other than vague suspicion? And remember, there's not the slightest suggestion she was involved in the actual murder. Even if they could prove Bob was killed there, the charges against her would be comparatively minor.'

'What about those thugs who helped Andrew – they know the truth.'

'They're under arrest. But they'll go to prison – and go to their graves – denying they went within ten miles of Bob that night. So they can hardly ever admit they know where he was killed.'

'So she's out of trouble?'

'More or less.'

'It's more than she deserves.'

'Now we're back to justice again,' he said.

Sherwood said: *Diwedd annwyl*, Malcolm, you took a risk barging into Hemmings' place like that without a scrap of real evidence!'

'Of course I did. It was crazy. I should have gone straight to the A.C. after Cochran came to see me, and let things take their usual course. But frankly, I was sick to death of the whole dirty business. Nothing had been going right with the case. Something had been holding me back the whole time. And I couldn't pin-point it.'

'Thompson?'

'Of course. Heaven alone knows how much he snarled things up – how much evidence he suppressed or how much false stuff he fed me. Anyway, by the time Cochran came to my room I was just about at the end of my tether. When I heard what he had to say, I saw the glimmer of a chance to clear up the whole thing there and then. So I decided to put my head down and go straight for the line. I might have got into a heap of trouble if it hadn't come off. But – well, it did come off. Though I hate to think what would have happened if Cochran hadn't been there.'

The Coroner said: '. . . we have heard expert evidence to the effect that one bullet had been fired from the pistol found on the floor near the body of the deceased; and that a bullet from the same pistol was found lodged in his brain and undoubtedly caused his death, the gun having been held close against his right temple when the shot was fired. We have now to decide how that shot came to be fired, and by whom.

'To my mind the evidence we have heard from Detective-Chief Superintendent Phillips, from the lady known as Mrs X, from the other witnesses, and from the tape recording – a recording which Mr Grant, a completely independent and unimpeachable witness, has sworn to be genuine and unedited, and which Mr Phillips has accepted as such – all this evidence proves beyond any reasonable doubt that Andrew Thompson was both a murderer and a blackmailer.

'Mrs X has told us that an attempt was made to blackmail her, and that she was expecting a visit from Inspector Palmer on the evening of October 22nd – the evening we now know he was murdered – that he never arrived at her house, and that she later enlisted the aid of the enquiry agent, Mr Sherwood. Mrs Palmer has told us how by means of a telephone call her husband had made she identified Mrs X as the lady he was going to visit, how she and Mrs X arranged a meeting, and how she persuaded Mrs X to talk to Inspector Thompson. Mr Sherwood has explained how he suspected Thompson and planned to trap him at that meeting. We have heard the recording containing Thompson's confession to the murder of Robert Palmer, made at that time. Mrs Palmer, Mrs X, Mr Sherwood, Mr Grant, and Colonel Forbes have all testified that Thompson made a murderous attack on Mrs Palmer – testimony which has been largely borne out by the evidence of the recording – that he was afterwards overpowered and, without being searched beforehand, was locked up in another room.

'Mr Sherwood and Colonel Forbes have further testified that while waiting for the police they heard the sound of a shot from the room in which Thompson had been shut up, that they ran to the room and found Thompson lying dead on the floor, a bullet hole in his temple and an automatic pistol on the floor near him. Mr Grant, who arrived half a minute later, confirms this.

'Finally, there is the fact that the only fingerprints found on the gun were Thompson's own.

'In view of all this evidence, I do not believe there can be any doubt that the deceased took his own life.'

Jill said: 'But why, Owen? Why was it so easy? I wasn't even asked what *I* was doing when Andrew died. It's incredible. Because I wasn't going to tell a lot of lies, you know. If I'd been pushed I'd have told the truth. But it just didn't come up. You and Dad didn't have to perjure yourselves to protect me, either. All the awkward questions were sort of blurred over. Why?'

'I can only guess, but look at it this way. The evidence left no room for any doubt of Thompson's guilt. And, given that, the police were probably very relieved to have him dead. Now Phillips may have suspected Thompson didn't shoot himself. But there was no earthly way he could ever prove it. And even if he had been able to, and you'd been brought to trial, no jury in the country would have convicted you. So what would be the point in the police making themselves awkward? A coroner works closely with the police, you know, and if they don't suggest foul play, as a rule he won't. In this case it was clearly in everybody's interest to smooth things over rather than stir them up.'

'So I've got nothing to worry about?'

'Not a thing.'

The Home Secretary asked: 'How long had it been going on?'

'About twelve years, sir,' Phillips said. 'Hemmings had been passed over for government office and was very bitter about it.

It must have been just money, or a desire for revenge that made him say yes to the approach – certainly nothing ideological.

'The whole system was brilliantly conceived – either by Hemmings or his masters, it isn't clear which. The basis of it was that virtually everybody has something he wants kept from somebody else. It may not be a secret that has to be kept from the world at large, but just from one person – hence it is often fairly easy to find out about. There are scores of examples in Hemmings' Lists. Naturally many of the people listed there have been guilty of various crimes, or mixed up in scandals of some kind. But the new thing about Hemmings' organisation was that the innocent could be vulnerable. The latest example to come to light is that of a certain scientist with a blind wife. They have a son in Australia. The man knew something. Hemmings wanted it. So he threatened to let the wife know that the letters supposedly from her son which her husband reads her each week, he writes himself. The son hasn't been in touch for three years.'

The Home Secretary shook his head. 'How horribly simple.'

'Hemmings certainly put a lot of work and thought into his organisation. He recruited a formidable team – including three journalists, several private investigators, at least two lawyers, three or four doctors, and people in the Inland Revenue, the Registrar-General's office, those with access to Service personnel files – and of course, one Scotland Yard detective. All in positions regularly to hear confidential information. Other people were employed casually, just for a single job – out-of-work actors and actresses, junkies, students, petty crooks. They might be hired to deliver a message, collect documents, make an initial approach to a victim in a pub or on a bus – that sort of thing.'

'These companies he controlled – where did they fit in?'

'He already had an interest in an accountancy firm. He saw the opportunities this would often provide for prying into people's financial affairs. So he brought Philip Harrington in, and put him in charge of that side of things. He realised the possibilities offered by P.R. work, so he bought Metropolitan Promotions and installed Maurice Parkstone in an important position. He started his own consumer research firm: this gave his employees opportunities to enter all kinds of places legitimately and ask detailed questions ordinary people couldn't ask. He took over a firm of bookmakers, so that he could make apparently legitimate tax-free payments to his employees. Among other things, incidentally, he invented a clever little gadget that enabled him to write quite featureless letters in ordinary ball pen. He did nearly all the secretarial work himself, and it was his pedantry in writing and punctuation that really started Inspector Palmer off on his investigations.'

'What about all that violence? It seems out of character.'

'He saw it was sometimes necessary, sir. So he got hold of the Storch brothers – probably through Thompson. They're plain, ordinary toughs. We think it was they who dumped Palmer's body, who helped Hemmings' wife to kidnap Lady Felicity Mannering, and who beat up a little crook called Harry Edwards, who'd somehow stepped on Hemmings' toes. That was an incident which interested Palmer a lot and he seems to have worked out what happened very accurately.

'Anyway, sir, the Storch boys are now behind bars. So are all the rest of Hemmings' mob. His cellar proved a treasure house. He kept records of everything – all his victims, all his minor employees – not of Dorothy or Thompson or his other chief associates, of course. But other than them – everybody.'

'He must have been crazy,' said the Home Secretary.

'Not really, sir. I mean, he *was* an M.P. – and an M.P.'s house would normally be as unlikely a place as one can imagine for a police search. And the office was completely hidden and inaccessible to everybody except Hemmings himself. The stuff had to be kept somewhere. He certainly couldn't have trusted any of his associates with it – because the contents of that cellar spelt control of the organisation. Also, he had to have constant easy access to it. So his own basement made into a strong-room was as good a choice as anywhere. He had all his plans made to get away quickly if he ever was suspected – and to set fire to everything before he left. But in the end he didn't get a chance.'

Cochran said: 'The weirdest thing about the whole case was that Johnny James should pick on Hemmings of all people to put the black on.'

'So Hemmings' complaint was perfectly genuine?' Sherwood asked.

'Perfectly. You see, he'd been living apart from his wife for years. And having an affair with Dorothy Lucas. But as long as it suited him to be an M.P. he had to keep up his image. So he didn't want a divorce. Then he decided to pack up politics. The point is that he then had no excuse not to get a divorce and marry Dorothy. But just about this time Johnny James must have somehow found out about Hemmings' and Dorothy's affair and managed to get some pictures of them.

'Poor Johnny. He must have been no end pleased with himself – getting the black on an M.P. The trouble was that he was too stupid to find out the true position. So he didn't know that by then Hemmings didn't give a damn who knew about Dorothy.'

'So when he got Johnny's call he just toddled off to the Yard like a model citizen?'

'Exactly. That must have given him a laugh, I should think. And I bet, too, it was a good excuse to get to meet Mr Palmer – he'd been building a reputation as a blackmail specialist, and it was a chance for Hemmings to size him up.

'The trouble was that Hemmings couldn't afford to have us look too closely into his own movements. So he had to tell Mr Palmer an obvious lie – that he didn't know where the photographs had been taken. That made Mr Palmer's job much more difficult. Hemmings must have realised very early on that largely because of his own secrecy we weren't going to be able to nab the blackmailer. That didn't suit him at all. His pride had been got at. So he got his organisation to work on it. I shouldn't imagine it was difficult for pros like them to trace Johnny James. It must have scared Johnny rigid to find out that a big criminal outfit were after his guts. He backed down straight away and didn't even collect the parcel that Hemmings had left on Hampstead Heath. We don't know exactly what happened then but somehow Hemmings' people got the pictures back. And then Hemmings made his big mistake. He was determined James should be punished. So he sent us a tip-off – which was one of the notes that later put Mr Palmer on his scent. Next, Hemmings had someone break into James's flat and plant Johnny's own folder containing the photos. Then he actually suggested we made a search. He slipped up there, too. He mentioned Johnny's flat. But how did he know Johnny lived in a *flat*? Something struck me as wrong at the time but I couldn't quite pin it down.'

*   *   *

Sherwood said: 'Bob had compiled a very impressive dossier and must have been getting pretty close to a break-through when I first entered the case. Cochran paid a routine call on me to ask if I'd had any blackmail victims approach me. I was able to tell him about a woman calling herself Jean Robinson, who'd asked for my help and who I'd sent away. Later that evening I 'phoned Bob and told him a couple of other things Jean Robinson had said. I was also able to describe a distinctive trick she had with her hands, which might help to identify her. Bob went home and, in the one big coincidence of the case, immediately saw this mannerism used on television by Diane Conway.

'Bob knew it was important to find somebody who was actually in contact with the blackmailers there and then. He probably looked up Conway and Romford in the 'phone book, but their number is unlisted. Now the police can obtain unlisted numbers but it's a complicated business, and an officer can't just get it from his home. And, of course, Bob realised that if he was to get Mrs Romford to talk, it might be vital to approach her unofficially, on the quiet. So he didn't want to make formal application for her number. However, policemen frequently get hold of ex-directory numbers quite legitimately in the course of their work – and I can assure you they don't just throw them away afterwards. Bob knew it was on the cards that someone at the Yard would know the number of a man like David Romford. And he did the obvious thing: rang through to Thompson, who was still on duty, and asked him if he could ask around and get hold of the number for him.

'It must have been a tremendous shock to Thompson and he had to think quickly. He had Mrs Romford's number himself, naturally. He didn't want to give it to Bob. But Thompson knew that if Bob didn't get hold of it quickly he'd be forced to make formal application for it. And Thompson didn't want that, either. So he told Bob he had it himself – probably said he'd been in touch with Romford in the past over some minor matter. Bob must have then told Thompson he was going to try to see Mrs Romford that very night if he possibly could.

'He got through to her, mentioning Jean Robinson. It shook her to discover somebody knew about her alias but she did eventually agree to see Bob. Before this, though, she asked him if he was a policeman and told him she didn't want anything to do with the police, because the man who was blackmailing her was one. That was another thing Thompson had boasted of to her, you see.'

Jill gave a gasp. 'So that's what it was gave Bob such a jolt!'

Sherwood nodded. 'And why he told you not to talk to anybody. He realised that time was vital and he rushed over to the Romfords' house almost immediately. But in the meantime Thompson had picked up the Storch brothers and managed to get there first . . .

'Now Hemmings swears he knew nothing about Bob's death beforehand. The police believe him. Thompson must have acted on his own initiative. There just wouldn't have been time to consult Hemmings – quite apart from Hemmings being in the debating chamber of the House of Commons from six-thirty onwards.

'The next development from my point of view was when you visited my office, Jill, and told me that Bob had rushed out of the house to interview a woman who had a particular mannerism with her hands, and who you'd since identified as Diane Conway, It was a bit of a bombshell, as you can imagine, to learn that it was the lead I'd given him that had led to his death. It had never occurred to me that he would have traced Jean Robinson so soon – or that none of his colleagues or superiors would know about it if he had done. I imagined that my little piece of information would be merely one of dozens he'd received, that it would have been duly noted in his case-records, and was not at all significant. That's why I had never bothered to see Phillips after the murder and report my conversation with Bob.

'But Jill's story made a big difference. I now knew I was very much involved. I also knew that my "Jean Robinson" was Mrs David Romford – and I understood what Bob had meant when he'd said to Jill that the whole thing was bigger than he'd thought.

'The story Jill told me was plainly fishy. There were only three possibilities: one, she was lying to me – which was clearly absurd; two, evidence was being sat on – either, as she suspected, to cover up a political scandal, or for matters of security; three, Thompson had lied to her. Now it was natural for you, Jill, to believe Thompson. But to me, knowing the Met as a body better than you did, the most likely explanation was that Thompson had lied to you. And there could only be one reason for that.'

'Then why didn't you go straight to the police with the whole story?' Colonel Forbes asked him.

'For two reasons, sir. Firstly, it was just possible Jill was right and I was wrong: that Thompson was perfectly straight, and that somebody else higher up was, not necessarily crooked or corrupt, but being subjected to political pressure. Or that things were more serious still and the Official Secrets Acts was involved. And if that was the case, I would have to tread very carefully. Either way I had to be sure of my facts before I went round to the Yard and started making noises about suppression of evidence. Such an accusation would have to be done very discreetly, ideally to just one man, and it would be just my luck if I picked on the man who'd actually done the suppressing.

'The second reason I didn't go to the police was that I felt I had to consider Mrs Romford. Clearly she was – or had been – in bad trouble. She'd come to me for help and I'd sent her away. Now again, it was possible that the police had already traced her, and that the political pressure was being applied on her behalf – as Jill suspected. But if Jill was wrong, then the police knew nothing about Mrs Romford – and she, it seemed, had good reason to want to keep things that way. Yet I couldn't think she'd done anything really wrong. And I happen, in addition, to be a great admirer of David Romford and, if the whole thing was political, I didn't want to do anything to jeopardise his career. So I decided that before I brought Mrs Romford's name to the attention of the police, I ought to give her a chance to tell me her story.

'I got her number from a very useful friend of mine in Fleet Street, rang through and said I wanted to speak to Mrs Romford concerning Jean Robinson. It must have seemed to her that history was horribly repeating itself, for Bob had previously done exactly the same thing. Anyway, she did agree to see me.

'I called there the same day and managed more or less to convince her she could trust me. Her story rang true and was consistent with everything else I knew. So I felt obliged to do what I could for her. She agreed to put herself in my hands. The description she was able to give me of Masters – his height, build, age and so on – fitted Thompson perfectly, and I was then convinced he was the maggot in the cheese. But I couldn't take my suspicions to Phillips and at the same time be sure of keeping Mrs Romford out of the picture.

'I had two duties: to help nail Thompson; and to get my client off the hook. I believed that I could combine these if I could present Phillips with positive proof of Thompson's guilt – for Phillips could hardly then refuse me one request in return: a chance to be the first to search the organisation's H.Q. when it was discovered and remove her file.

'I then worked out a plan to trap Thompson. I knew the only way would be to catch him off guard and panic him into a rash move. So when you came to see me again the next day, Jill, I told you enough about Mrs Romford to be sure you would want to talk to her. My advice to Mrs Romford was to wait for you to contact her, agree to meet you – and then give you an edited version of the truth.'

'She knew who I was – from the first time I called her?'

'Yes. The whole object was to spur you into immediately calling Thompson.'

'How could you be sure I would?'

'I couldn't be sure. But you'd have to tell someone what you'd discovered. You distrusted the police as a whole but you still had faith in him. And I was convinced you wouldn't be able to resist proving to him you'd been right about the person Bob had seen on television. But if you hadn't suggested it, Mrs Romford was going to try to manœuvre you into it – ask if you knew of a trustworthy policeman she might talk to unofficially, and if you could arrange it.'

Jill said: 'You advised me to go home. You didn't mean it, did you?'

'I did, Jill. I hoped you would go – for your own sake. If you had, I would have had to work out some other plan. But I was sure you wouldn't go – whatever I said.'

'But why didn't you tell me what you suspected – and let me help you openly?'

'I didn't think you'd credit the possibility of Thompson's guilt unless you heard it from his own lips. And I thought that if I told you, you might well go and ask him straight out for an explanation. And that would have been fatal – perhaps literally. But even if you did believe me, I couldn't see you acting out my plan to trap him. You'd have been too upset. To lure him out you'd have to be genuine when you spoke to him on the 'phone.

'I banked on three successive shocks forcing Thompson into a mistake,' he went on. 'First, the discovery that you were in London all along, when he'd thought you were safely away in the States; second, finding out that you'd traced Mrs Romford and knew Bob had been killed in her house; and third, being confronted with that splendid theatrical accusation from her in your presence. He'd clearly have to do something quickly and it was odds on he'd give himself away.'

'What I don't understand,' Felicity said, 'is how Diane recognised him as Mr Masters so quickly – when she'd never even seen Masters' face.'

'She didn't recognise him. My instructions to her were to denounce whoever it was Jill brought into the room. My chief worry, of course, was Jill's safety. When she'd told Thompson what she knew, two weeks earlier, she must have been in real danger. I think anyone but Jill would have been killed immediately. But then she apparently believed his story of the lead being a dead-end and said she was going back to the States. So he thought he was safe – for the moment. And next he started planning to pin the murder on someone else. He knew the fact that Jill might talk would always hang over him – until she was satisfied the killer had been convicted. Once she was, he could be sure she'd let the matter drop. He might even have got her promise never to speak of it: I'm sure he could have thought up a plausible reason for asking.

'Anyway, that's how I imagine his mind worked. And I knew that if he discovered what she was really up to, she'd be in grave peril. So I arranged to have her watched all the time. I was worried about you, Jill. I knew you had nobody close to you in London. So I 'phoned your parents. Your mother told me the Colonel was actually over here, and where he was staying. I went and told him everything – including the fact that you were in danger and I was planning to put you in possibly even greater danger. His attitude was that you wouldn't thank anyone who missed out on a chance to expose the killer just because of a possible risk to you, and that anyway not much harm could come to you as long as he was around.

'So then for three days there was nothing to do but wait for you to make a move. I knew it could only be a matter of days before you got round to calling Mrs Romford. During that time one of my people was never far from you – not even when you followed Miss Mannering out to the country.'

Jill stared. 'You had someone tailing me then?'

'Yes, on a motor-cycle. As you followed Miss Mannering, he followed your taxi. He got to the clearing in the wood just in time to see the rout of the enemy.'

Jill said: 'That figure I saw skulking about in the trees after the others had gone. Remember, Felicity?'

Felicity nodded.

'That whole incident puzzled me no end when I had his report,' Sherwood said.

'What was the object of it – just sheer revenge?' Felicity asked him.

'I think so. You'd humiliated Dorothy Lucas and hurt her badly. Over the next year she must have built up an intense hatred for you. But her work for the organisation kept her pretty busy, and I don't suppose she had any chance for a long time to do anything about getting her own back. Then, after the murder, Hemmings seems to have decided to shut up shop for a while – until the pressure was off a bit. And for the first time Dorothy, who'd now married him, had some free time. So she planned her little surprise. Whether Hemmings had anything to do with it I don't know. I should think not. But of course the Storch boys would be quite used to taking orders from Dorothy. Interesting that she wore a Ku Klux Klan-type mask, like Thompson, and spoke in a whisper throughout. I'd guess from that that he'd given her a full account of his technique with Mrs Romford.'

Felicity shivered. 'I was lucky, wasn't I? If Jill hadn't been around . . .'

'Very lucky. Dorothy Hemmings is a thoroughly vicious piece of goods. Hemmings, I'd say, was in the business almost solely for the money. But she enjoyed her work. Anyway, Miss Mannering, say the word to Phillips and he'll add abduction and malicious wounding to all the other charges against her.'

Felicity looked wistful. 'It's very tempting. But Charles would hate the publicity. And they've got plenty against her without my evidence, haven't they?'

'Oh yes. She'll go down for a very long time.'

'Then I'll content myself with going to the trial as a spectator and letting her see me sneering at her from the public gallery. But if anything should go wrong with the prosecution's case, then I'll let the police use my evidence.'

There was silence for some seconds. Then Jill said: 'Finish the story, Owen.'

'There's not much more. I continued to have you watched. I got the key to the empty house and I told Mrs Romford to let me know the second she heard from you. She 'phoned me on the Sunday morning. I had the last-minute idea of getting an independent witness and eventually lighted on Mr Grant. After lunch I picked up him and the Colonel and took them to the house. Mrs Romford joined us later. I'd already had discreet enquiries made into Thompson's habits and learned that he was nearly always at home on a Sunday afternoon. So then it was just a matter of waiting – and praying things would work out.'

17

Two days later Sherwood, Cochran, and Felicity saw Jill and her father off at London Airport.

Sherwood took Jill's hand. 'Good luck, *cariad*. I won't say keep in touch. I hope you manage to forget us, and England, and all that's happened – just like you wanted.'

Jill shook her head. 'I'll be back.'

He raised his eyebrows.

Felicity said: 'But I thought...'

'I know what I said. But I think Bob's child ought to be raised in England, don't you?'

They stared at her blankly. Then Sherwood said: 'No – really? Oh, wonderful! I couldn't be more pleased. Congratulations.'

Cochran said: 'Great.'

Felicity said: 'Oh, darling, can I be a godmother? It would really prove I was down to bottom gear. To make godmother could be my crowning achievement. Can I? Please?'

Jill said: 'I'm not sure wanting a god-child as a status symbol is the purest of motives.'

'But darling, I'd be just perfect. There's not a single temptation I haven't personally experienced. I could warn the poor little devil against every possible iniquity.'

Jill laughed. 'Well, I'll think about it.' Then, more seriously, she said: 'It's odd, you know. I'd really intended to put England and Bob right out of my mind. I knew I couldn't do it until the case was closed. I thought that *then* I'd be able to start forgetting. But even before – before Andrew died I was beginning to realise I might not be able to. And now – well, I've got no chance at all, have I? A bit of Bob will always be with me.'

'Do you mind?' Sherwood asked her.

She smiled. 'What do you think?'

'When will you come back?' Felicity asked.

'I don't know. Two – three – four years. It depends. I want him born...'

'*Him?*' her father interrupted.

'Him,' she repeated firmly. 'I want him born in the States. I want to be with my mother. I want him off to a good start. But I know Bob would have wanted him raised in England. And I owe Bob that.' She looked at Sherwood. 'It's a kind of debt, you see.'

'Point taken,' he said.

'Probably I shan't feel much like leaving America when the time comes. But I will. Because over here he'll have a name to live up to.'

'Especially if he joins the police,' said Cochran.

'I shan't try to stop him,' Jill said.

They watched Jill and her father cross the tarmac. From the plane steps she turned to wave. Sherwood waved back.

Cochran glanced at him. 'As somebody once remarked: "nice girl".'

'As somebody once replied: "the best",' said Owen Sherwood.

*If you have enjoyed this book, you might
wish to join the Walker British Mystery Society.*

*For information, please send a postcard or
letter to:*

Paperback Mystery Editor

**Walker & Company
720 Fifth Avenue
New York, NY 10019**